Don,

Thanks for taking
the time to read my
book & write a review!
Hope you enjoyed it!

Brian Spielbauer

PRAISE FOR

THE LEGACY OF FAITH

"*Originally, I was honored to be asked to be one of the first to read Brian Spielbauer's book "The Legacy of Faith." Then, before the book was delivered, I wondered if I really wanted to do it or not. I mean, read a book about a guy's family coming to America? How boring was that going to be? But a promise is a promise, and I had said I would do it. I could not have been more wrong. This book kept me involved the entire time. The story of Johann Baptiste Tschohl traveling with his family from Lichtenstein to Iowa in the 1840s is a story you do not want to miss. It is informational and historical, but it also involves action, romance, and danger. This should be required reading for anyone studying immigration of the period or anyone that just wants a great read.*"

Kevin Oeth
Mayor of Fayette, Missouri

"*Brian captures the strains, struggles, decisions made, and the perseverance it took for a family to strike out for the adventure of a lifetime. Those decisions produced a legacy for generations that followed.*"

Don Mackey

"*Mr. Spielbauer presents a fascinating story of a migrant family's emigration to the United States. From his research, he traces his family's migration to the settlement of Guttenberg, a German community located in Iowa along the Mississippi River. An interesting read with interesting side stories about their struggles to get to their destination. Looking forward to a sequel about the arrival of the family and the problems and successes they face at their new location.*"

Howard Hubbell,
Retired High School History Teacher, Guttenberg, Iowa

"I loved the book. I just finished it, and I couldn't put it down. I remember many of these names from my Dad talking about them before he passed. My older siblings (Arnie, Joe, Rose, Frank) know them better. Still, in my opinion, the book is well-written, interesting, and a masterful blend of real-life people and the historical setting in which they lived."

Tom Spielbauer,
Amarillo, Texas

"I absolutely treasured following the separate journeys of the Tschohl, Rohner, and Spielbauer families as they each placed their trust in a trek of a lifetime that took them from central Europe to a small river town nestled in the bluffs of the Mississippi River, Guttenberg, Iowa. This historical fiction book was an extremely entertaining read as the author enabled me to gain an insight into settling in America that I had not considered before; personal stories of real people and the feelings and faith that must have been evident when taking part in a trip such as this. As I read the adventures involved in the long travel to Guttenberg, I could not put off reading this story. I am fortunate to have been raised in this small German town, and after reading this book, I find myself taking in the scenery of the Mississippi River Valley. In an instant, I can see the valley through the eyes of people traveling up the river for the first time to find hope and security in an unknown time. It is an exhilarating perspective to be able to experience and is due to following these families in their journey in The Legacy of Faith."

Sue Meinecke
Spring Valley, Minnesota

"I thoroughly enjoyed reading this book. The travels of these families made me appreciate how difficult life and travel were for those who came before us. The challenges they faced were immense but not insurmountable. After reading Mr. Spielbauer's book about their travel to America to establish new lives, I am drawn to spend more time learning the stories of my own family members."

Diane Frauchiger
Madison, Wisconsin

"This book is a great story of real family members traveling from Central Europe to America and to where they eventually settle, Guttenberg, Iowa. I loved following these characters across Lichtenstein, Austria, Bavaria, and France to set sail from Le Havre and across the Atlantic Ocean. The book then chronicles their journeys as they arrived in New Orleans / New York and traveled across America to the Midwest. Finally, they arrive in the small town of Guttenberg, Iowa, where they settled and built a life.

Their journey is easy to follow, and I enjoyed the people that they met along the way. It is interesting to learn about their lives, relationships, interactions, and survival of these families. One can easily determine the large amount of faith they had in God, in each other, and relatives to leave a familiar life and eventually begin a new life in a new world unknown to them.

Once I started this book, it was difficult to put down. I wanted to keep reading to see what would happen, who would cross their paths, and where each family would arrive next."

Michelle Frazier
Byron, Illinois

"Mr. Spielbauer has artfully crafted a beautiful family history in his The Legacy of Faith. Reading it was a privilege. From the first chapter, I felt a kinship develop to a family I am a stranger to, and I found myself proud of each of them and rooting for them. Every scene, every set of harrowing circumstances, and surprises were all carefully written to make the reader feel present in those moments. I was moved by the strength and determination that never wavered and by the compass of love that guided a family's journey. When I finished, I felt I had been given a gift. I look forward to reuniting with this remarkable family when Mr. Spielbauer continues his most intriguing and satisfying account of their legacy."

Jenny Fortel
Columbia Missouri

My love of researching the Tschohl family history has been a joy. I've loved learning the genealogy of their journey to North America, and I have traced their family back to Christian Tschohl, who was born around 1700.

Brian brought life and color to the Tschohl's journey from Liechtenstein. This book is a fun read. I particularly liked the descriptions of how they traveled together and said their goodbyes. *The Tschohls were a strong family. Thanks, Brian."*

Betty Tschohl Weingartner
Edina, Minnesota

"The greatest legacy that one can pass on to one's children and grandchildren is not money or other material things that one accumulates in one's life, but rather a legacy of character and faith."

- Billy Graham

THE LEGACY of FAITH

Brian Spielbauer

Concordis
Publishing

**Concordis
Publishing**

28160 McBean Parkway, Unit 25201
Valencia, CA 91354

concordispublishing.com

First Concordis Publishing Hardcover edition March 2021

For information about special discounts for bulk purchases, please contact Concordis Publishing Special Sales at 1-310-650-0213 or rodney@concordispublishing.com.

DESIGNED BY RODNEY V. EARLE

Manufactured in the United States of America

10 9 8 7 6 5 4 3 2 1

Library of Congress Cataloging-in-Publishing Data Pending

ISBN: 978-0-578-86794-6 (Hardcover)
ISBN: 978-0-578-86307-8 (Softcover)

To the many descendants of Johann Tschohl, Mathias Rohner, and George and Mary Pankraz Spielbauer. I hope you enjoy this novel, which is based upon intertwining family stories. May you gain a greater appreciation for the sacrifice and perseverance our ancestors exhibited and to the faith that played a significant part in their day-to-day endeavors and carried them through.

Each of us has our own challenges that we face. Even though they are far different from the struggles our ancestors faced, they are still just as challenging today. They cause us to doubt ourselves, to question the presence and role of God in our lives and make us feel as though we are alone at times. We are not alone.

We have our family, we have those that have gone before us and watch over us from above, and if we have stayed true to the faith of our fathers, we have a strong religious belief in the inevitable victory that is to come. That legacy is ours to achieve, and more importantly, it is ours to pass on.

CONTENTS

DEDICATION

I dedicate this book to my mother, Jackie Wessels Spielbauer. She passed away on May 5th, 2019, after dealing with Multiple Sclerosis for many years. She always smiled and never complained. She was the best mom anyone could ask for, and I think of her daily. A lot of hearts broke that day, but I know where she is now. My mom is with God in Heaven, and I know she is with the many angels of our family and others who watch over us as we carry on their legacy.

ACKNOWLEDGMENTS

I have several important acknowledgments to make. The first is to Betty Jane Tschohl Weingartner of Edina, Minnesota, a descendant of Ignaz Tschohl, brother of John Baptiste Johll (Tschohl, Tshol). When one begins a journey he or she is meant to be on, I believe things come into his or her life unexpectedly to aid the journey. These surprises help them on their way and are a sign of, I believe, God's intention and urging of that journey. Betty did a lot of work deeply researching the Tschohl family, and it was invaluable to my book, particularly the parts focused on the Tschohls. Thank you, Betty, and I hope you greatly enjoy this book!

Next, I need to acknowledge my Aunt Hilda Spielbauer Brooks, formerly of Marshalltown, Iowa, and Uncle Arnie Spielbauer, formerly of Liberty, Illinois. Both supported my writing and showed particular interest in my effort for the Legacy of Faith. Regrettably, for us that remain, both of them passed within months of each other in the Fall of 2019. As with my mom, their resting place is secure. I have received many inspirational messages and hints as I finished this story, and I know I will continue to do so for the upcoming sequels.

Hilda wrote her book, *Living Arrows*, which illustrated her immediate family as they grew up in Guttenberg, Iowa during the depression. It is a 'must-read' for anyone yearning for the Spielbauer family's stories and life in and around Guttenberg. I suspect the same story could be replicated in many towns of that era of the Great Depression. Her story and courage to write was, and remains, an inspiration to my writing. Her research into that time was an invaluable resource for this current story. I wish her husband and children the best as they continue to carry on her caring and loving legacy.

Arnie took research to an entirely different level! Before the internet, this man sent letters and called all over the country, even to Liechtenstein and Bavaria, to research his family history. He needed evidence, not insinuation. I was the benefactor of his research and the willing acceptor of all things family history. He was a quiet man of many talents and not boastful in the least (and he certainly accomplished many things of which one could boast). Sadly, Arnie passed away on October 12th, 2019. I cannot thank him enough for his help and wish his family the best as they continue on.

I also need to thank the people of Guttenberg, Iowa. Thank you for supporting my writing, the character you hold, and the many characters you have produced! It was a great place to grow up, and I had amazing friends. Guttenberg is a remarkable place that I hope can hold onto the same feelings that Hilda so amazingly described in her book, and of which I hope to do justice in mine.

I would be remiss (and scolded!) if I didn't thank my beautiful wife Jennifer and my wonderful daughters, Sydney and Allie. We have accomplished a lot as a family, and I love watching us grow and evolve. Thank you for allowing me the time to write and do my author activities. Your support is vital, and I will always cherish it. I love you all!

Lastly, I want to thank my parents, Frank and Jackie. You gave our family a terrific home to grow up in. We all had the start we needed to get us where we wanted to go in life, and I'm not sure what more a kid can ask for. Thank you!

INTRODUCTION

Over Christmas break, 2017, I sat and talked with my dad one night. I cannot remember why, exactly, but he started to tell me a story about our family. I had never heard it before, but I was immediately eager for more. He told me about his grandparents and even older generations, and the stories of their coming to America. I don't know why I had never heard it, but one truth has become a fact to me over the years: The Spielbauer family is not boastful, and in fact, we are quite stingy with the information. This is especially true for items that could lead to anything, dare I say, flamboyant. Even harder to get are facts that could be considered scandalous.

The family stories my dad told me that night had been handed down, one generation to the next in anything but an intentional way. Mostly they were shared after beer and cards during family get-togethers. The stories were about how the different family branches left the old country to come to America and the many trials they faced after arriving. I have made significant efforts to verify these stories, but my efforts pale in comparison to those made before I began my search. While some have been verified, others seem determined to remain a mystery. Perhaps they are better left so.

These stories, combined and began in this historical fiction novel, are here to be a testament to the faith that our forebearers had. Imagine the courage it took to take the long and perilous trip from Europe to America in the mid-1800s. It's a testament to the determination they needed to persevere through hardships. I fear people today wouldn't have the fortitude to withstand the common difficulties our ancestors dealt with, and they probably did so with little thought or complaint.

We need to remember the faith of our fathers. Their courage, determination, and strength are also ours, as is their deeply held faith in God and his plans for our future. Our ability to overcome the obstacles we face is equal to theirs, for that is the legacy they left for us.

Their faith, however, is not naturally given from one generation to the next. Children do not receive it like eye-color or height. It's harder than that, and it's far more important. We must intentionally teach our belief and trust in God to our children to enable them the ability to cultivate this precious resource for living daily life and overcome the many challenges we encounter. If we have done that for our children, then we have indeed left them a Legacy of Faith.

GUTTENBERG, IOWA
UNITED STATES

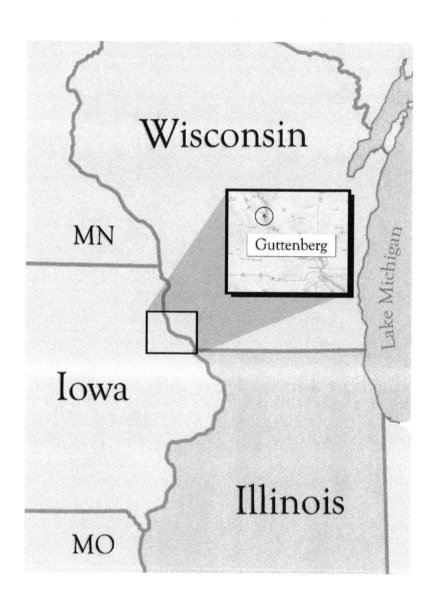

TIMELINE

Johann Baptiste Tschohl	Year	World
	1803	Louisiana Purchase
	1833	End of the Black Hawk Wars. Iowa opens up to settlers.
	1843	Western Settlement Society purchases land in Prairie La Porte.
Johann Tschohl's 3 daughters, along with Franz Michael Vogt travel to Gutenberg as the first group from Liechtenstein.	1845	
	1846	12.28 Iowa becomes a state.
Scholastika comes to Amerika.	1850	John Leanard of the Western Settlement Society purchases Block 76. Donates Lot 1 and 2 for a church. The first mass in held in 1851.
	1853	A new brick structure is build for St. Mary's Church.
	1853	Father Winegar, a renowned Missionary, blesses a cross at the Original St. Mary's Church, and 'Cross of Light' appears in the sky midday for 45 minutes.
2.11, Tschohls depart Balzers, Liechtenstein.	1855	
4.21, Tschohls arrive in New Orleans.	1855	
5.8, Tschohls arrived in Guttenberg.	1855	
	1860	Clemens Kappen builds the first hearse in Clayton County.
10.18, John Baptist Tschohl joins the war as a paid replacement.	1864	
Mathias Rohner		**World**
	1861	Civil War Begins.
	1862	Steuben Guard of Guttenberg, an all German regiment, joins the war as Company D of the Iowa 27th Regiment.
Mathias Rohner swims Lake Constance to escape war in Austria.	1865	
	1865	Civil War Ends.
	1867	A rift occurs in St. Mary's Church about the location for a new church, with close to half the families leaving.
Mathias Rohner works for and lives with George Weist, according to the Census.	1870	
	1871	The first train reaches Guttenberg after the town voted to raise $30,000 to entice the railroad.
George Spielbauer, Mary Pankraz		**World**
Joseph, their son, is born.	1868	
	1870	November, Bavaria joins the North German Federation.
	1871	Jan. 18th, Ludwig refuses to attend an event, his brother Otto and uncle Luipold attend to represent Bavaria.
Mary and Joseph arrive in Iowa.	1872	
	1874	The foundation of the new St. Mary's church was laid, at its current block of location.

THE LEGACY of FAITH:

THE JOURNEY

Of

Johann Baptiste Tschohl

Josef Tschohl

Ignatius (Ignaz) Tschohl

Bernhard (Louis) Tschohl

John Baptiste (Johnnie) Tschohl

Date:	February 11, 1855
Origin:	Balzers, Liechtenstein
Route:	Le Havre, France
	New Orleans, Louisiana, USA
	Guttenberg, Iowa, USA

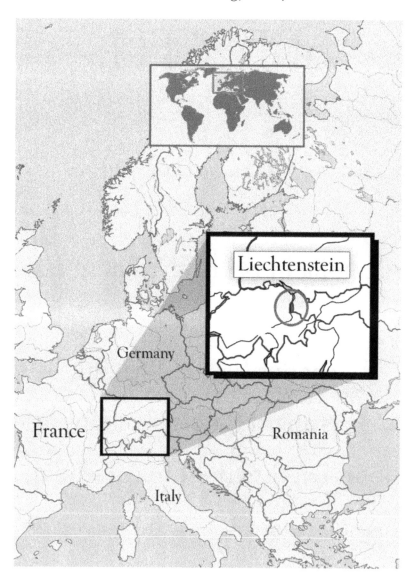

TIMELINE

Johann Baptiste Tschohl	Year	World
	1803	Louisiana Purchase
	1833	End of the Black Hawk Wars. Iowa opens up to settlers.
	1843	Western Settlement Society purchases land in Prairie La Porte.
Johann Tschohl's 3 daughters, along with Franz Michael Vogt travel to Gutenberg as the first group from Liechtenstein.	1845	
	1846	12.28, Iowa becomes a state.
Scholastika comes to Amerika.	1850	John Leanard of the Western Settlement Society purchases Block 76. Donates Lot 1 and 2 for a church. The first mass in held in 1851.
	1853	A new brick structure is build for St. Mary's Church.
	1853	Father Winegar, a renowned Missionary, blesses a cross at the Original St. Mary's Church, and 'Cross of Light' appears in the sky midday for 45 minutes.
2.11, Tschohls depart Balzers, Liechtenstein.	1855	
4.21, Tschohls arrive in New Orleans.	1855	
5.8, Tschohls arrived in Guttenberg.	1855	
	1860	Clemens Kappen builds the first hearse in Clayton County.
10.18, John Baptist Tschohl joins the war as a paid replacement.	1864	

CHAPTER ONE

LIECHTENSTEIN

The gravediggers threw the brittle crusts of dirt, frozen from the oncoming winter, onto the wooden coffin. The many attendees of the funeral pulled their long wool coats tightly about them as they failed in their valiant attempt to keep out the bitter winds. Johann, whose beloved wife was just laid to rest, stood stoically by his sons. The four boys stood like sentinels around the lonely grave. Johann's collar flapped helplessly in the breeze as his two youngest sons each clutched one of his hands. Johnnie was just six years old. Though Bernhard was fifteen, this was his first funeral, at least of someone he cared for so much.

Johann felt their fear for what lay ahead and dared not take the selfish time to adjust his coat or scarf. He looked to the row of tombstones that marked his first wife and their children, of whom God had already called home. "How many more of my family will pass before my demise?" he thought. "Please, Lord, watch over and keep safe my daughters who have gone to Amerika. I pray that I may see them again."

Johann, who fathered eleven children overall with two different wives, knew death as much as anyone. Its bitter sting was plentiful. Its target spared no house or family during this time of immense need. Of his eleven children, three failed to reach even one month of age before the Lord called them home. No one revered and feared the Lord more than Johann Baptiste Tschohl, but each death sprouted the same question in his heart, "If the Lord does not make mistakes, then how can a child be given and then taken away so fast? Was the good Lord

1

correcting a mistake? Was there no Lord at all?" He knew not to question God or put him to the test, but these thoughts troubled him. Johann desired nothing less than to trust the Lord with all his heart, soul, and mind, but days like this day severely tested his faith.

The pain of losing a child struck him hard, and Johann had already buried three of his children. His first wife, Katharina Foser, died shortly after she gave birth to her last-born, Bernhard. Her death left Johann with eight surviving children and the tough business of the flour mill and farming. He worked tirelessly to provide for them and the many who endured the tough times in Balzers, Liechtenstein during the 1840s. Many depended on his goodwill for their families' survival. Whether he chose not to charge them for his milling services or provided flour to the hungry for little or nothing, Johann often gave to his community. In each eye of those at the funeral, Johann recognized a friend from the town, or at the very least, a well-wisher who benefitted from his giving nature.

However, this day, it was not the death of a child or his first wife that brought him again to death's doorway. Three years had passed since his first wife's death before Johann found love again. He married Katharina Frick, a widowed woman whose previous husband had died during the Egyptian-Ottoman War, who came to work for Johann and take care of his growing family. They needed a kind mother, as Johann was a hard man by all measures. He was also self-aware and knew his shortcomings well.

Johann took his position in the community to heart. The responsibility of it all wore on him, and only his deep faith carried him from one day to the next. He thanked the Lord for bringing Katharina into his life when he most needed a partner and deeply loved her. Together, they provided for his children, though his daughters left for Amerika two years into their marriage.

He and Katharina married in 1843, and at the age of forty-five in 1847, she bore Johann a son, John Baptist Tschohl.

Katharina sadly passed on October 26th, 1854, again leaving him alone once again to raise his family.

Katharina was much younger than Johann, and he was certain he would never outlive her. The pain as he watched her pass through her grueling sickness, and then as he buried her this day, wrenched his soul.

"What will we do, father?" Johnnie's innocent little voice lifted to his father's weathered ears.

Johann looked down at his son's tearful face. "Son," Johann consoled, "we will be fine. God has taken your mother, and we could not wish for a better place for her." He tried to comfort his youngest, but it was not his usual position.

Johnnie looked at the coffin, which the gravediggers had already completely covered as they hurried to fill the grave. Johann knew they had other work to do and that the bitter cold pushed them to finish, but he wished they could have waited a bit longer to start their business of filling the hole.

"It is so cold, father. Will mama be cold?" The pain in his Johnnie's voice strained Johann's heart. Though Johann buried many in his time, this was Johnnie's first. He let go of Bernhard's hand and reached for Johnnie's face. He turned the soiled cheeks away from the burial.

"Do you believe in God?" Johann asked. Johnnie could not answer but nodded yes. "If so, then you know your mother's kind soul is with him in Heaven. It is not cold there. It is always like a warm summer day. She is smiling and watching over us. She is praying to God for our lives, just as she did every night. Do you remember her praying for us?"

"Yes, father," Johnnie answered. "I prayed with her."

Johann smiled. "I know you did, and after you were off to bed, I prayed with her, too. God must have needed someone who could pray, and there was no one better."

A slight smile crept onto Johnnie's face.

"What are you thinking of?" Johann asked, intrigued by his son's grin.

3

"Mother is walking through the tall grass and picking flowers for our table on a sunny day. She loved to do that," Johnnie answered happily.

Johann embraced his son. With his other sons Josef, Ignaz, and Bernhard, he turned from the grave to begin their long and lonely walk home. Before he left, Johann received condolences from several families, but three waited until the end.

"We are sorry for your loss. Katharina was a tremendous woman who has no doubt made her way to Heaven," Maria Kaufmann said as she clutched her husband John's hand. She hugged each of the boys in turn, but she took extra time with Johnnie.

"We will talk soon," John said to Johann before he let them pass.

The next family to offer their condolences was the Niggs, Anton, and Thomasia. "Your daughters will be very sad to hear the news. I know it is soon, but if you are going to go to Amerika with us, now is the time," Herr Nigg said as he took Johann's hand.

"Not now, Anton. For God's sake, give him time," Thomasia scolded her husband. She then hugged each of the children and then Johann. "When you are ready, and not a moment sooner."

"Thank you," Johann replied. "It weighs heavily on my mind."

Alois and Theresia Buchel patiently waited in the wings. "I am going back to Gutenberg, but this time I am taking my family with me. It is a beautiful place, and I hope you will go also," Alois said. "There is still time for you to take the same ship, but you will need to make a decision quickly."

"And you believe it is wise for us to do so?" Johann asked.

"Yes. It is a wonderful place, full of opportunity. It will be the last trip I ever make," Alois answered. "The only reason

I came back was to get my family. Gutenberg is a remarkable place for hardworking men like ourselves!"

"Thank you all for what you have done. I will talk with each of you soon," Johann replied. He then turned and walked away with his sons.

"Father," his son Josef began, but Johann cut him short.

"Not now, Josef. Please, give me time to think."

Johann felt his son's despair. Their steps together were heavy as they moved toward an uncertain future. The boys often heard their father talk with the other men of Balzers about traveling to Amerika and whether it was better to stay where they were. The family spoke little as they went and passed the vacant countryside as ghostly specters.

Alois Buchel had recently returned to get his family. Theresia, Johann's oldest daughter, and her husband, Franz Michael Vogt, made the trip in 1845. Maria's sisters Juliana and Franziska also joined her. The fourth sister, Scholastika Appolonisa, left for Amerika in 1850 and made the trip alone.

Johann let Bernhard take Johnnie ahead while he walked with Josef and Ignaz. Johann asked, "Do you boys remember when your own mother passed?"

"Yes, father," Josef answered.

"It was not as cold as today, but it was very tough. Please watch out for Johnnie and Bernhard. Bernhard was just a baby when your mother left us, so Katharina is the only mother he has ever known. These will be tough days for the both of them."

"We will, father," Ignaz assured.

"Katharina was very good to all of us," Josef added. He kicked at a rock as he strolled along.

"What will we do now?" Ignaz ventured.

"We know what you are considering, father," Josef added.

Johann looked to his sons. He wanted to answer, but a lump developed in his throat that did not allow him to speak. He lowered his head and walked away from his oldest children, but he knew he would need to answer the question soon.

They finally arrived at their home. Johnnie looked around the empty house and again broke into tears as he ran to his bed. Bernhard rushed to console him. "What is wrong? Are you hurt?" Bernhard asked.

"I thought mother would be here. I do not know why, but I did. She is gone forever, is she not?" Johnnie confessed to his brother.

"Yes," Bernhard confirmed. "But we are still here, and we will take care of you." Johann was proud of his son, particularly as Bernhard helped with something that would be hard even for him to do.

"Are we going to Amerika?" Josef asked as Johann closed the door. Johann knew the questions would not cease until he answered them.

"Yes," Johann resolutely answered as he sat hard on the old wooden chair. "Ignaz, get the fire going." He then locked eyes with his oldest son, "We are selling everything we have and going to Amerika." He took a drink of his whiskey and then picked up a parchment that lay on the table. The yellowed paper had lain there for well over a year. He looked to Josef and said, "Please read it to me again."

Johann handed the paper to Josef. His hands shook from the sadness of the day's events and from the worry about the path he was about to set forth for them.

Josef took the paper. "Western Settlement Society of Cincinnati. Good earth for sale around the new German city of Gutenberg, Iowa. Farmland is plentiful, a thoroughly German city in the Heart of Amerika." Josef read the paper as he had done a hundred times at anyone's request, and twice that amount for his own satisfaction.

Johann's first wife had refused to go. His second wife dearly desired to leave for a better future. At first, they wanted to wait until Johnnie was older, and then the illness that set in on her in her final years prevented it.

"Is that where Maria and the others are?" Ignaz, aged nineteen, asked. The few letters they received from Johann's daughters had long ago sparked Ignaz's imagination.

"Son, the only thing greater than your interest in going to Amerika is your lack of knowledge about how long and dangerous the trip will be. This is no easy decision," Johann responded. "But yes, that is where they are. According to Alois, they are well-established and living just across the river from Gutenberg. The town is on the banks of a mighty river that divides Amerika in half." Johann saw the excitement in all their eyes as each of his four sons heard the words again.

"Is it bigger than our Rhine?" Bernhard asked. He sat up on the bed with his arm still around Johnnie.

"From what I have learned, it is, but that is hard to imagine. We will see, for we are selling the farm, the flour mill, and all we have. We are going to Amerika, to a place called Gutenberg, Iowa. We will take only what will fit on our wagon." Johann had not said the words before, but in doing so, he felt his strength increase. His son's smiles greeted his message as they were ready for the journey before them. "We will not travel alone, either. The Kaufmanns and Niggs are going with us. If we purchase our tickets in time, we might be on the same ship as the Buchel family."

As their father, resolute in word and deed, said, the remainder of the Tschohl family followed the same path Johann's daughters traveled ten years earlier. Johann said, "Many times, your mother and I marveled at the bravery of our daughters, but especially Scholastika. The letters that have come back to us bring hope for a better life."

"I am excited to see Scholastika again and meet her husband," Josef replied.

"I will be glad to see all of them, too. It has been so long," Johann said. "I admire all of you for your determination. Tomorrow morning, I am taking John Kaufmann and Anton Nigg to purchase our tickets for the voyage."

✝

Johann and his sons set out their things for the sale. Winter was close to over, and four months had passed since they buried Katharina. They were leaving within the week, and all that was left was to sell their belongings.

"I do not want to sell everything!" Johnnie burst into tears. They streamed defiantly down his face. Johann grew tired of his son's hysterics, which happened far too often for his worn patience, but Johnnie seemed helpless in controlling them.

"We cannot take it with us," Ignaz asserted sharply. Johann saw a lack of compassion in Ignaz, and he wished for his son to be better. In truth, the bond between their deceased stepmother and Johnnie made the older boys jealous.

"Watch your temper," Johann warned his middle son. "I have seen this happen too many times before, and I wish to head it off now." It was too late.

"Tell Johnnie to quit whining all of the time. All of us are going through the same thing. He needs to toughen up and quit crying!" Ignaz challenged his father.

Johann gave no ground.

"I do not cry all of the time!" Johnnie bawled as he ran and kicked Ignaz in the shin. Tears of anger streamed down his dirty face as his youthful rage boiled. Before Johann could reach them, Josef grabbed the injured Ignaz while Bernhard corralled the crying Johnnie. Johann's strong voice stopped them cold. "Listen to me carefully," he said. "We have been through too much, and I know this is difficult for you, but we are leaving here forever, and we will do so with dignity! We will not spend our final moments in Balzers bickering!" He then looked directly at Josef. "When Ignaz and I return, all of these things need to be placed outside for the sale."

"Yes, father," Josef dutifully answered. He let go of his brother. Ignaz shot a stern look of disdain at Johnnie before he turned to follow his father out the door. Johann stalked past the barn that needed repair and into the open fields that were still a month away from planting. He kept walking, and Ignaz submissively followed at a safe distance. Johann resisted the urge to reach for a switch to discipline his son, which he was certain Ignaz expected.

Johann turned; his face wrenched not in anger but twisted by an immense sadness. "Ignaz, I have buried two wives and three children, which we will soon leave behind. I have worked tirelessly to provide my family with their basic needs while I also helped as many as I could through these tough times—" Johann stopped. He was unable to finish his thoughts. He then gathered himself and began anew. "Son," his shaky voice quivered as his lower jaw struggled to hold tight, "you have had an unfair life. Your mother passed when you were young, and I have driven you and your brothers hard. I wish that you had a better person than I to model compassion for others. Your mother would have done a marvelous job. She loved you so, as she did your brothers and sisters, but you were her favorite. Johnnie was his mother's favorite, and she had a hard time relating to the rest of you. She tried hard. God bless her soul." Johann struggled to continue.

Ignaz's tears began to flow. Johann never allowed his children to see this side of him before, and Ignaz did not know what to do. To Johann's surprise, Ignaz walked to his father and embraced him, something he had not done since he was just a small boy.

Johann accepted the embrace, calmed his voice, and said, "I need your help to get through this. I know God has a plan for our family other than to bury the ones we love. He will guide us and allow us to prosper." Johann stepped back and looked into his son's eyes.

Ignaz looked directly back as a grown man. "I will do what you need and take care of my brothers, especially Johnnie. I am sorry."

"Great things lay ahead for us, but we must stick together. Trust in God, and trust in me," Johann encouraged.

"Yes, father. I know you are right," Ignaz answered. They walked back to their home, but this time alongside each other as men.

When they returned, everything was set out, just as Johann had instructed. The Kaufmanns and Niggs had arrived with a few last things of their own to sell. The first people from Balzers came to purchase their desires. Josef, Bernhard, and Johnnie stared as Ignaz, and their father walked up. Ignaz wiped away the last of the tears from his eyes. Johann could tell from his son's looks that they believed he whipped Ignaz. It saddened Johann that he never gave them a reason to suspect anything else. Johnnie held his backside as if to protect himself from what he believed might come his way. Johann smiled at the three and put them at ease. He then patted Ignaz on the back as he addressed the newly-arrived people who arrived at the sale.

"Welcome!" he boasted. "Please look over our items, and make sure to look in the barn as well. The home, the barn, and the land itself have already been purchased. Only the items we have laid out before you and in the barn remain for sale."

An older man, Herr Ledermann, who was rich in spirit but poor in every other measurable way, talked to the heads of the three departing families. "Herr Tschohl, Herr Kaufmann, and Herr Nigg; is it true that you are going to the Amerika? And if so, just what do you hope to find there that you cannot find here? Herr Buchel came back, and you will too!"

The questioning of Johann's intentions did not sit well with him, but he was quite used to the challenges. Johann Tschohl was a well-known businessman and an upstanding member of the community. "The good people of Balzers see your decision to leave as traitorous!" Herr Ledermann accused.

"Herr Ledermann, Herr Buchel left again last week to return to Gutenberg, in Amerika, in case you did not know."

"Is that true?" Herr Ledermann asked.

Johann then continued his retort. "Despite the constant wars our nation seems intent on fighting, the yearly flooding that is determined to ruin my fields, the growing taxes that make running my flour mill impossible, and the death that is hell-bent on stalking every woman I have ever loved, I do want to stay here. However, the grim possibilities for my children's futures drive my need to find them a better one. That, Herr Ledermann, is exactly what I intend to do." Johann stared into the old man's eyes, but Herr Ledermann carried no fear of Johann.

"Well then, Herr Tschohl," Herr Ledermann began as he glanced at his sons for a moment. He then looked back to Johann and leaned in close to him as he shielded his words from his family. "I do not want the others to hear, but do you have room for one more?"

"Pardon, Herr Ledermann, but would that not make you a traitor also?" Johann chided.

"Well, yes," Herr Ledermann began, "but a living traitor is better than a dead loyalist. Do you not agree?"

Johann laughed and looked to see the man was quite serious. "Herr Ledermann, I have enough money only for my family. I am sorry." The old man scowled at Johann and stamped his cane into the hard ground. Without another word, he turned and began his long walk home. Soon others came to the sale, some to wish the three families Godspeed as they departed, while others only came to find a needed item. Being of some wealth compared to the others of Balzers, many were eager to see what was for sale.

Each of the boys cringed as the people bought their things. The people bargained for every item the boys held dear, though Johann did his best to get the highest amount. Eventually, everything went, though most of it for only half of what the boys thought it should. All that remained was the luggage, clothes, and food that Johann and his boys would take with them. Before the sun went down on their final day in Balzers, everyone and everything was gone. Johann walked into his home to see that Ignaz had started a fire in the hearth. The kerosene lamp sold first, so the fire provided the only light they would have for the evening. It was a dim scene.

"Fear not, sons, as the Lord is on our side. I believe He desires for our family to be together again and to thrive in the new world." Johann knew his sons were worried, and he did his best to comfort them.

As they did every night, the five knelt in a circle to pray the rosary. Before they began, Johann spoke again. "We are going on a journey to the United States of Amerika. If God is willing, we will see your sisters again and start a new life. I pray that each of you does great things in this new world. It is a place where your hard work and intent will carry you as far as you desire. Do not let the sadness of our parting overshadow the excitement of our adventure." Johann looked to each of his sons, who listened intently to his every word.

"Yes, father," they answered, each in turn. Johann led them in their prayers, and they settled on the hardwood floor with just a few blankets. They rested for the night as dreams of their journey and the new world danced in their minds.

CHAPTER TWO

AUF WIEDERSEHEN

Johann opened his eyes to see that his sons were awake before he was, perhaps for the first time. They tidied up from their sleep, dressed, and readied for their departure. Josef cooked their last meal over the fire, and the Tschohl family ate their final breakfast in Liechtenstein.

"The horse and wagon are ready, father," Ignaz proudly stated.

"And our bags will be loaded soon," Bernhard added. "The salted pork, sauerkraut, potatoes, flour, and apples are packed. We will have plenty of all of them to last for several months."

"And I am going to clean the plates," Johnnie piped in. "I want to help too!"

Johann looked at his sons again as he ate his last bites of food. "I am proud of all of you," he said, and then he put his hand on Johnnie's leg. "Johnnie, how about I help you do the plates so we can get going?"

Johnnie laughed, "I have never seen you help do the wash before. Mother would like to see this!" The boys laughed at the thought and grabbed their few remaining things. After the plates were clean and loaded for the trip, they took one last look around their empty home.

"This is the only home I have ever known. It never seemed so large," Josef said as he looked around. Johann set his hand on Ignaz's shoulder, and the boys bowed their heads. "Dear God, protect us and keep our three families safe. We also pray for the departed souls of our mothers and the safety of

Theresia, Juliana, Franziska, and Scholastika. Let them know we are coming to see them and watch over all of us until we arrive."

"Let us go," Ignaz compelled as he stood in the open door. "I am too excited to wait any longer!"

As they clambered up and into the wagon, Johnnie questioned Ignaz. "What are my sisters like? Will they like me?"

Ignaz thought for a moment and then responded, "I had forgotten that you were born after the girls left. Only Scholastika has seen you, and you were just a baby. They are all very nice and are very much like your mother."

Johann smiled proudly at Ignaz as he heard the discussion. Ignaz continued, "They will love you, just as all of us do." He put his arm around Johnnie, who fidgeted nervously.

Many of the residents of Balzers waved at them as they traveled through the town one last time, but several refused.

"Father, why do some of them not wave at us?" Bernhard asked.

"They fear us. The well-wishers are content where they are and wish us to find the same contentment wherever we choose. To the rest, we only serve to remind them of what they could do if only they dared to act. They are sad about their situation and would rather we stay here and shared in their sadness. We will not do that."

Then they came upon the home of Herr Ledermann, the man from the sale the day before. The carriage of the undertaker sat outside, and Johann pulled over. A man came to the wagon.

"Herr Ledermann has finally left this earth. He would advise you to stay here, Herr Tschohl, and avoid death on this ill-fated journey!" The man's warning stare and raised brow met Johann's determined eye.

The hostile words stung the boys' ears. "I did not consider that we could die on this trip," Bernhard uttered to Ignaz.

Johann's deep laugh stopped the man's tempered look. "I doubt it," he answered sharply. "Just yesterday, Herr Ledermann begged to go with us!" Johann then reached inside his pocket, pulled out a coin, and then flipped it to the man. "Make sure Herr Ledermann is buried well. It looks as if he escaped Balzers the same day we did."

"Ha!" Johann barked as he cracked the whip and urged his horses forward. They rode away from the scene, and Johnnie scrambled out of Ignaz's arms to sit just behind his father. "Are we going to die?" he asked hysterically.

Johann chose his words carefully. His sons listened intently. "Yes, Johnnie, we are all going to die. I do not know when, but we are going to die someday. My only question to all of you is, are we going to live?"

"We *are* living," Josef answered. "These past few days, you have been acting strangely, father."

Johann smiled, "You boys have been through a lot, but I have as well. These events have changed me, Josef." Johann scanned the town as they passed through. Every sad face buoyed his confidence in what they were doing. "We are alive, but so are the people back there who did not wave. But are they living? Those people are too scared to take the steps that lay squarely before them and beckon them ahead. Those who lack the courage to seek their happiness are not living. They are merely alive. Herr Ledermann wanted to live, and he desired adventure. But he had neither the health nor wealth to pursue it. To him, death was a welcome blessing."

The boys heard their father and knew he was right. Soon the wagon reached the edge of town. That is where the Kaufmanns and Niggs waited. Johann waved to his friends as they rode up, eager to depart. Johann told them there was one thing he needed to do before they left, and it was something Johann did not look forward to. The only sounds were the horses' feet and the wagon's wheels. Johann pulled them to a stop and locked the wagon's wheel. He slowly climbed down, and his sons hesitantly followed. Ignaz lifted Johnnie out and set him on the ground.

"Please give us a moment," Johann asked of the other two families. They opened the gate to a barren, tomb-marked yard. Row upon row of etched stones lined it from end to end. Johann did not enjoy visiting the cemetery. The pain for each of his beloved that he buried there was too much. He never wanted his children to see him cry, so the only time he visited the cemetery was late at night. He made those sad pilgrimages alone. Other than rare occasions, he only returned when he needed to bury another family member.

Johann led his reluctant followers slowly through the quiet cemetery until they found the marker for his wives' graves. Buried next to both of them were their three siblings, all in a row.

The three older boys stood in silence and stared at the grave of their mother, Katharina Foser Tschohl.

"I do not know what to feel," Bernhard said as he looked to Josef. "I do not even know what she looked like."

Josef placed his arm around Bernhard, "You do not have to feel anything. Just pray for her and know that she loved you."

"I feel bad because I miss Johnnie's mother more," Bernhard admitted.

"You do not have to feel bad. Our mother would not want that. She would have been very thankful that we had two mothers who cared for us," Josef consoled.

"Your mothers would be very proud of each of you," Johann said.

They looked at the tombstones of their two brothers and sister, all of whom died within months of their birth. Every family knew how precious life was, for each bore the scars of deaths rendered far too soon.

"Where is Johnnie?" Ignaz asked as he turned to look for his brother. "What are you doing?"

"I am coming!" Johnnie yelled. His handed-down pant legs fell past his boots as they always did, and Johnnie tripped as he ran. His armful of carefully-picked rocks scattered onto the weeds and dead grass.

"Now is not the time!" Johann scowled as he picked up his son by the arm. Then he saw Johnnie's face and the tears that streamed down it. "Are you hurt?"

"No, I had to get something for mama!" Johnnie answered as he pulled away from his father and scrambled to pick up the rocks again. His brothers watched as Johnnie feverishly picked up every single rock, even as several more fell again. He then bolted past them and perfectly laid each one in front of the marker of his mother's grave. He also placed several on the graves of the babies who passed. As he dashed back to the rest that fell, he told them in his trembling voice, "She should have flowers, but I could not find any. I picked the best rocks I could find. I hope she is not disappointed." The boys stood in awe of their little brother, and Bernhard went to help Johnnie with the rest.

As Bernhard put his rocks down next to Johnnie's, his younger brother stopped him. "No, those are for *your* mother," he said. Bernhard stopped and stared at Johnnie. Johnnie's kind gesture to think of both mothers took Johann by surprise. Bernhard carefully placed the rocks on his mother's grave, just as Johnnie had done. Bernhard then put his arm around Johnnie as they stopped and prayed.

Johann waited a few moments in silence. He cherished the memories of both women he loved dearly. Both had given him so much. "It is time to go," he said. He then turned and walked to the wagon, with Ignaz and Josef following directly behind.

"Thank you for getting the rocks for my mother," Bernhard said. Johnnie smiled back at his brother. Then he reached down and took one of the rocks. "I am going to keep this one with me always so I can remember her."

Bernhard smiled as Johnnie got up and raced back to the wagon, rock in hand. After taking a few steps, Bernhard stopped and turned towards the grave. He also took one of the stones from each tombstone and kissed both markers before returning to the wagon.

The other two families waited patiently for the Tschohls. "It is time to go," Josef Nigg announced, "but I think we should pray first. Please take a hand." The three families all reached for another's hand. Together with Anton and Thomasia Nigg were their older children, Anne, and Alois, both over the age of twenty. Also with them were their younger children Johann, Maria, Franz Michael, and Crezentia. John and Maria Kaufmann brought their two younger sons, Josef and Johann. Together they prayed for their safety on the long trip, for the safety of the Buchel family who left before them, for their relatives who stayed in Balzers, and for those who departed for Amerika long before them. After the short prayer, they mounted their wagons and prepared for the long ride to Le Havre, France.

The horses and wagons jolted forth at the crack of the whip, and the echo carried off into the leafless trees. Anton Nigg led the way as the Tschohls, and their companions left Balzers and never returned.

CHAPTER THREE

AMIENS

The road to Le Havre, France, was long, and for the unprepared traveler, quite dangerous. Hordes of hopeful travelers who sought a better life in the new world frequented the main roads. So, too, did the unscrupulous ruffians who sought to take advantage of the weak or dumb. Johann Tschohl, along with the three families, were neither.

Though Johann expected the border soldiers in France to check their wagon thoroughly, their demeanor to him, his children, and their friends still ruffled him.

"Des billets!" the soldier barked to Johann, who reached the checkpoint first. "Des billets!"

Johann knew enough French to understand the request. He reached inside his coat, pulled out the tickets, and handed them down to the guard. The guards were not supposed to allow immigrants to cross the border without reason. The intent of the journey was obvious to the guards, as so many passed this point every day. The vast majority headed to the ports of Bremen or Hamburg in Germany, but Johann chose to depart from Le Havre, France.

The guard handed the tickets back as he sneered at Johann, "Aller, poubelle!"

Johann tipped his hat to the man and smiled. The guard laughed as Johann roused the horses, and the wagon jutted forth again. The guards treated the Kaufmanns and Niggs similarly.

"What did he say, father?" Johnnie asked.

"Have a good journey," Johann answered. Johnnie turned and waved at the guards, who did not return the gesture.

"Is that really what he said?" Josef asked as he leaned in close to Johann.

Johann simply shrugged his shoulders, "I honestly have no idea what he said."

"Why do they look at us so poorly?" Josef asked.

"They do not consider us well. You must remember that we have fought many wars with the French. They do not want us in their land, and to be honest, I would not want them in ours. One of the reasons we are leaving is that I fear more wars will come, and I do not want my sons dying in any of them. Do not be surprised that we are treated so, and do not expect it to change. Alois warned us that it would be like this."

"What if we did not have tickets? Would they have shot us?" Bernhard asked.

"No, I do not think so. If we did not have tickets, I am sure that they would let us go if I paid them enough. In all of my years running the mill, I have learned many lessons. One of those lessons is that people are greedy. Every transaction is a deal, and each side wants to feel as though they have won." Johann enjoyed telling his sons his thoughts on life, which he never felt he had time to do before.

A month had passed since they first left Balzers, and the three families were deep into France but still a few days away from their destination. While many who saw them looked down on the travelers, others showed them great kindness. A clean barn was a far better place to sleep than the covered wagon, especially during the cold and damp spring.

Johann eagerly exchanged hard work for hot meals and a dry place to sleep. Even the French, who hated Germans like no other, needed help getting things done. The Niggs and Kaufmanns fared similarly. However, on the trip, each child of all three families seemed determined to get sick.

"I am tired of riding in this wagon!" Johnnie squirmed as they began another long day of travel.

"Quiet, son. Bernhard feels poorly," Johann said as he reached for Johnnie. "Maybe you should sit with me."

"Yes, I love to sit by you and Josef in the front," Johnnie answered.

Ignaz leaned forward and asked his father, "Should I give Bernhard more of the whiskey?"

"Yes, but not too much. Cover him to keep him warm." Johann feared losing Bernhard and hoped his fever would break soon. Maria and Thomasia both took turns tending to Bernhard, but they had their own young children to care for as well. The cold journey with far fewer hot meals and warm places to sleep than were needed took its toll. "I am just glad you have not gotten sick," Johann said to Johnnie. Then to Josef, he said, "We need to find an inn and get a warm place for Bernhard to sleep."

"Do we have the money for that?" Josef asked.

"Quit worrying about the money!" Johann snapped. He felt Johnnie go rigid next to him. He remembered his own father's temper and how frightened he was of the man. Johann did not want his sons feeling the same way about him. He placed his arm around Johnnie and grabbed Josef's arm to reassure him. "Yes, we will be fine after we sell the horses and the wagon. You must trust me. We will have plenty to get us to Gutenberg. If we need to, we will work our way there as we go and earn what we need, just as we always have."

Josef smiled at his father. "We will make it."

Johnnie relaxed as the two softened up, and he leaned into his father's warm coat.

Tickets for the trip cost more than Johann guessed, as did the taxes and many other things on the way. "I am accustomed to growing my food and selling the surplus to others. Purchasing it on the road is far more costly than I thought it would be," Johann said to Josef. "I am glad our only real need is fresh meat."

Nonetheless, he needed to get Bernhard a warm place to sleep, even if he needed to pay for it. "Wrap him in the blankets and keep the cold wind from his face." Johann prayed to Jesus and both of Bernhard's mothers to look over him and keep him safe.

Before the end of the day, and as Bernhard faded fast, they came upon Amiens, France. The large city was still three days from Le Havre. As they approached the city's limits, and just outside the city wall, they stopped at the first inn they came to. Families of all levels of wealth lined the road, and each hoped to secure a place for the evening.

"This will do," Johann gruffed as he pulled the wagon to a stop. Johann pushed the horses hard on the day's trip, and they were ready for rest, food, and water.

Josef asked, "Are you sure, father? This place looks very nice. Did you see the carriages and teams of horses?"

"Son, let me worry about such things. Just look after your brothers." Johann's words bit hard on Josef, especially after their conversation earlier. Johann did not let his sons know their level of wealth, which far exceeded the carriage style in which they rode. Johann was a humble man. He did not wish to flash his money in Balzers and certainly would not do it for strangers on this journey. He was, however, annoyed at Josef's unending concern that they would not have enough money.

"Wait here. I will be right back," Johann barked as he jumped down. He waved to Anton and John to join him. He then pulled his hat over his head tightly and adjusted his suspenders as he was determined to make a favorable impression. Several hands tried to work many carriages and horses, but they failed miserably in their haphazard attempt. The boss ordered them about, and the Tschohl boys laughed at the scene that played out before them.

Johann stopped his **walk** to take a hard look back at his sons, who straightened up quickly. A horse reared and knocked down one of its handlers, and the boys could not contain their laughter again.

Their merriment quickly ended as their father strode up stern and confident. He took the reins of the wildest horse from the inept handler, and he promptly corralled the stallion. His strong hand and gruff voice obliged the horse to fall in line. What started as hostility toward the horse quickly turned into nurturing whispers from man to beast. Anton and John did likewise to the other wild steeds, and soon the three rugged men took control and began clearing the horses and wagons. The crowd watched in amazement, and several of the onlookers cheered for the victors. The sons did not cheer, as they had seen their father take charge many times.

Johann handed the reins over to John and tracked toward the boss, and he pulled the man aside. The man listened intently to Johann. The two quickly struck a deal, which they sealed with a sturdy handshake.

"What is father speaking with him about?" Ignaz asked. "I thought we were going to stay here."

"Father knows what he is doing," Josef replied sternly.

"Now you sound like him," Ignaz jeered.

Johann quickly turned back to his sons. "It looks like it is time for us to go to work," Josef said as he stood up from his seat.

"How do you know?" Johnnie asked.

As Johann got within range, his orders fell hard and fast. "Josef, pull our wagons back there next to the barn. You and Ignaz get Bernhard comfortable and hurry up about it! We need to get these horses and carriages in order. Johnnie, you start with the carriages back there and get them cleaned up. You will get lashings in front of God and everyone if your brothers need to go over them again!" Johann quickly assumed his old hard-driving self. His boys responded, and each jumped to their assigned task.

23

Anton's son Alois helped with the horses, and his daughter Anne helped Johnnie clean the carriages. The wives took care of the little ones and put their things in the barn.

The boys did not hesitate or question. "You know what 'in front of God and everyone' means, right?" Josef asked Johnnie as they crossed paths.

"Yes!" Johnnie meekly answered as he ran his hand over his backside. "All too well!"

In no time, Anton and John took the horses and wagons to the back of the Inn, where Josef lined them up next to the barn. Ignaz watered and fed the horses, and Johnnie cleaned and shined the carriages, with Anne's help. Alois helped Bernhard to the barn and made a bed in a hay pile that lay just inside the door.

Josef barked at the hired hands. "You are dismissed! Maybe you should go help in the house or somewhere else, but stay out of our way!"

The hands stood dumbfounded, but Johnnie shooed them off. "You cannot even clean the carriages properly! Move on, or I shall whip you right here in front of God and everyone!" The three brothers laughed as the hands waddled off. The Tschohl brothers had thoroughly embarrassed them.

Bernhard slept uneasily in the hay, but he slowly began to warm in the dry bedding. The boss Johann spoke to was the keeper of the inn. Johann's offer of help in exchange for a place to stay and hot meals for the three families proved to be an excellent deal for the innkeeper. It did not take the men long to clear the horses and carriages, and shortly after, the keeper came out with his two men who had attempted to handle the horses before Johann, John, and Anton arrived. The Innkeeper changed their roles from outside help to waiters. Each grimaced as they handed the hot plates to the three smirking boys and two men. The keeper did the same to Johann.

"I thank you for your help!" the keeper said. Then a girl appeared from the back of the inn, and she carried yet another plate. "Father," she said to the keeper, "did you say there was one more?" Josef and Ignaz quickly noticed how fetching she was. They hurriedly arranged their shirts and trousers, which their father saw and smiled. Josef spat in his hand and rubbed it through his hair to smooth it out. Johann thought back to when he was their age and the first time he saw Katharina Foser.

"Bernhard is in the barn and not feeling well at all," Johann said. "Please leave the plate—"

Before he could say another word, the girl rushed past him and into the barn with the warm plate of food. Josef and Ignaz quickly scampered behind her, and each fought to be first. Ignaz won.

"Can I go, too?" Johnnie asked.

"No, you should just stay right here. I think Bernhard is getting plenty of attention." Johann smiled at his youngest. The girl's father grimaced. Johann said to him, "Your daughter is beautiful."

"Thank you. Her name is Lucienne, and she takes after her mother; God rest her soul," the innkeeper answered. The pain was easy to see on his face. He wiped his dark memories away and extended his hand to Johann, "I am Guion, the Innkeeper."

Johann accepted the invitation. "I am Johann. We are from Balzers, Liechtenstein, and on our way to Amerika. This is Herr John Kaufmann and Herr Anton Nigg. I am sorry for your loss. I have buried two wives, so I know your pain well." Guion accepted the kind words.

The girl's urgent voice interrupted them. "Father, he needs medicine! Can you bring some?"

"We have no medicine for him," Maria admitted, her concern evident.

Josef yelled to his father, "Bernhard is sweating fiercely!"

Johann quickly walked past the others as he feared the loss of another child. He saw his sick son surrounded by the other three. Sweat ran off his skin. Johann moved Josef and Ignaz aside and placed his hand on Bernhard's head. "Bernhard, can you hear me?" Johann asked, but Bernhard did not respond.

"We need to get him out of this barn and to a real bed," Lucienne insisted.

Johann ordered his sons, "Get him up. He cannot stay here any longer." He was hard to grasp, as sweat had drenched his shirt. Guion rushed back to them with a small box. He set it down for Lucienne, and she quickly opened it and looked for what she wanted.

"Where is the willow bark?" she mumbled to herself before she found her item. She looked at Josef. "Fetch me water, please."

Josef ran to the well and quickly hoisted a bucket of water. A wooden cup hung there. He filled it and ran back to the barn. Lucienne took the cup and mixed in willow bark.

"What is that for?" Johnnie inquired with concern.

Lucienne smiled at the little boy. "This is willow bark. It will ease his fever."

Johann lifted his son's head, and Lucienne poured a small amount of the drink into Bernhard's mouth. "He needs a warm bed, father," Lucienne lamented. "He will die out here in the cold!"

"We are full, dear. I am sorry, but I cannot make someone leave," Guion said.

"Then he shall have my bed," Lucienne answered defiantly, as she was determined to get Bernhard inside. Before Guion could argue, Lucienne moved forward with her plan. "Can you help me, please?" she asked Josef.

"Thomasia," Maria interjected, "please look after mine, and I will make sure Bernhard is taken care of."

"Of course. We shall also pray for him," Thomasia answered as she pulled the younger kids into the barn.

26

Johann, Josef, and Ignaz hoisted Bernhard and hurried him across the yard to the backside of the Inn. They followed Lucienne as she led them straight to her room. She went to the bed, moved a dress to the side, and withdrew the covers as the boys set Bernhard on the bed. She removed his boots and socks, rolled up her sleeves, and went to work. Maria helped her as they tried their best to save Bernhard.

"Should we cover him up?" Johnnie asked.

Lucienne bent down to address him, "Not until I clean him up a bit."

Johnnie's eyes widened, and he looked hard at his father. "She is going to see him—"

Josef covered Johnnie's mouth quickly, which Johann appreciated.

"Johann, all of you should leave. We will take good care of Bernhard," Maria said as she shooed them out. They did as ordered and stepped out into the hallway.

"Boys, that is Lucienne in there with Bernhard, and this is her father, Guion," Johann said. He then turned to Guion, "These are my boys. Josef, Ignaz, Johnnie, and the one in the bed is Bernhard. How can we repay you?" Johann asked. "We will work for as long as is needed to cover the cost."

"Please continue to help with the horses and carriages, and make sure they are ready in the morning. After that, Lucienne will bring you breakfast. That will repay us for our services, yes?" Guion asked.

Johann accepted the offer and thanked Guion. Lucienne stepped into the hallway to fetch some warm water. She said to Johann as she left, "There is one more thing you will need to do. Start a fire near the barn and boil three large tubs of water for bathing. One is for the men, one for the women and children, and one is for your clothes. You all smell horrible, though I doubt the night in the barn will help any." Her sharp words were without humor.

Johann smiled. "You remind me of my first wife. Yes, we shall do that," he conceded. Johann and each of the boys took a moment to thank Guion. They did as Lucienne instructed, and in little time Josef had the water boiling for baths and clothes. Johnnie again marveled as Lucienne walked to the barn with Bernhard's clothes, and she was ready to wash their soiled laundry. Maria and Thomasia helped with the laundry and washing the children, and each thanked Lucienne sincerely. "May God bless you for your help. It is hard to keep clean on such a journey."

"You are going to Amerika, are you not?" Lucienne asked.

"Yes," Maria answered.

"Then may God bless and keep all of you safe throughout," Lucienne replied.

"She saw Bernhard without clothes!" Johnnie whispered to Ignaz, who covered his brother's mouth again, but far too late.

"How is Bernhard?" Ignaz asked Lucienne as he carried their dirty clothes to the three women. Maria immediately reached for the first shirt and dipped it into the hot water. She then rubbed it with the lye soap and scrubbed it on the washing board before she dipped and wrung it again. She did this several times before she hung it to dry.

"He is getting better," Lucienne said with a smile as she continued to wash the clothes. "His fever has broken, and he is resting." Johann and his scantily-clad sons kept the fires going, ever more eager to do so with the cold temperatures and little clothing. They also helped Lucienne clean their clothes, and each took turns bathing as the water cooled quickly. By the time Johann was finally able to take his wash, the water was cold and filthy. The fire and the cold night breeze dried the clothes. Before they bedded down for the night, they were all as clean as they could be.

After they dressed, Johann said to Lucienne, "You speak German well."

"We get a lot of travelers leaving for Amerika. It helps for our business," Lucienne answered.

"Can you tell me what 'aller poubelle' means?" Johann asked. "A French guard said it to me."

Lucienne hesitated. "It is not nice. I would rather not repeat it."

Johann suspected as much. "Please tell me. After all, you did not say it."

Lucienne paused but then offered the meaning. "Go trash," she said.

"The sooner we board the boat, the better," Johann replied. He saw the look on Josef and Ignaz's faces and the bitterness they gained for the people of France.

"Please do not judge us all by the acts of a few," Lucienne asked. "I, too, am French, as is my father. I hope we have cast a better light on our country than others have."

"You have been kind to us, as have many on our journey through France. The soldiers are the ones who have treated us poorly, and that is to be understood. You make a good representation of your country, and we thank you for your kindness," Johann answered.

"Thank you," Lucienne replied. "I am going back inside now to check on Bernhard. I bid you good night."

✝

"Did we really smell that badly?" Johnnie asked his father. "I did not notice it at all."

"Yes!" Maria and Thomasia answered at the same time.

Johann smiled back as he thought of the many baths orchestrated by his two previous wives. "Women have a way of knowing such things. It is best to trust them and do as they bid you," Johann explained. Johann took a moment to pray for his departed wives and the health of his ailing son. He also prayed the trying times weren't a sign from God that they were going against His will. Lastly, he thanked God for the people who were helping them on their way and for the Kaufmanns and Niggs who traveled with them. Just before he fell asleep, Johann again set his mind to the task of bringing his family together once more in Gutenberg. He went to sleep, hoping Bernhard would be better in the morning.

CHAPTER FOUR

LUCIENNE

Bernhard stirred. Even before he opened his weary eyes, he knew his fever was gone. Then he noticed the soft sensation of the hand that held his. "Mother?" he asked softly. He thought he was still dreaming.

"No, Bernhard. I am Lucienne." The voice was pleasant, but the answer was completely unexpected.

Bernhard jolted awake and sat up quickly. Too quickly. Blood rushed to his head. That, combined with the vision of the beautiful girl before him, was far too much for him.

Lucienne held his hand tightly and placed her other hand on his. "Are you feeling better?" she asked and then reached to touch his head.

Bernhard knew not why, but he leaned away, which stopped her reach.

"I am sorry. Have I startled you?" Lucienne asked.

She was the loveliest girl Bernhard had ever seen, and the sound of her voice was like that of the most beautiful song to reach his unworthy ears. "No! I mean, y–yes," Bernhard stammered. He gathered himself, took a deep breath, and then tried to speak again. "No, you did not startle me. And yes, I think I am feeling better," Bernhard explained as he slid back down into the bed. The waking dream before him owned his thoughts.

"May I check your temperature?" Lucienne said as she locked onto his gaze.

"Yes," Bernhard bashfully approved, as he was eager to feel her touch.

Lucienne reached over him and placed her hand on his forehead. The sickly sweat from the day prior appeared to melt from him. Her hand was so soft. Bernhard closed his eyes. He was determined to remember that feeling for the rest of his days.

After a few moments, Lucienne removed her hand and leaned toward Bernhard again while still holding his hand. "You seem to have recovered nicely. I would think, after a few days, you shall be good as new." Bernhard did not hear a word she said as he intently studied every curve and contour of her face. The sparkle in her eye lit a fire in his heart and flooded his body. "You were quite sick when they brought you in here," Lucienne explained.

"The last I remember; I was carried into the barn. Where are my brothers and my father?" Bernhard had forgotten until that moment the journey they were on and his family altogether.

"They are in the barn. Your family has been very helpful in taking care of the horses and carriages. Would you like something to eat?" Lucienne asked nicely.

Bernhard's hunger rushed forward at the mention of food. "Yes, please! And if you do not mind, where are my clothes?" Bernhard also just realized he only wore a shirt.

Lucienne smiled at him again, and Bernhard noticed her blush a beautiful pink hue. "I shall get you some breakfast. The rest of your clothes are over there. I will return in a short while." Lucienne flitted out of the room and closed the door softly.

"Wait!" Bernard called. "What is your name?"

She opened the door again. "I am Lucienne, and I have already told you that once! And you are Mr. Louis Bernhard Tschohl, and you and your family are on your way to Amerika. Your little brother told me everything about you. I shall return soon." With another smile that lingered on her pretty face, she whisked out of the room and closed the door. Her beauty and charm entranced Bernhard, and he had no desire to leave in the least. He slowly stood and dressed. The fresh smell of his clothes told him they were clean, and for the first time in a long time, with soap.

The door opened behind him far sooner than he expected. "Lucienne," he said as he whirled around, but Josef's mocking voice slapped him hard.

"No, I am not Lucienne," Josef said. Bernhard's disappointment at the gruff reply quickly turned as his brothers and father walked in. He was happy to see them and noticed the relief on their faces that he was awake.

"How are you feeling?" Johann asked.

"I am much better," Bernhard answered.

Johann heard enough and replied, "Good, then we must be going. It will take a tight schedule for us to catch our ship on time. We do not want to miss it." Bernhard was not as eager to leave as before. He felt silly for having such strong feelings for a girl he just met, for he did not even know if she felt the same.

Lucienne brought Bernhard's food in. Guion was right behind her, as he also came to check the health of the young man. "Bernhard, your food is ready. Please eat."

"It is good to see you up, lad!" her father added.

Johann greeted Guion. "I thank you and your daughter for helping us. We have seen several boards on your inn and barn that need tending. The work will take us past midday. Will you accept that in exchange for your help with Bernhard?" Johann asked the innkeeper.

"That would be more than enough. I, too, have seen the need, but I have neither the time nor the skills for such repairs. Thank you," Guion replied.

Lucienne set Bernhard's food down and then whispered to her father. Guion then turned to Johann. "Mr. Tschohl, would you and your family consider staying on with us? You could take care of the animals, carriages, and buildings. With the extra help, I could expand the inn. We could do great business together. What do you say?"

Bernhard watched Lucienne as she stared at him with hopeful eyes, and he was confident she held the same feelings for him as he did her. He thought for a moment that he would not have to find a way to stay behind.

"I thank you for your kind offer, but my four daughters live in Amerika, and that is where we shall go. I promised their dying mother that one day I would make our family whole again, and that is what I intend to do." Johann's fast answer shut the window on their hopes.

Guion smiled and thanked Johann. His look turned as he noticed his daughter's disappointed frown. Lucienne shakily set the tray of food down for Bernhard and hastily left the room. Bernhard watched her go. He desired to follow her, but he was not sure what to do.

Johann looked to his sons and said, "We have work to do, and the sooner we get it done, the sooner we can leave. Bernhard, take your time with your meal and then join us. We will be outside working, and we will need you so we can depart." Johann's stark voice pulled Bernhard from his trance.

"Yes, father," Bernhard answered dutifully. He had never before considered disobeying his father, but perhaps the time was soon to come.

They left, and Bernhard's ravenous hunger from moments ago had vanished. He fiddled with his food as a different desire replaced his appetite for food. Then the door slowly opened again. Lucienne rushed in, much to Bernhard's delight.

"Are you going, too?" her troubled voice asked. She sat next to him and reached for his hand.

"My father has said we are going. He is a man of resolve and is not one to be questioned." Bernhard replied. He set his food aside and stood to talk with her. He then pulled Lucienne to her feet.

"I have spoken with my father, and his offer still stands if any of you want to stay, or if even only one of you wants to stay. Will you please consider it?" Lucienne asked as she reached for Bernhard's other hand.

Bernhard let go, but only to embrace her fully. He had never held a girl before like this. He felt her hold him tightly, and her tears wetted his neck. His new feelings for Lucienne quashed the dread of telling his father he wanted to stay.

"I have only just met you," Bernhard began, "but I do wish to stay here to help you and your father."

Lucienne raised her arms and placed her hands around his neck.

"I will talk to my father," Bernhard whispered to her. His face was very near to hers. The idea of kissing a girl—a girl that wanted to kiss him back—had never entered his mind. He was very close to her, but he dared not kiss her in case he needed to leave her. Bernhard relentingly left Lucienne behind in the empty room. He muttered to himself as he walked down the steps of the inn. "I need to find a way to convince my father to let me stay."

Bernhard went to work. He completely forgot his sickness of the day before. They quickly mended the barn and inn while Anton and John fixed several patches of the roof that would soon give way to the rain. Ignaz readied their horses and wagon, and Johann went to say goodbye to Guion. "Father, can I speak with you?" Bernhard asked.

"It can wait until we are on the road. I had hoped to be on our way by now," Johann answered as he walked past Bernhard.

"No, father, it cannot wait," Bernhard's voice commanded.

Bernhard's determined voice stopped Johann. "What is it, then?" Johann asked. His quick turn, squinted eyes, and tight lips announced his agitation at the further delay.

Bernhard looked at Lucienne. She trembled in the doorway of the inn. Bernhard walked past his father, as he could not address him in front of the others. He was pleased but surprised to hear Johann follow him. Bernhard felt his father's anger. Bernhard led him past his three brothers, who sat on the wagon with a look of dismay on their faces.

Around the corner of the barn and out of sight of the others, Bernhard turned to speak. "Father, I do not wish to go with you and the others." Johann's pained look was difficult for Bernhard to see.

"No, son. I promised your mother that I would get this entire family to Amerika, and that is what I shall do. You cannot stay!" Johann commanded. His jaw quivered.

Bernhard did not back down. "I love you, father, and my brothers and sisters, too, but I wish to stay."

"For a girl? One you just met?" Johann questioned. "Do we mean so little to you that a girl you have known for only one day changes your mind? Get in the wagon, son. We are leaving." Johann turned to walk away. Bernhard refused to follow.

"Why did you let my sisters leave for Amerika?" Bernhard asked. Johann stopped, slowly turned back, and dropped his head. "Did you let them go so they could pursue *their* paths?" Bernhard continued. "Was it so they could reach for *their* dreams? You even let Scholastika go across the ocean on her own. Please, father, I wish to stay and seek my path with Lucienne. Do not make me choose."

Johann looked around the corner at the others who waited by the wagon, which included Guion and Lucienne. He saw Lucienne nervously chewing her nails. Her eyes were swollen and red. Then he looked back at Bernhard, and tears filled his own eyes. "I will not make you choose, Bernhard, but I cannot save you from the choice. We are leaving, and Lucienne is not." He walked to Bernhard and embraced his son. "You are free to make your decision, with my blessing to whichever path you take. But we are leaving for Amerika, immediately."

Bernhard could not believe his ears. He rejoiced for a moment, but then a feeling of trepidation filled him as he considered what was leaving him should he choose to stay.

"What are you going to do?" Johann asked as they turned to walk back to the wagon.

"I do not know," Bernhard solemnly answered. His legs shook, and they were barely able to carry him. "This is the biggest decision of my life, and I only have twenty steps left to figure it out." Johann smiled and placed his arm around his son's broad shoulders.

When they arrived at the wagon, everyone stood to wait for Bernhard's decision. Johann boarded the wagon and sat next to Josef. He was ready to depart. Bernhard walked up to Lucienne. Her teary eyes brightened pleasantly above her welcoming smile. "Lucienne, my father has blessed my decision, whichever I choose."

At Bernhard's first words, Johann said to Josef, "Let us go."

"But father!" Josef protested.

"Go!" Johann ordered. Josef released the wagon's brake and flicked the whip at the horses. The horses surged forth, and the wagon began to roll away. The Kaufmanns and Niggs followed his lead.

Maria Kauffman protested, "Surely we are not..." John held his hand to quell her.

Lucienne threw her arms around Bernhard, "You are staying!"

"Father, wait for Bernhard!" Johnnie squealed. "We cannot leave him!"

Bernhard saw the wagon begin to depart. He looked back to the beautiful girl in his arms. "I cannot leave them. They are my brothers. Thank you for all you have done for me. I shall never forget you."

Lucienne sobbed. Bernhard let her go and took one step to leave. Then, unable to leave without doing so, he turned back and kissed Lucienne deeply. He held her tight as they kissed.

Guion turned away and murmured, "The pain is sharp, but Lucienne will love again."

Filled with overwhelming pain, Bernhard released Lucienne. He grabbed his pack and ran past the first two wagons toward his father's wagon, which still had not traveled far.

"Goodbye, Louis," Lucienne uttered quietly before she withered into her father's soothing arms.

"Wait, father!" Johnnie yelled. "He is coming!"

Johann turned and smiled as his son approached, though he did not allow Josef to slow the wagon.

Bernhard climbed into the back with Ignaz's help. "I am so glad you are back!" Johnnie screamed as he leaped into Bernhard's lap.

Bernhard turned and leaned between Johann and Josef. He read his father's happy smile, but then he looked at Josef. To his surprise, Josef wore a glum look on his face as he ushered the wagon forward.

"What is wrong, Josef? Do you not feel well?" Bernhard asked.

Josef sat up and looked at Bernhard for a moment before he looked back at his father. "Bernhard, you are a dummkopf! I would have stayed!"

Johann smiled but did not reply. Bernhard looked back at the inn and saw Guion consoling Lucienne. He sat back down into the wagon and put his arm around Johnnie. "I shall never forget you, Lucienne," Bernhard said softly.

Johann looked to the road ahead. He then leaned over to Josef and whispered, "I would have stayed, too."

CHAPTER FIVE

LE HAVRE

Johann rode the last few hours of their journey in silence. Though he was glad Bernhard chose to come with them, Johann was uncertain his son made the correct choice. Johann lived long enough to know love was rare, and its power was stronger than any force. He pictured his son as he kissed Lucienne goodbye and knew her pain as they parted. Johann then looked back into the wagon and saw Bernhard staring into the distance. He knew his son's thoughts and prayed that Bernhard had made the correct choice.

Bernhard sat up and leaned toward his father. "I want you to call me Louis from now on. It reminds me of my mother."

"I can do that, son. It will take some reminding, though," Johann replied.

Louis smiled and said, "I want to see Amerika and my sisters again, but I think I shall return here someday."

"That is up to you, Louis," Johann stated. He made sure to say his name correctly. "If you desire, I will take you back there, even now if you like. She seemed like a very nice girl."

Louis smiled, "Yes, she was. There are others, though, right, father?"

"Yes, many more," Johann comforted. "You shall find another. I do not doubt that. So will Lucienne. I promise."

✝

Johann woke early the next morning as a strange smell greeted his nose. Though he had smelled it before, it was one he could not identify right away. As he sat up and took another deep breath, he remembered just what it was.

"What is that smell, father?" Johnnie asked. He looked around the woods as if something would appear.

"It is the smell of the sea," Johann responded as he remembered days long past. "We will be there soon." Johann was happy to continue the journey, but he did not look forward to the long ocean voyage. He spent his entire life on land, save for an occasional fishing trip. He trusted his feet to keep him sturdy, but the journey across the ocean was nothing short of an act of faith. His fear of it prevented him from taking his family across years ago.

"Have you been to the ocean before?" Josef asked as he loaded their things in the wagon.

"Once," Johann said. "When I was young, I traveled with my father to the port of Bremen. It was long ago." Though the boys asked often, Johann was not quick to speak of his youth. He and his father did not get along well, and his father was very tough on him. These brief glimpses into his past were all the boys had to go on.

"But we are going to see it today. Before midday, I would guess we will be in Le Havre, and then we will need to find the docks." Johann ushered the boys back into the wagon, which they had grown to loathe.

They stopped for one last break, and the three fathers huddled together. "We made the journey fairly fast," John said. "We will likely spend a few weeks in Le Havre as we wait for our ship to depart."

"Yes, but anything could have happened on our trip to cause more delays. Thankfully, we only had a few. I would rather wait in Le Havre than to miss our vessel," Johann replied.

"Absolutely," Anton agreed. "Remember, we will need to stay close together as we enter Le Havre. The Surete watch everything closely. We must avoid taking issue with them. Men get killed for that."

"Yes. Alois said that foreigners who travel alone can have bad things happen to them. We need to remain close. I will come in last, but keep watch that we do not get separated," John replied. The three then mounted their wagons for the last leg of the land journey to Le Havre.

"I am tired of riding in this wagon! When will we be in Amerika?" Johnnie whined as Johann whisked the horses into motion.

Johann laughed. His burst of joy was quite unexpected, and it usually made the boys uncomfortable as it happened so seldom. "Johnnie, this trip has only just begun! We will sell the wagon and horses this evening and find a place to stay for a few weeks until our boat departs these shores to Amerika. The trip across the ocean will take a month or more. Then we will spend several more weeks traveling up the Mississippi River. Should we all survive the entire journey, we will end up in our Gutenberg, Iowa. Then, and only then, will we find a place for our new home and finally reunite our family."

The boys in the back kneeled intently as they listened to their father. He spoke of the trip's details seldomly, but when he did, the boys absorbed every word. "The trip across the ocean is going to last a month?" Louis asked as he looked at his brothers in complete awe.

Johann worried that the length of the trip might make Louis rethink leaving Lucienne.

"A month? I cannot be on a boat for that long," Johnnie responded with a disbelieving chuckle.

"A month or more," Johann corrected. He turned so that his sons could see his eyes and ensure they understood that he was not joking. Johnnie's mouth hung wide open. Louis's face was blank and dismayed.

"I am excited about the adventure across the ocean. There is nothing that will stop us from getting to Amerika!" Josef boasted.

"Nothing! Once we arrive, we shall work hard to clear our lands and earn our take. We will have large families and plenty of what we need!" Ignaz added as he dreamed of their futures. "Who lives there now?" he asked.

"It is mostly open land from what I have heard, and free for the taking. I sincerely doubt it is free but cheap at the least. Indians used to live there, but they are mostly gone now." Johann's knowledge of Amerika was limited by what he learned from the few letters from the families who journeyed there before.

"What is an Indian?" Johnnie asked.

"They are the people who lived there before people like us arrived. There is too much land there for them, and they need our help to manage it, I presume," Johann replied.

"Well then, they will be glad when we arrive," Ignaz boasted. He seldom showed excitement about things, so Johann noticed. "No one will be able to clear the land as fast as we can! We will build another mill and start over. As Louis gets older, we will start a large farm and mill flour and lumber. Is that not right, father?"

Johann smiled, "Yes, that is correct, Ignaz. You pulled the words right from my dreams."

"Well, what am I going to do?" Johnnie interjected. "You are leaving me out of everything!"

"For a little while longer, you will be too young. But when the time comes, you shall take your place and start a farm, work at the mill, or do whatever your heart calls you to do, son. We are going to Amerika, and anything we dream can come true." Johann's excitement for the journey heightened with every word and every dream his sons shared.

Johann proudly watched as each of the boys sat in silence. They tried to picture what they would see as they went about their journey. Then, as they rounded the top of a hill, a sight beheld them that spoke of the wondrous things that lay ahead. Below them was the city of Le Havre.

As they stood on the ridge, a strange sight filled Ignaz's eyes. "What is that?" he asked. He pointed to the trail that ran narrowly along the river.

A loud, hearty whistle filled the air, which startled Johnnie, and he coiled into his father's arms. A vast column of smoke erupted from a giant metal beast that rushed along the trail. Johann smiled, and he turned Johnnie's head to look. "It is a train. It carries people and goods. It is nothing to be frightened of."

The boys had heard of trains before, but this was the first one they had ever seen. They were amazed at how large it was as it chugged along. It seemed an hour passed before it was gone. Josef cracked his whip, and the horses moved along again toward the city before them. As they approached the outskirts of Le Havre, they came to a long line of carriages waiting to enter the city. Men, the armed officials Alois called Surete, went from wagon to wagon. They searched each one, though Johann could not imagine what it was they were looking for. Three of these men approached Johann. "Papiers!"

Johann presented their voyage tickets to a man, and he scrutinized them. The Surete walked around the wagon and suspiciously looked at everything inside, particularly the two boys. "Stay on this road, German! Straight through town and to your boat. Stay down by the docks until you board and be gone! You must sell anything you do not intend to take with you on the ship, and you must sell it by the docks and nowhere else! Do you understand?" The man was rude, and Johann saw Josef begin to move on the surly man. Johann reached over and stopped Josef's fist.

"Yes. We shall do that. Thank you." Johann uttered with a small smile. He took the tickets back and urged the horses forward.

As they rode forward, Josef protested, "Father, how could you—"

Johann raised his hand and stopped his son. "Not now. Watch as we go to ensure the Kaufmanns and Niggs get through."

Josef did as he was told. With the same poor treatment, the other two families passed the Surete checkpoint. The wise leader of the Tschohl family saw the looks of disgust from the Surete as they continued through the outskirts of the town. The Surete questioned and bullied many of the immigrants who wished to enter the city. They guessed the nature of Josef's angered look and hoped for the opportunity to correct it as they fingered their clubs.

"Stay yourself," Johann's stern tone cautioned Josef. "This is not Balzers, and we are not locals. We are in their land, and we will be until we leave. They do not consider us well here, and all of us will do good to remember that!" His words efficiently carried to Ignaz and Louis, who knelt directly behind the seat where Johann sat with Johnnie.

Josef also noticed the many men on the ground, and one in particular, who curiously took notes of the carriages as they passed. He carried an uneasy feeling as they entered Le Havre. They were determined to stay clear of the Surete during their extended stay.

CHAPTER SIX

THE TRADING BARN

The three families rolled through the French port's busy streets, and the boys gawked at the scenes that surrounded them. There were women dressed in their finest clothes, both on the streets and upon the balconies which overlooked the endless trail of wagons. Men crisscrossed their path, and they often forced the wagons to a stop as they strolled boastfully between them.

"Watch our things!" Johann commanded his sons as he saw the small children who darted by the stopped wagons. They quickly stole anything they could get their hands on from the overloaded wagons. The boys sat in corners of the wagon and shooed away the little kids as they skirted past. They were careful not to lock eyes with the older men as they feared starting a fight. The three families stayed very close in the hopes of staving off unpleasant issues.

The narrow road was only wide enough for one wagon at a time. Johann felt the buildings on both sides pinch closer as they went. When they passed the side streets, Johann noticed they were even more narrow and often open only for walking traffic. People filled the condensed and dark walkways. Some looked to sell what they had, while others only looked for the more sheltered areas for their shady business. Johnnie stared down each side street and took note of the hordes of people who scurried up and down them. They quickly darted in and out of stores. "What are all of these people doing here?" he asked Ignaz.

"They live here," Ignaz answered with sharp disdain.

"Ignaz, you are just as amazed at the city as he is. Please leave Johnnie alone," Johann defended.

"Yes, father," Ignaz dutifully answered.

"Where are their gardens and pigs? How do they eat?" Johnnie asked. "Where are the children? And where do they play?"

"You ask too many questions," Ignaz quipped, which brought another stern look from their father.

Anytime their wagon stopped, which mostly occurred due to the traffic, people clambered around the immigrant's wagons to sell them things.

"I cannot believe they speak German," Josef said.

"Many German-speaking people come through this port. They would not make much money if they could not speak to us," Johann replied.

Some of the men tried to sell food, while others offered them a place to stay. A few ladies came to the wagon, each suggestively dressed. They tempted the wide-eyed young men with a sensual opportunity. Two came at once, and one put her hand on Josef's leg while the other placed hers on Ignaz's face.

"Boys, would you like to come to the inn for a while?" one asked as they giggled and smiled at the boys.

"These young men are not what you are looking for!" Johann shouted. "Begone!" He took the whip from Josef and ushered the horses on again. The embarrassed boys held on as the wagon jolted forth. "Those are not the kind of women you want. You must trust me on this," he said to his sons as they rolled on.

"They are not like Lucienne in any way," Louis agreed.

Josef turned to roll his eyes at Ignaz, but his brother's gaze was still thoroughly planted on the two ladies they left behind. The ladies turned their attention to the Kaufmann's wagon and Anton and Alois. Before they started their offer, Thomasia stood to shoo them off. It was a brief encounter.

They approached another knoll, the last one, which led down to the ocean. The docks, which consisted of a patchwork of wooden poles and planks in perfect order, lay neatly before them.

"Oh, my," Johann uttered as he took in the vision of the immense ocean beyond. It was the first time the boys saw the expression of amazement and perhaps a hint of fear on their father's face. The boys also took in the daunting sight, all except Josef, who was busy as he kept the horses slow and under control as they trod down the dangerously steep cobbled path.

"We are going to cross that?" Johnnie asked. Johann turned and expected to see his son's worried face. Instead, the biggest smile he ever saw greeted him. "I cannot wait! Are we leaving today?"

"No, we will be here for some time before we leave. I was unsure how long it would take us to get here, and we could not be late. We will find work to keep us busy until the ship departs in early April." Johann seized the moment to address all of his sons. "I am uncertain about a lot of things in our future and just what adventures lie before us. But I count on our work ethic and good people who appreciate such a thing, to get us whatever we need. Wherever we go, I am confident we will be able to provide for ourselves."

"Yes, father," they answered in unison.

The surefooted horses worked hard to keep the heavily-laden wagons steady as they reached the bottom of the hill. Eventually, the wooden docks replaced the cobbled stone. Families, goods waiting to be loaded, and goods that had just been unloaded cluttered the busy docks. Families clung close to their precious food and items as each waited to board their ship to Amerika.

"How long have these families been here? They've built homes along the docks," Josef said in disbelief.

"We would be out a lot of money if we missed our boat, Josef. We had no choice but to arrive early and wait," Johann answered.

The Tschohls took in the saddened looks of all the people who waited. "Do they have nothing to do?" Louis asked.

"There is always something to do," Johann replied. "I have never held much faith in a man who sought rest above work. I am afraid I would simply wither away."

A large man who was well over six and a half feet tall, and the girth of three men, stood before them. His large hand blocked their path and ordered the wagon to stop. "Boarding a boat, German?" the man yelled over the noisy mess on the dock.

"Yes, we—" Johann started but was interrupted.

"Take your wagon over to the barn!" he ordered as he pointed to the large barn along the hill. "I do not care about any of your other thoughts. Sell your horses and wagon there, and then come back here to see me, and I will sell you a place to stay until your boats depart." His surly demeanor ruffled Johann, but again he remembered his larger goal.

"I would seek work for me and my—" Johann started to say but was interrupted again.

"German!" the man shouted as he stepped closer to Johann, "We do not hire stinking Germans on this dock! You will do as you are told! You'll do it *when* you are told, and then you will board your ship and depart! Start trouble, and you will never live to see your trip. Do you understand?" The man peered into Johann's eyes and challenged him to offer up a fight. He readied his mighty fists, which hung clenched by his side, and eagerly awaited their call. "Challenge me, German. I dare you. Many stubborn Germans have before, and each one lost. None of them lived to continue their journey," the man spat through gnashed, dirty teeth.

Johann looked at Josef. He could see the anger again that boiled within his son. "Go!" he ordered Josef, who quickly ushered the horses forward. They left the man behind and rode toward the barns ahead.

"Father," Ignaz protested. "We should have fought that man!"

Again, Johann's raised hand told Ignaz and his other sons to keep quiet. "Go slow," Johann said. "We need to make sure the Kaufmanns and Niggs get through." After a few tense

48

moments, the others also made it past the man. All three wagons continued through the makeshift village of refugees, who no doubt had seen that same play many times. All the challengers lost, and the rest chose to swallow their pride for another day. Then they reached the cobbled path of land again. As they arrived at the barn, Johann dismounted and left the boys behind. "Stay here. Speak to no one and yell for help if you need it, and no fighting!"

"But father, why do we allow them to treat us like this?" Ignaz argued.

Johann stopped his walk and spun quickly around to address his sons. "Lean close to me and listen, as I am not going to repeat this!" His harsh voice pulled his sons in tight. "These men do this every day. I promise you the guards at the city entrance note every wagon and what it has in it. Then they relay that information to the men down here so they know what to expect and what should be sold. They are all in this together, and they take advantage of us at every turn. This, however, is not our war. Our fight to survive will begin when we depart this shore. Any fight that prevents us from doing so is a waste of time. Do you hear me?"

"Yes, father," Josef answered for his brothers. Johann turned to find Anton and John standing behind him.

"I have a mind to teach that man some manners," Anton stated as his anger rushed forward.

"No, Anton," John replied. "Johann is right. These men matter not. There is no winning here. Do what we must, and let us get on the ship and continue." The two followed Johann as he walked quickly toward the building to sell their horses and wagon.

Johann entered the noisy barn, which was crammed with immigrants from front to back. The three waited at the end of one of the four long lines as the many immigrants traded for the best price for the horses and wagons that they could not take with them. The men who ran business knew quite well the Germans had no chance for fair trade.

An outburst ahead erupted over the usual commotion. At the front, a man argued over the trade price, which interrupted Anton's complaining about the guards outside and the many who despised their very existence in Le Havre.

"That is not half of what those horses are worth!" the German up front argued as he emphatically slammed his fist down on the wooden counter. All grew quiet as the man behind the thick wooden bar stood up and yelled back, "That is what I offer! Take it or leave it!" The German reached for the other man, but his hands barely moved before two henchmen rushed through the crowd and hammered the man with their clubs. The German collapsed, but the men continued to beat him. The man's wife and two daughters stepped forward and protested. "Leave him alone!" After the men stopped beating her husband, the woman and her daughters helped him off the dirty floor.

All in the room stood aside, as each was afraid to challenge the men carrying clubs. "This is not the first time those henchmen have done this," Anton seethed. Johann, Anton, and John walked forth to help the man up, while many others stayed back out of fear.

"Thank you," the wife whispered to Johann as tears rushed down her face.

"Are you trading or not?" the man behind the bar belched toward the beaten man and his wife. Johann shot the man a stern look. The man with the club who stood closest to Johann stuck his club in Johann's back.

"Think twice," the man uttered. Johann again was angered, but the soft touch of the wife's hand stayed him.

"Yes, we will trade," the woman said. The strength she carried impressed Johann as she walked back up to the large man at the counter. Her grace defied his look of disdain. She walked proudly to the counter and reached for the money the man offered.

The man threw it on the counter below her hand. He sneered back at her. "Anything left on that wagon in ten minutes is ours!" The woman stared boldly at the large man.

"We should go now," Johann urged. He pulled the woman away and broke the glare between the two.

"They will take our things. There is no way we can unload the wagon," she answered as tears continued down her cheeks.

"We will do it for you," Johann assured. "Do not worry. Anton, hold our place. We shall be right back."

The woman turned back to her husband as their daughter and son helped him to his feet. "I do not fear them," the woman uttered as she left the barn. "God will have His day."

"Let us get your family out of here and get your things," Johann said as he helped them get outside the dingy barn.

As they left, Johann motioned for his sons to get down quickly. "Help them get their things off the wagon, and hurry. Place it over there, and then do the same with ours." Johann turned and went back inside the trading building.

"Hold on!" the large man from earlier yelled. He marched over to Johann. "That spot you are referring to rents for two francs a week!" The man huffed hard in Johann's face.

Johann clenched his fist and grit his teeth, "This has been a hard day, and I am—"

"Here, father," Josef interrupted as he stepped between them. "I believe you were looking for your coins."

Johann looked at Josef for a moment and then back to the gruff man. He took the coins from Josef and handed several to the man. "Here is your payment, and that is for all three families in that spot for the next three weeks. Agreed?"

The man did not look at the coins. "I need two more coins per week!" Johann straightened again, but Josef grabbed the bag and quickly counted out six more. "Here you go, sir. Thank you," Josef said as he turned Johann away from the man. "Father, you must remember what you told us."

"What happened?" Ignaz asked as Josef and Johann came close.

"He decided to start a fight that did not matter," Johann explained as he rethought the past few moments. He looked at Josef, then back at Ignaz, and added, "There is never just one of them."

"I will help out here. Sell mine if I do not get back in time," John said. They quickly went to work and unloaded the wagon. John and Louis handed the luggage down to Josef and Ignaz. Ignaz hefted a large bag and turned to see a girl from one of the other families standing before him. Tears filled her eyes.

"Thank you for helping us," the girl said as her soft voice trembled in the cold wind.

Ignaz smiled back. "My father will tack us hard if we do not get your things unloaded. Please tell us where you want them."

"You and your family are so kind. Please set them over here," she said as she led him to the side of the dock. Ignaz, loaded down with several bags, followed her.

"Not again," Josef said as he took a bag from Louis. "What is it with you two?" he scolded as he turned back to Ignaz. Louis saw Ignaz with the girl. He smiled.

Ignaz set the bags down and turned to the girl. "What is your—" he began to ask but was cut off by Josef.

"Ignaz! The minutes are ticking away! We must hurry, or others will steal their things! Perhaps we could talk later and work harder now?"

Ignaz lowered his head, kicked an invisible rock at his feet, and then turned and went back to his work. The girl and her family took care of their injured father as they watched the boys work. One of the older sons helped unload, and the last of the bags were unloaded just in time. The men from inside came to take the wagon. They did not speak a word, but they glared down their noses at the Germans with disgust. They each spat at the four German families. The gruff men took great pains to ensure all of the chaw they had in their jaws ended up all over the German family's things. They then took the horse and wagon and rode off.

As Johann re-entered the barn, ready to sell his things, the large man behind the counter stood for all to see. His booming shouts at everyone resonated through the whole building. "You *will* take what we offer, or you *will* leave the docks! You *will* pay what we tell you to stay here, or you *will* leave the docks! You *will* do as we tell you, or you *will* leave the docks! And if you fail to do any of these things when we tell you, you *will* get the same beating that man did!" He then jumped down and yelled, "Next!" The next traveler inched cautiously forward to accept his dreadful offer.

The men firmly established order in the jittery room. The men behind the counters offered tragically low prices to the immigrants—even lower than before—as they dared any of them to say something.

"We cannot accept that low of a price!" Anton grimaced to Johann.

"We have no other option. Questioning their price earns a clubbing. We are going to accept the offer, and together, we will make it through to Amerika," Johann corrected in a stern voice.

"You are right, but someone must do something about this place," Anton protested as it became his turn to step up for his trade. "None of this is fair!"

"This is not our war," Johann uttered under the din.

John finally arrived back in line. "Their wagon is emptied. Ours will be as well before we get out of here if I know your boys at all. You should be proud of them."

"I am very proud, but right now, we need to get through this mess. Take their offer, whatever it is. You go before me." Johann needed to make sure they all got through, so he went last.

Johann peered out the open door and watched the trail of empty wagons and horses that trailed away from the barn. The endless dance of trade continued. Anton clenched his teeth tightly. He held the money for his wagon tightly in his fist, and his knuckles turned white with anger. He looked toward Johann, who only shook his head to encourage Anton to keep walking. John scratched his head and almost smirked at Johann as he walked out. Johann finally emerged from the barn with his money, far less than half of what his trade should have earned. Anton and John waited outside the door and shared a laugh. "What's so funny?" Johann asked.

"Anton here took a pretty hard turn, but I did quite well," John said. "My wagon is broken. It was the axle, which had been grinding fiercely as we drew closer. It snapped just as we came to a stop, and now that wagon is worthless!" He could not stop his laughter under his breath, even as the guards took notice of the very unusual happy moment on the dreary docks.

"Let us go," Johann said. "And quell your laughter. This man is hurt badly, and his family will not appreciate your story. I am just thankful I was able to sell the mill before we left, and for a fair price at that," he said. Though he told no one, he brought a small fortune to start over in the new world. He prayed to reach Amerika in one piece, and he hoped his family could start anew. At each turn of the trip, he offered a prayer to his dearly departed to thank them for getting them this far and asked for their prayers going forward.

"Thank you," the wife of the injured man said as Johann approached.

Johann smiled weakly but then saw that her cheeks were wet with tears. "How is your husband?" he asked.

"He is not good. He is resting, but it is starting to rain, and we have nowhere to go. We do not know what will become of us. We depended on my husband to get us through, but now he cannot help us."

She bowed her head as if in prayer, but the expression she wore was one of pure defeat. Her two older daughters wore glassy-eyed faces with dripping noses and downturned mouths. Then Johann saw her six other children huddled together. The youngest had not yet seen a year of life.

"Do not worry. We shall take care of you until your husband is better. What boat are you waiting for?" Johann asked.

"We are on the Serampore," she answered.

"Good! We sail on that one as well. We will find it in the morning and settle in until we depart," Johann affirmed for everyone. "We need to get your husband out of the elements. We will put up a tent. This is Anton Nigg and John Kaufmann," he said, motioning toward them with an open hand. "Together, we shall see you through."

"We are so grateful to you," the woman said. Her face changed as if the sun had shone on it for the first time. She embraced each of them. Thomasia and Maria approached with newfound hope on their faces and introduced themselves. Johann's sons had never seen a woman other than their mothers embrace their father.

Johann noticed their open mouths and wide eyes and ushered them on. "Get to work!"

Along with the other men, Johann and his sons carried their things off to the side as the rain came down harder. Anton started a small fire with the dry wood they carried with them. They all hunkered down for the night. The women made a stew as they crowded under the small awning. The smallest of them sat on the inside, closest to the fire. Each family stayed in their own section. The only dissenters were the children, and they made quick friends with each other. Johann watched as Ignaz traded frequent glances with the oldest girl from the other family.

"My name is Mariana Schmit. These are my children, Elizabeth, Anna, Jacob, Magda, Johannes, Barbara, Marie, and my youngest is called Christine. My husband's name is Richard."

"Thank you, Mariana. I am Johann, and these are my sons, Josef, Ignaz, Bernhard—I beg your pardon—Louis, and Johnnie." Anton and John introduced their children also. Johann continued, "We need to stick together, at least until your husband is better. Hopefully, he will rise with the sun in the morning." That evening, the families huddled close and said their prayers. They also said special prayers for the healing of Richard, who moved little in the night.

CHAPTER SEVEN

ELIZABETH

"How is your father?" Ignaz asked Elizabeth. She was so pretty, and Ignaz felt horribly for their impoverished situation. He would do anything he could to help her.

"He is hurt badly, but my mother thinks he will be better in the morning. I wish I had her confidence because I am not so sure," she confessed. Elizabeth looked at her father, "He has moved so little since we laid him down to rest."

"I am sure he will improve by morning," Ignaz reassured.

Elizabeth turned her head shyly to Ignaz and asked, "Your name is Ignaz?"

Ignaz's face grew rosy in the dark rainy night. "Yes. It sounds nice when you say it," he admitted. Though the four families sat around them, it was as if they were all alone. "It is short for Ignatius. Ignatius Tschohl."

"Well, Ignaz," Elizabeth said with a smile as she put her hand out for him to shake. "I thank you for helping us. We would be out in the freezing rain alone if not for your help."

Ignaz trembled and shook her hand. He was reluctant to let it go as the sincerity of her voice washed over him. "Your hand is so cold," he said as he sat closer to her and shared his blanket.

"Thank you," she said as she accepted and placed her hands on his leg to warm them. Her eyes twinkled with the dwindling light of the fire. The others had already gone to sleep.

"You are welcome, Elizabeth," Ignaz answered back. "Where are you and your family going?"

"A place called Prairie Du Rocher, Illinois. It will be a long journey up the Mississippi River."

Ignaz smiled as he thought of the time he would have to get to know Elizabeth. "We are going to Gutenberg, Iowa. I am not certain, but I think we will be traveling even farther up the river than you."

Elizabeth smiled again. Her dark hair had mostly fallen out of her bun by the end of the long day. "Well then, we shall be together quite some time. I suppose we should go to sleep, though, so we can be ready for what greets us tomorrow. Thank you again for your help. I should hate to think of how much worse off we would be without you and your families." Elizabeth handed the blanket back to Ignaz, stood for a moment, and looked down at him. Ignaz was not sure what to do, but he wanted to kiss her. The moment awkwardly passed, and Elizabeth dropped her gaze and looked for a place to sleep. "Good night, Ignaz. I am glad you are here."

Ignaz watched as Elizabeth stepped over several of her brothers and found a spot next to her little sister. Ignaz turned and sat next to Louis. He stared at the fire a little longer and then stoked it with another piece of wood. He turned to lay down and saw Louis, who smiled and blinked exaggeratedly at him.

"What?" Ignaz asked.

"You should have kissed her," Louis mumbled with a grin. Then he rolled over and went to sleep.

Ignaz positioned himself and silently pledged, "I will not let that chance pass me again."

Ignaz woke early. He looked up to see Mariana as she sobbed into her hands. Thomasia and Maria consoled her as the three fathers stood close by. Elizabeth woke at the same moment, "Mother, what has happened?" Mariana fell into

Maria's arms, "Richard is dead! They killed him! I woke to see if he was all right, but he was cold already!" Elizabeth rushed to her mother's side at the sound of the dreadful news.

"What are we going to do?" Mariana cried as the ocean waves continually washed hard against the docks below. They marked the endless march of time that acknowledged neither birth nor death.

Johann woke Josef. Along with John and Anton, they carried the already stiff body of Richard Schmit away. Johann found a Surete, a kind one, and pleaded Richard's case to the man. The Surete kept Mariana calm and walked her away from the growing multitude of people who came to look at the dead man.

"I am sorry for your loss, but you have a family to think about. Death happens every day down here at the hands of those who run the docks. Take your husband and bury him. Leave this place as soon as you can. If you raise an inquiry, there is going to be more killing. Do you understand me?"

"I have little time for false hope that these men will be held accountable. I understand," she said. Her disdain was evident to anyone within earshot.

"What am I to do?" Mariana asked herself as she looked toward her children. Her children cried at the loss of their father. Elizabeth corralled them and led them in prayers for their father's passed soul. Worry consumed all of them.

"I do not know how we will get to our family. I did not get half of the money I had hoped for when I traded the horses." Her wispy voice gave way to tears as she buried her head in Johann's chest. "I cannot let my children see me like this." The Surete walked away from Marianna and the many curious eyes which studied the scene.

Johann pulled Mariana gently away. "We will help you get to your family. I promise."

"But how? You have your own families to worry about," Mariana said.

"We have grown men to do work and women to watch the children and help as needed. We will make it to our destinations, God willing," John consoled.

"Yes, we will make it," Anton added.

Mariana could not answer but shook her head in appreciation and agreement. The men carried Richard off and buried him in the local cemetery. Several priests who waited to travel to Amerika presided over the service. The four families said tearful farewells to Richard and lent their support to the Schmits.

Ignaz thought back to his two mothers, brothers, and sister his family left behind. "I understand father's desire to keep our family together. I will do all I can to help the Schmits reach their destination," he said to Josef.

Ignaz and his family prayed for the Schmits, for they knew too well the pain at the loss of a parent. In the following days, they took good care of Mariana and her family. The men found a good place for them to set up their camp, and the women helped with the cooking. It was not long before Mariana and Elizabeth again helped with the cooking and laundry. Ignaz marveled at the determination that rose in Mariana as she keenly focused on getting her family to Prairie Du Rocher, Illinois.

With the women taking up their duties, Ignaz, his father, and brothers, Jacob, John, and Anton, searched for work. They did this to keep busy but also to make more money to help fund their trip. It did not take long, for work was plentiful around the docks. What was not plentiful was a man willing to do the work and those willing to pay well for it. Though their pay was low, and at times nonexistent, the men toiled joyfully. Not only did they enjoy the work, but they also enjoyed learning a new trade and the workings of a boat.

One day, Johann's sons helped unload a load of freshly-caught fish. As they hefted the catch from the boat, each boy wore a frown that Johann knew all too well. "What is wrong?" Johann asked his sons.

"These fish!" Ignaz exclaimed. "They stink! I am glad for the work, but I shall be much happier when I no longer have to smell these cursed fish!"

Johann laughed, which did little to brighten Ignaz's foul mood. As they reached the weigh station, Jacob tripped on a loose board and dumped the fish he carried onto the dock.

"German! You will pay for those spoiled fish!" one of the dockhands scolded as he reached for his club. Jacob cowered and waited for the club to strike his back.

"Arretez!" a voice shouted from the ship. Another Frenchmen, the one who hired the Tschohls, yelled at the man with the club.

Hearing the order, he held his club up high but turned to see who dared yell at him so. An argument ensued between the two as they fought over the discipline of the young German boy. Johann helped Jacob to his feet, and they quickly picked up the fish. The man who hired the Tschohls ended the argument, "When you break his head open, are you going to haul the fish in yourself? Are you going to scrub the fish cleaning stations or wash cholera and lice-infected cabins after the trips across the ocean?" The dockhand then thought twice about smashing the boy and returned the club to his belt.

"I did not think so!" the boss yelled.

The dockhand walked away and spat in Jacob's direction. Jacob began to smirk, but the boss stepped into his face. "And you! If you ever drop the fish again, *I* will be the one who splits your head open!" he yelled, even though he was close enough to the boy's face that Jacob could smell the rank tobacco rotting the man's teeth. He let Jacob and the Tschohls know for certain the pecking order on the dock and that they were the ones on the bottom.

✝

Ignaz's feelings for Elizabeth continued to grow. But the only family member he felt comfortable talking to about Elizabeth was Louis.

"What are you waiting for?" Louis asked. "Tell her you like her and kiss her already."

"It just never seems to be the right time. There are always so many people around," Ignaz replied with his chin on his chest.

"So? There is nowhere for us to go. If you want to wait until we are not around, you are never going to be able to tell her anything," Louis argued.

"I will find the right time," Ignaz said as the two went about their day.

The families prayed together every morning and night, and in all other ways, the families lived as normally as they could.

"This is so much fun," Johnnie said to his father. "I have never been around so many kids who are my age. We get to play together every day!"

"I am glad you have playmates, particularly for when we board the ship. It will be a very long trip," Johann said to his youngest.

"I get more excited each day, father," Johnnie replied as he ran off with his friends.

Another day passed. Ignaz still did not confess his feelings for Elizabeth. The night came and went, and Ignaz said nothing. He tossed and turned in his sleep as the thoughts of Elizabeth pounded in his head. "I am going to tell her tomorrow, no matter what," Ignaz promised to Louis.

"Sure you will," Louis mocked as they lay down to sleep.

The next morning started as usual, as Johann woke the boys for their breakfast. Ignaz took his plate from Elizabeth, with her usual smile as the firelight sparkled in her eyes.

"Good morning," Ignaz grumbled. His voice was still hoarse from his sleep.

Elizabeth giggled and went for the next plate. Another opportunity had passed, but Ignaz already knew just when he would make his move.

"Thank you for breakfast. You do not need to do this for us," Johann said to Mariana.

She turned sharply to him, "I will never be able to repay you for what you have done for me and mine, so please allow us to do these small things. They provide us something to do while we wait. I will not sit uselessly around like many in this filthy place. They wait for handouts when they could easily do for themselves, just as you and your sons have."

Ignaz added, "You are right. Many are just sitting on the dock, wasting days of their lives that they will never get back." The Tschohls, Schmits, Kaufmanns, and Niggs praised their Lord through their work and refused to waste the talents given them.

Ignaz sat up as Elizabeth brought him a rare second plate, which he eagerly accepted. "There is just a little left. Ignaz, would you like it?"

"She always brings yours first, and now today she brings you a second plate? You see that, do you not?" Josef asked Ignaz.

"What do you mean?" Ignaz asked back.

Josef leaned toward him. "We all know you like her and that she likes you. It is obvious! If you do not say something to her soon, I will," Josef stated.

"You would say something to her for me?" Ignaz asked. He was surprised to hear Josef's offer. "I would be very appreciative if you did so."

"No, Ignaz, I will not ask for you. I would ask for me," Josef threatened with a smile. Ignaz had all the motivation he needed to seek her hand.

After breakfast, Johann and the boys went off to do their work. Most often, it included unloading the newly arrived boats from Amerika. The boats carried few passengers, but they were loaded down with riches of all kinds from the new world, each ready for sale in France. The boats needed to be full for the trips to ride the storms that frequented the northern Atlantic. On the way to Amerika, they were full of passengers. But on the return trips, they were loaded with cargo from the new world.

One of the men walked off the boat, and he swore to the rest, "I will never sail again! We should not be alive!" He stomped off and left the others to contemplate their next move.

"What happened?" Josef asked.

"It is none of your business!" the first sailor yelled at him as he jabbed at Josef with a cane he limped on.

"Are you sailing to Amerika, boy?" a second sailor asked as he draped his arm around Josef. Ignaz and his father watched carefully, ready to step in. Johann nodded to Josef to answer.

"Yes," Josef gulped.

"Then, you best say your prayers! 'Cause, it is just as likely you will see the bottom of the ocean than it is that you will see the new land!" The man spat his words, along with his chaw, onto Josef's face.

"Stop yer yappin' and unload the boat! Johann, if you want to talk, find you and your sons another labor!" their boss yelled.

Johann grabbed Josef from the sailor's grip and pulled him to a large number of boxes and barrels that needed to be unloaded. "Stupid Germans!" the sailor spat again. Then he ambled off through the crowd on the docks who crooned to hear news from the new world and to see the rumored fight.

It took Johann and his crew most of the morning and early afternoon to unload the boat. After they finished, the boss ordered them done for the day, but not before admonishing them for the morning's incident. "I told you not to talk to the sailors! You are here to work, not to hear the gossip from the boats!"

"It will not happen again," Johann replied. He then gave a hard look to Josef, who could not carry the stare. Johann and the boys marched off the boat and headed back to their tent home. The hard work did them good and kept them strong, while many grew weak as they withered on the docks.

"I am sorry, father," Josef offered as they marched.

"Do not speak of it again as our ship leaves tomorrow. We only need to last one more evening," Johann answered back.

After dinner, as usual, Marianna asked her daughter, "Elizabeth, please fetch some clean water to do the dishes." Elizabeth grabbed the washtub and took the long walk to the fountain that supplied the only clean water to the dock.

Ignaz looked to Josef as he thought of his brother's words from earlier in the morning. He could not go another day without speaking to Elizabeth about his feelings for her, and this was the opportunity he had waited for. After a few painful moments of delay, he stood and announced, "I am going for a walk."

Ignaz hurried to catch up to Elizabeth on her trek. "Why does she have to walk so fast?" he muttered to himself as he rushed through the crowd. He marveled at Elizabeth's smile that made everyone around her feel as though the sun was shining, just for them. She seemed to dance as she moved around the docks as if she had not a care in the world. Elizabeth strolled like a princess in a castle, not as the poor German immigrant that she was on the crowded and filthy docks. "I do not know how, but I think she feels the same about me," he thought. "I will not lay down for one more night without telling her of my love for her."

Ignaz quickened his pace as his hopes ushered him on ever faster. His heart raced, his excitement for what was to come rushed uncontrollably. He did not notice the many people, both those living on the docks who waited for their boat and the lurkers, the sailors who hung about in-between their voyages. The lurkers always eyed the German girls. The parents of the families that waited often warned their daughters of the dirty men and their despicable thoughts that were all too easy to read. Their desire for younger women was only surpassed by their interest in drinking large amounts of alcohol.

Ignaz tromped through the area where the lurkers held court. He detested the thought of Elizabeth walking past them every night. He quite easily guessed the thoughts of the detestable men at the sight of his lovely Elizabeth. "I am glad she will never need to walk through this dingy lot of men again," Ignaz whispered to himself as he bumped into one of the lurkers.

"Watch where you are goin', boy!" the drunken man warned. Ignaz ignored the man, who quickly returned to his mug of ale.

As Ignaz continued past the reveling mob, he came to the area where everyone drew their water. Several other girls were there, getting water for their nightly dishes, but Ignaz did not see Elizabeth. He became even more nervous for her and continued down the dock. Then he came to a darker place on the pier, well away from the usual crowd. He tripped over a tub that lay hidden in the shadowed darkness. It was a tub he easily recognized.

"Do not fight this girl. It will not last long!" Ignaz heard the muffled threat coming from under the stairs that led to the street above. He slowly walked toward the sound as worry climbed high in his mind for Elizabeth.

Then he heard a quickly muffled scream. "Elizabeth!" he uttered in horror. He rushed into the darkness to save her, completely unsure of what awaited him. Under the stairs, he saw a mountain of a man who shoved Elizabeth against the wall. She fought back and tried to free herself from the coveting hands that pawed at her.

Ignaz reached with both hands and violently ripped at the man's shoulder. His pull spun the man off Elizabeth. As the man flipped backward, Ignaz saw Elizabeth fall to the ground.

"Run, Elizabeth!" Ignaz yelled. "Get to safety!" She was too stunned to move and cowered against the wall in fear.

Then the man stood. "Boy, who are you to deny me the girl? You will pay for that!" the sailor grinned. The man searched the darkness of the dock but did not find what he looked for. Then he quickly turned back to Ignaz, "Well, I guess I am just going to have to beat you to death!"

As the man stepped forward, Ignaz planted his feet firmly and delivered a mighty punch to the man's jaw. The sailor stepped back, stunned from the blow.

He quickly regained himself, with his grin smashed away by Ignaz. Ignaz tried again, but the man blocked his punch and delivered a blow of his own that knocked Ignaz off his feet. Ignaz's head bounced off the wooden planks, and he felt blood run freely down his face. His head spun from the pain, and he did not recover fast enough as the grotesque man straddled him with his fist raised high in the air.

Ignaz saw the hammer-like hand that crushed down, but he could not move. The last thing he saw was Elizabeth as she slowly stood behind the man. She held something that glinted in her little hand. Then another fist smashed him to the other side of his head, and he passed out.

CHAPTER EIGHT

THE ESCAPE

"What is taking them so long?" Mariana asked as she fidgeted with her baby. "They should have been back by now."

Johann smiled, "I just hope Ignaz finally found enough courage to talk with Elizabeth. He must be very nervous. We will go to find them and make sure all is well. John and Anton, let us go."

Johann led them down the dock, which bustled with excitement as everyone who would be boarding the Serampore the next morning prepared to depart. Many had been there quite a while and so had a lot of packing to do. Anton and John followed Johann as he weaved through the masses. Soon they passed the busiest area. "Look for them. They could be anywhere along here," he said.

No sooner did he finish his words than Elizabeth rushed through the mob of people. She fell into one person and then into the next as she stumbled toward Johann. She held her tattered clothes as blood dripped from her lip. She also had a blood-soaked strap of cloth wrapped around her hand. The frantic look on her face told Johann something was very wrong.

"What happened?" Johann exclaimed as Elizabeth ran into his arms. His concern for Ignaz erupted as he waited for Elizabeth to speak of his son.

"Ignaz is beaten badly, Herr Tschohl! Back around the corner!" Elizabeth screamed. Though Johann tried to silence her, it did little good as others around them began to listen. She wriggled in his arms and quivered in fear.

"John," Johann said, "take her back to our tent. But do not rush. We do not want to draw attention. We will find Ignaz and be back soon. Wait for us there." John took Elizabeth under his arm and did as he was told. Despite her whimpering, which he tried to conceal, few paid them any heed as they made their way back. Upon seeing her mother at the tent, Elizabeth broke down and fell into her embrace.

"Elizabeth, what has happened?" Marianna asked.

"I killed him, Mama. I killed him!" Elizabeth whimpered. She then laid down, and Marianna covered her up. She sat next to her daughter and consoled her frightful state. "Please, God," Elizabeth prayed, "please keep Ignaz safe!"

Johann and Anton rushed forward until they came upon the scene. Ignaz tried to sit up in the darkness. The other man's dead body lay close to him on the shadowed dock. "Dear God," Johann uttered as they ran close.

"Father," Ignaz mumbled. "Is Elizabeth all right?"

"She will be fine, son," Johann answered as he slid Ignaz up against the wall in the darkness. He looked at the dead body. "Anton, get a large rock and some string, quickly!"

Anton did as he was told, with each requested item easy to find along the dock. Johann tended to his son, who seemed only bruised and battered, and with no further injuries.

"Help me," Johann said to Anton as he went to the dead body. "Pull him closer to the edge."

Johann read the dreadful look on Anton's face. "Do it!"

He and Anton each grabbed a leg of the body and pulled it across the dock's wooden planks to the edge of the pier. It was well before midnight, but little moved on this part of the dock. Johann took the rope and tied one end to the man's leg and the other to the rock.

"Johann, what are we doing?" Anton asked.

"Saving my son and Elizabeth!" Johann barked as he continued his deed. He quickly lowered the rock into the water, and then the two did the same with the man's body. "Lower it as far as possible to limit the splash." He did as Johann instructed. When Johann nodded, Anton let go of the already cold arm, and the man's body silently slipped into the water with the smallest of splashes and disappeared into the cold depths below. The man was one of the sailors who had just arrived the day before. As it disappeared into the cold water, the image of the man burned into Johann's memory.

Anton sat up. The recent events whirled around his mind, and he got sick on the dock. Johann grabbed him hard by the neck, "Stop that! We need to stay strong to get out of here together!"

Anton wiped his face and sat up. "Yes," he replied.

Johann yanked him to his feet, and the two rushed back to Ignaz, who was still propped up in the darkness. Johann took a rag and washed Ignaz's beaten face as good as he could. He then took off his hat and pulled it tight over Ignaz's head. They lifted Ignaz and mostly carried him the distance back to the tent.

"Everyone is watching us," Anton worried as they went.

"No, they are not. They are drunk and about to sleep. They will not even remember us by morning," Johann assured. "They will think Ignaz is just another drunken sailor."

As they entered the tent, Marianna rushed to them. "My God, what has happened?" Johann laid his son down, and they quickly covered him up. Elizabeth still cowered in the corner and refused to come from her hiding place. "Please tell me what happened!" Marianna pleaded.

"A man attacked Elizabeth, and I think Ignaz killed him. The man was very large, and there is no doubt what his intentions were with Elizabeth." Johann then turned to Elizabeth and asked, "Is that what happened?"

"Mama," Elizabeth's small voice crept from the corner.

Marianna ran to her. "Yes, dear, what is it?"

Elizabeth looked around as Johann, Anton, John, Josef, and Jacob looked at her, as all eagerly waited for her response. "Ignaz did not kill that man. I did." As she finished her confession, Elizabeth fell into her mother's arms once again.

Marianna tried desperately to stifle her daughter as she wailed, but she could not.

The four families nursed Ignaz and Elizabeth the rest of the morning as they readied their things to depart. They prayed for the soul of the departed man, but more so to depart Le Havre before anyone discovered the body. They tried to sleep for the last few hours, though it was nearly impossible.

Johann sat by the fire as Marianna held Elizabeth. Ignaz slept uneasily. "He is going to take a long time to heal, as will Elizabeth," Johann said. "I pray for our safety and that we might escape this day without losing anyone."

"I will pray that, too," Marianna said as she reached for Johann's hand as they prayed together.

As the sun rose on the 22nd day of March 1855, Johann watched the usual ebb and flow of the docks, which loaded with the hopeful families who awaited their boat's departure. It had been so from the first day of their arrival. This day was different, though. This was their day to leave. Johann never expected that tragic events would eclipse the excitement of this day.

The sun rose over the smooth ocean waters. It seemed like a usual day to all except for the four families, who tried to hurry without alarming anyone to their urgency—the aching moments ticked by ever so slowly. Only the oldest of their group was aware of the precarious nature of their nervous wait.

Stories abounded of the ships that did not reach their targeted destination and the awful conditions endured by many of the trips to Amerika. The most recent ship to sink was the RMS Tayleur.

"She was an iron ship, my lads! If she can sink, any of them can!" a crickety old sailor bellowed to any who would listen, though it appeared no one was. He limped up and down the docks and spread fear into the hopeful hearts of the immigrants who awaited their turn to try the seas. Despite the foreboding message, they and the many other families could not wait to depart. The unwelcoming tolerance of the hard-handed rulers of the docks only furthered their eagerness to leave. That, along with the hope that the dead would stay gone long enough for the doers of the deed to slip away.

"Today is the day. Is that right, father?" Johnnie asked as he woke to see Johann as he stuffed the last of their things into barrels for the trip.

"Yes, son. Today is the day," Johann answered. He knew he would need to fight his desire to snap at any of the thousand questions the youngest would rain upon him that day. Though Johann was ready to depart, his concern over Ignaz and Elizabeth overshadowed his every move and consideration. The journey would be difficult, but there was no time to think about it.

Johann prayed for their quick departure and safety on the trip. He hoped they could somehow reach their destination in New Orleans. The excited and the nervous crowded the dock as they impatiently waited for the whistle to signal for them to begin loading their things. The crew had worked feverishly over the past weeks to prepare the boat, and they made many small repairs to the vessel they knew so well. The men had recruited Johann, Josef, Ignaz, Louis, John, Anton, and their new friend Jacob Schmit to help with the preparation, so they knew well the cramped conditions they would soon experience.

Though the boat sat empty for well over a month, the horrid smell below dwindled little from the refuse left behind through the many transatlantic trips the boat had made.

"Karl!" a sailor bellowed out over the crowd as he stomped past. He was one of the men from the previous day, a partner of the dead man. Johann and Marianna stood as the men stomped past. They hoped to hide the sight of the injured Ignaz and Elizabeth just behind them. "You!" the man snarled as he looked to Josef.

"Yes?" Josef asked. He dared not to look directly at the man.

"Have you seen Karl, the sailor you spoke with yesterday?" The sailor peered at Josef untrustingly.

"No. I have not." Josef looked down and turned from the dirty man. The man looked with disdain about the small camp. Another sailor yelled, "Come on! He probably got drunk and is in town. Let us go look for him!" The two marched off. They climbed off the dock and entered the city proper.

Johann looked to Josef with approval, and the two spoke no more.

The families anxiously lined up, courteous of those who made an effort to get there first. "Father, we should have gotten in line sooner," Louis lamented. "We will not get a good place on the boat." Ignaz stirred behind them and sat up. Louis and the youngest children noticed him for the first time.

"What happened?" Johnnie blurted.

"He fell last night, down some steps. He will be fine," Josef explained. Louis noticed his father's concerned look and asked no further questions.

"It is not polite to stare," Johann said to Johnnie. Then he knelt by Ignaz. "Can you walk to the boat?" Ignaz looked around until he finally saw Elizabeth. She stared at him from the other side of the fire, and when their eyes met, she rushed to him, and they held each other tight.

"Yes, we will make it. But let us go last, so we do not have to stand in line," Ignaz replied. Elizabeth would not let go of his hand.

Johann finally got back to answer Louis's question. "The men on the crew told us to get in line in the middle, son. The first people do not get to pick their place. The crew forces them to the very bottom of the boat. We will get the better spot without getting what is left over," Johann informed quietly.

Jacob nodded his agreement as he protectively placed his hands on his mother and sisters. He leaned over Ignaz. "Thank you for what you did for Elizabeth," he said. He then looked to

Johann. "And thank you for what you have done for all of us. We would not have made it this far without you. For now, we just need to get on the boat safely."

The whistle finally blew, and the men allowed the people to load the boat. Each family needed several trips to load their things for the crossing. They needed not only their personal items but also food for the entire trip.

The Tschohls finally marched onto the Serampore, and they led the other three families to the middle deck of the ship. The Serampore was a large wooden brigadier sailing ship, with two large masts that held the many sails which would carry them across the ocean. Rigging strung from the masts to all sides of the boat. The rigging gave support to the masts and provided the rope ladders the sailors used to climb when needed to untangle a rope or mast. It would take several trips to load everything, and Ignaz and Elizabeth waited until the very end. Ignaz pulled his clothing and hat tight as he tried to hide his battered face.

"I cannot do this. What if someone sees us and we get caught?" Elizabeth worried to Ignaz.

"Put your dreadful memories away for the moment. We do not have far to go. We will make it," Ignaz comforted.

Elizabeth steadied Ignaz and asked, "How can you be sure?"

"Because God wants us on that boat," Ignaz answered her with a slight smile.

Mariana took care of her brood and Johnnie as the men loaded their things.

"This boat is huge!" Johnnie yelled. Neither he nor Barbara paused at the smell that turned everyone else's nose. "I cannot wait to go!" Johnnie screamed as he ran back and forth between the crowded mass of people who vied for a place to keep their many things.

By mid-afternoon, the people had loaded the last of their belongings, and the captain made the final call before departure. The men of the four families moved fast to help as many as they could to load their stores. They worked to the point of exhaustion, but they refused to relent until all in the boat were ready to sail. Ignaz and Elizabeth walked on last.

The remaining immigrants crowded the frenzied dock as they fought for the new places the departing families left open. Many of the families that boarded had things that they could not take with them, which they left behind for whoever wanted them. No one noticed the beaten man as he slowly ambled past him or her, as Elizabeth carried most of his weight.

After they reached the boat, they handed their tickets over to the man who collected them. Johann saw Johnnie as he stood still. His head was crooked back as he stared at the giant pole which held the massive posts from which the sails hung. "What are you looking at?" Johann asked.

"Father, this boat is so big. How is this post held up?"

"Well, let us see for a moment. Do you see those long lines from the top? They go to the front, back, and sides to keep the mast, this post, from falling over. The ropes running everywhere and holding the sails are called the rigging. We do not want to get caught up in any of that. This is called a Brigadier ship, so there are two masts. The foremast is the one closer to the front of the boat. This one is the mainmast, and it is much taller," Johann explained.

"And what is that?" Johnnie asked as he pointed to another section of the deck, the highest one, that sat on the back of the boat.

"That is called the aft-castle."

"A castle? Can we stay in there?" Johnnie asked excitedly.

"No, son. That is for the captain. The steps that go up both sides of his quarters lead to a small deck where the wheel is for steering the boat. Only the sailors are allowed up there. We can come out here on this open deck and breathe the fresh air from time to time. How does that sound?" Johann asked.

"That sounds wonderful. This is going to be a great trip. Do you think that is so?" Johnnie asked as Johann took his hand, and they walked toward the steps that led below. A massive hatch lay open close to the stairs, which was covered during storms.

"It will be interesting, to say the least," Johann answered as he took Johann to Marianna.

"There you are! I have been looking for you," Marianna scolded as she led Johnnie down.

"Aww, I was having fun..." Johnnie's voice trailed off as the two went below.

Then a commotion started on the dock behind them even as the sailors removed the loading ramp. The Surete whistles blew down the way, and it came from the direction of the fight the night before.

"Keep going. Pay it no heed," Elizabeth urged as Ignaz stiffened. At her words, he continued his painful trudge to the lower deck.

The captain yelled his orders to depart. "Hoist the anchor! Raise the mainsail!" The crew churned the wheel that raised the anchor, while others loosened the ropes that tied the boat to the dock. The dockworkers used long wooden poles to shove the ship away, and two smaller boats with crews of men helped pull the Serampore further from the dock. More crew members hoisted the mainsail, which the breeze quickly filled. The combined power of the men who paddled and the wind quickly moved the boat away from the shore.

Johann emerged from the hull as he heard the whistles. As he passed Ignaz, he placed his reassuring hand on his son's shoulder. "Not far now, son. Just down a few steps, and you can rest." Johann stood on the deck as the boat floated farther away. It left the dock, and his family's troubles, behind.

Wind billowed the sails and pushed the boat on. The Surete rushed about the dock yelling, "Muertre! Muertre!"

One of the sailors looked to their captain and asked, "What is he saying?"

"He is yelling *murder*. Someone must have been killed," the captain answered with little concern. He curiously watched the scene back on the dock as his ship hurried away. The Surete hailed the Serampore to return.

"Should we stop?" the sailor asked.

The captain's look changed to that of anger. "No, you muzzy bastard! It was probably one of you that did it, and be damned to hell whoever did! But I need all of you for this journey! Continue!"

CHAPTER NINE

THE SERAMPORE

Relief overtook Johann as the boat continued its slow pull away from Le Havre. He saw the sailor from earlier, who stared at him from the dock through the waving crowd. The people on the docks did not care for the Surete or the sailors. They cared even less for the French men who controlled their life while they waited. "Does he know what happened?" Johann thought to himself. "I guess I will never know."

The passengers aboard the Serampore fought the others to climb above the lower decks as they hoped to wave goodbye to those left behind. There were few to wave to, however, for everyone they knew made the trip with them. The only people still on the dock waited for their boat to make the same journey. Many of the passengers stopped to pray, and each thanked God for getting them this far. They also prayed for safety for the dangerous voyage ahead.

"Head back below! There is work to be done, and you will not be in our way twice!" the captain scolded. The passengers retreated below deck and assumed the positions they would hold for several weeks.

"Do you mind if I stay above a while longer?" Johann asked one of the sailors he knew.

"You and your sons may do so. Just stay out of our way and be ready if we call on you to help," the sailor answered. Johann was one of the fortunate few allowed above the lower decks. He earned his stature by the weeks of work he, Anton, John, and their sons did for the sailors. He stayed out of the men's way and said goodbye to the only land he had ever known.

"May God watch over the souls of my dearly departed, and I pray for the men who man this ship. May their hard work and knowledge carry us over the ocean to Amerika. I also pray for forgiveness of what Elizabeth did to protect my son from that man who sought to defile her and for God's grace on his wretched soul. Amen."

"Do you believe we shall ever return?" Louis asked as he snuck up behind Johann.

"I do not see it for me, but only God knows." Johann knew the reason for Louis's questioning thoughts.

Louis stared into the west, but the ocean was all he could see before him and beyond. The wind buffeted his face, and then he looked to the sail above. "How can the wind blow in our face and still fill the sail and push us forward?" Louis asked.

Johann appreciated his inquiring mind. "We do not travel in a straight line toward Amerika, which is why the trip takes so long. The wind only needs to hit a little of the sail to fill it, which is why the angles the captain takes are very important." Johann learned a lot in a short time as he helped with the boat, and he was a man who enjoyed engineering things.

"Father?" Louis began.

"What, son?"

"What happened to Elizabeth and Ignaz?" Louis asked. He took his gaze off the horizon and looked to Johann.

Even though they were on the boat and had no fear of anyone ever finding out what occurred, Johann whispered to his son as the winds blew past them, "A bad man attacked Elizabeth, and Ignaz tried to save her. The man was large, and he beat Ignaz badly. I believe Elizabeth stabbed the man to save Ignaz."

Tears filled Louis's eyes as he considered the events. "How can people be so evil? Did she kill him?"

"I believe she did. We must never speak of this. Do you understand?" Johann stared into his son's eyes as he needed him to realize the importance of the request.

"Yes, father. I understand." Louis sat for a moment. He then stood again, "I am going below to check on Ignaz."

"I will be there shortly. Remember, son. Say nothing." Johann was still concerned for others to find out.

Louis climbed back below.

As he sat there, Johann continued to watch the shrinking shore behind them, and he considered what he left behind. "How long will this journey take?" Johann asked a sailor as the land finally disappeared behind them, and the sun slowly set in front.

"Thirty days or more," the man gruffly answered.

"Unbelievable," Johann responded. He stood and went below to find his place by the Schmits, Niggs, and Kaufmanns. The area below was stuffed with people and their things jammed into one corner or another. Johann weaved his way around the various groups and the many hammocks strung from the posts. Marianna, Marie, and Thomasia made them dinner, and as always, they prayed before they ate. The murmur of prayer was a constant but welcome presence in the lower decks. Only the faithful dared the dangerous journey.

The four families shared the mid-level of the boat with the majority of the passengers. It consisted of a large room with many poles that supported the strength of the vessel. Each pole ran from floor to ceiling, through each of the decks. Hammocks strung from pole to pole, with several stacked on top of the others. The families took turns with everything, from using the hammocks to taking time on the deck to cooking in the inadequate kitchens. On most days, they were lucky to get one hot meal, and each family made sure to ration their food to last the many days across the sea.

Marianna, Thomasia, and Maria watched the children and tried their best to keep them fed, cleaned, and occupied. They prayed and fretted over every cough and runny nose, for many took ill on the trip. The rolling sea did not help, as many became sick from the churning waters. During the storms, of which there were several, all huddled together in prayer that their small boat would survive the squalls that terrified the northern Atlantic every spring. Inevitably, the storms passed, and the boats found smooth waters to sail again. While it was good to get fresh air from above, it was also frightening to see how tiny their boat was in the great and large expanse of the ocean. They believed more than ever that only the hand of God would safely get them across the Atlantic.

"Johann and Marianna, how long have you been married?" Catherine Ley, a fellow passenger from Bavaria, asked. She and her family occupied a spot very close to the Tschohls and Schmits.

Thomasia and Maria both laughed at the suggestion. Marianna smiled back at her two new friends and then looked to Johann. He stepped forward and placed a calming hand on Marianna, "We have been together for a long time."

Catherine smiled, "Your family is wonderful. You are truly blessed to have so many children, and they are so well behaved."

"Thank you," Marianna said after Catherine went back to her own family. She turned to Johann, "Thank you. I am not sure why, but that is hard for me to answer."

"Do not worry. We will get you and your family safely to Prairie Du Rocher. If people mistake us for being a large family, that is fine by me," Johann reassured.

Marianna wrapped her arms around Johann, "Thank you again, for everything." She then went back to her unending duties of watching her family, and Johnnie too.

The four families were inseparable on the trip. They made a wall with their barrels and trunks, which marked their small part of the ship. Each family did so to define what was theirs.

At the end of their first week on the boat, Johann saw a detestable man who looked through their barrels. Marianna squealed out of fear of the poor looking traveler, who pretended not to notice the others who watched him.

"Hey!" Anton bellowed as he stood tall. The man smiled a two-toothed grin at Anton, which challenged him to stop the intruder. John and Johann stood behind Anton.

"What are you going to do?" the man scoffed. He had already spoiled two other families' food stores. He took what he wanted and alerted them that he would be back. Johann watched this occur and hoped to avoid it himself. He quickly found out he could not. "These are ours. You should be off!" Anton argued.

The fattened man scowled back, "My name is Christoph, and I takes what I wants!" Christoph reached his dirty hand into the barrel with the salted pork. Anton was not looking for a fight, but he tightened his fists.

Christoph raised his handful of pork to his mouth, but Anton's massive fist beat the salted food to the finish. The blow knocked Christoph back, but he was far from done. He gurgled in excitement, "Everyone will see that challenging me will get you killed! Come, man! Fight me!" He swung a fist toward Anton and hit him solidly in the ear. The pain shot through Anton and dizzied him. Christoph hit him again with the other fist, and Anton fell hard to the steerage floor. Passengers scrambled to get out of the way of the brawl, but the crowded conditions left little room to move.

With Anton discarded, Christoph turned and yelled, "Anyone else want to try to stop me? Let us have it out now and be done with it!"

Johnnie broke free from Elizabeth and yelled, "Leave us alone, you chowder-headed rum-gagger son of a b—"

"Johnnie!" Elizabeth chastised as she covered his mouth as quickly as she could. Johnnie fought wildly to get free, but Elizabeth would not allow it.

Johann and John came forth, and Christoph again reached into the barrel. Johann stood before him, "Put that down!" John stood with Johann. Josef, Jacob, and Louis stood with them too.

Christoph smiled and raised his hands to grab John, but Johann slammed his fisted hand into the back of Christoph's head. Christoph turned to see his attacker. Johann quickly followed the previous blow with an even more ferocious blast to Christoph, which knocked him back again. Johann's fuming look drove his arm forward as the third sledgehammer blow knocked Christoph clear off his feet. The fat man landed hard on the wooden floor. Christoph tried once more to stand, but the fourth and final fisted-hand pounded him into submission.

Johann knelt low over Christoph, "Do not come back here, not even by accident! You will take no more from the families on this boat!" He then stood tall over the awestruck steerage passengers. "Do not come here looking for food or drink! I cannot stand freeloaders, nor do I care for those too dumb to prepare for such a trip!" The message was clear to all as Johann's boys drug the largest of the bullies away. John, Maria, and Thomasia went to help Anton, who started to sit up.

"Anton, are you all right?" Thomasia asked.

"Yes, dear. I am glad I could distract him to give Johann a chance to take him on," Anton replied. Blood from a cut on his forehead ran down the side of his face.

With Christoph taken care of, Johann turned his attention to his youngest son. "Johnnie, come here."

Johnnie skulked as he walked over. "Yes, father?" he asked as fear dripped from his eyes. "I am sorry I used those words."

"Where did you hear them?" Johann said as he took a stern look at his sons, who in turn gave each other admonishing looks.

"I..." Johnnie sheepishly began. "I heard one of the sailors use the words."

"Do you know what they mean?" Johann asked as he brought Johnnie into his arms.

"No. I just knew they were bad, and I wanted that man to go away. I am sorry," Johnnie confessed.

"All right, son. Just make sure you never use them again. Do you understand?"

"Yes, father. I promise not to do that again," Johnnie answered. Johann hugged him and went on.

Marianna and her family stayed even closer to the other three families after, and their kids no longer ran through the steerage as they played. Johann sent the warning that this was a dangerous journey, and not only for the trip across the ocean.

In the coming days, Ignaz grew stronger and was able to stand and walk on his own. He and Elizabeth stayed together the entire trip, with no need to state their feelings aloud. They helped each other get through their darkest time, and the two families seldom spoke of the evil events back on the dock in Le Havre.

†

Johann and the other men of the four families found work on the top deck with the sailors, who already knew of the hard-working Tschohls. The captain refused to pay them, not even in food. "Why are we doing this if we are not getting paid?" Ignaz asked as he coiled up the last of the rope.

"We are not doing it for them. We are doing it for us," Johann explained. He walked near to Ignaz to keep their discussion quiet. "The work keeps us strong, and clean air does us good. I fear for the little ones below and those who sleep all day through this journey. Many will not make it, while others will emerge with no strength to survive the new world. But we will come out of this strong and ready when the trial meets us."

Ignaz thought for a moment. To Johann's surprise, Ignaz undid a pile of rope he had just wound up.

"What are you doing?" Johann barked. He feared his son's anger over events at the dock ruined his obedient spirit.

"I will make sure this is the best-coiled rope the ship's men have ever seen. I do not want them to think they can find

85

someone better!" Ignaz replied as he carefully placed each loop of rope in the perfect place.

Johann smiled as he saw the old Ignaz slowly coming back to life. "You are spending a lot of time with Elizabeth. Is she doing better?"

Ignaz's smile disappeared while he finished the rope. "Yes, she is. She does not like to speak of it and has never told me what she did. I know, though. I hate that I was not able to save her. If I had been stronger, she would never have had to do that." The pain in his voice hurt Johann.

"Son, you cannot blame yourself. If not for you, it would have been far worse, and she might be dead now. You saved her, and you save her more every day that you spend with her."

"I hope you are right," Ignaz replied. He finished the rope, laid it on the pile, and went back below.

✝

On an ill-fated morning, Johann climbed the ladder to walk the deck. He had befriended several of the sailors, who allowed their 'workers,' as they called Johann, Anton, John, and their sons, to come on deck whenever they wanted. They knew Johann and the rest would do what they asked and were knowledgeable enough to handle themselves on the boat.

"Worker!" one barked. Johann walked to him. He noticed the scowl on the man's weathered face. "You best be on your guard! The red dawn announces a wicked day before us and whispers of a mighty storm that could attack us this eve. Warn those below to get air today. If I am right, it will be several days before they can drink the cool air again."

Johann witnessed the urgency in the man's face. "This is no idle banter. Do you hear me?" the man asked. Johann nodded and went back below, and he took the extra rope the man gave him.

"Josef, take this rope and tie our things tight. Give the rest to Anton and John for their things. A storm is coming, and I think it will far exceed what we have seen so far." Johann then went to the center of the steerage and announced, "Everyone, a storm approaches. It would be good for us to get fresh air today, as it may be several more days before we can again. Take turns, and do not linger too long on deck." The passengers respected Johann and listened intently to what he said.

"How bad will it be?" Josef asked.

"Just do as I said and tie our things down so that at least something can survive this storm to help the others when this is over." Johann slowly went back above as Josef, Ignaz, Louis, and Jacob began to move their items. They took their time so they would not scare the others and were thorough in their deed in the hopes that their food would survive the storm.

Just after midday, one of the ship's crew came below, which they never did. His presence brought everyone to quiet. "A storm comes! Find your place and hold on!" A stir came over the crowd, many of which had nothing to hold on to and no way to protect themselves from what approached, as they only took the space that was left when they boarded. Johann found some extra rope and handed it out in the steerage for the others to tie their things. Several even tied themselves to the large poles in the center of the boat.

The churning seas began to rock the boat in the late afternoon. It foretold the truth of the sailor's words. Though it was slow at first, the pace quickened as night came. Johann stood at the top of the stairs and watched the storm as it descended upon them.

"It is eerie to watch a storm fall on you from so far away and yet be completely unable to move to miss it," Johann thought to himself as he helplessly witnessed the storm's vicious attack. The sailors rushed about and clung to the ropes that lined the boat to keep the churning seas from washing them off.

"Lock the hatches, Johann! If they open, the boat will flood, and we will all go down!" It was the first time one of the sailors called him by name. Johann hurriedly returned below just as the sailors closed the hatches, with the last dim light shut out of the coffin-like compartment below. He locked the latch to the entrance, as instructed.

"The sails have been lowered, and everyone has gone inside for the storm. They believe it will be terrible," Johann informed his family over the smallest of candlelight. "We need to brace ourselves in the cubbies, as we may get turned over. We men will stay out to leave you all some room."

"I will stay out with you," Josef offered.

"No, you need to go in to help brace the younger ones. Anton and John will help me," Johann ordered. Josef obeyed.

Marianna did as Johann said. Elizabeth and Anna went into the cubby with Ignaz, Louis, and Johnnie. Josef went into the other with Marianna and the rest of her children to keep them from tumbling around. "Let us pray before we try to sleep," Marianna said as she sat by the youngest. Together they huddled between the lower and top bed boards to brace themselves for the storm. The faithful offered prayers throughout the cabin in the hopes God would spare their lives. Several of the unfaithful joined them as they saw the urgency of the moment.

Many already suffered from the early stages of cholera and typhus, which ran unabated on most of the immigrant ships. Johann did not allow his family to drink the water offered to them by the crew and only drank the wine he brought with them. He also made sure his family ate at least one apple every day in his feeble attempt to keep them in good health. Their sullen looks stayed in Johann's mind long after he ordered the last of the candles put out.

Johann jammed several trunks and barrels into the opening of the compartments so none of his family would fall out.

"When I was still onshore, I heard dreadful stories of boats turning over in the storms and the many innocent children who were crushed in the turmoil. We need to keep our families safe," Johann said to John and Anton. They did the same with their own things to keep their families safe.

The storm did not disappoint as it thrashed the little ship around in the amazing and unrelenting waves of water. The people in the main part of the steerage fell back and forth with the waves and rolled into each other. Prayers for help mixed with wails of pain filled the cabin. Water seeped through the many holes and rained on the forlorn below. Johann, John, and Anton held tight to a post. Darkness filled the cabin as Johann allowed no lights out of fear of a fire that could erupt in the tumult. Things crashed about that no one bothered to tie down, which then slammed into the people who didn't have cubbies in which to block themselves.

Painful screams and cries of the women and children lost in the darkness scorched Johann's ears, though he was helpless to lend aid. Sickness took many as their senses were unable to withstand the rocking and twisting of the ship. "We are going straight to the bottom!" a lone voice screamed.

A crack of thunder—one of many—pounded the boat as the hatch nearest Johann broke open. The fantastic light from the storm interrupted the darkness and offered a brief glimpse of the suffering and wreckage wrought below. In the fleeting moments, many of the lost were found and quickly gathered back in by the families who searched for them. Enemies of the day relented their ills to help others as all came together in their desperate attempt to survive the tumult of the storm.

A wave crashed over the boat, and its mass of water poured into the open hatch. It seemed to Johann as if the entire volume of the ocean rushed in. Water covered their feet, and Johann thought of those sad people in the lower deck and the water that had to be pooling down there.

"They will drown for sure," Johann thought to himself. He knew what he needed to do as he remembered the sailor's foreboding words about the open hatch. "God help me," Johann uttered. He released his tight hold on the pole and dove for the ladder as the boat churned again. He missed his moving target and landed on the hard surface where a large pool of water stood only a moment ago. He quickly bounced to his feet and lunged again for the sturdy ladder, and grabbed hold. He struggled with all his strength to climb to the hatch as the boat continued to pitch. He also fought the water that crashed down on him from the opening, which sought to thwart his valiant attempt to close the hatch.

The freezing froth bit hard on Johann, but he struggled through the mess and climbed one difficult rung at a time. As he finally reached the top, the water saw its defeat by the determined Johann, and it diminished as the boat violently twisted in yet another direction. Johann stood for a moment. His head peeked out of steerage as he eyed the wicked storm. The winds howled all around as if they were deciding which way to blow. A magnificent stream of lightning lit up the sky and slowly spider-webbed across the darkened landscape. Quiet stole the moment. It was as if God had raised his hand and ordered a halt to both the storm and ocean. A monstrous wave of water rose before Johann, taller than any building or mountain he had ever seen. It towered in front of him, and Johann indeed knew the incredible power of God. The wave stood still. Then, in the next moment, a grumble of anger erupted. A churning swell came forth and violently twisted the boat once again. The mountainous wave rolled over the top of the helpless vessel as the wave pummeled it.

Johann dove back in just in time, pulled the hatch secure, and locked it again before the wave toppled the vessel. The Serampore, and all inside, turned top over bottom. The chaos caused the passengers to lose their hold and threw them about. Several, both the young and old, died in that single churn. The invisible mass of people, trunks, and barrels that crashed about crushed the casualties. Johann fell hard against the support post he had held tightly onto moments earlier, as a loose trunk smashed him against the solid post. He knew no more of the storm which knocked him out cold.

CHAPTER TEN

NEW ORLEANS

Johann woke as a cold, wet rag was applied to his forehead startled him. The trunk the storm had loosened and whipped around the hull gashed his right eye, and Marianna tended to him as he lay still in one of the cubbies.

"Shh," Marianna calmed him. "Do not worry. Thanks to God, we made it through the terrible storm. From what we are told, Johann, you saved us all!"

"The hatch..." Johann moaned. "I had to close it..." His thoughts trailed off as he remembered climbing the ladder and latching the hatch just before the enormous wave crashed down on them. He woke completely and sat up. "The wave will never leave my memory. It is proof there is both a God and a devil. Only a power so great could have summoned such a monster and something so terrible." He groaned as he thought about it.

A man peered at him through the darkness. "Who is that?" Johann asked. Seeing Johann awake, the man turned and yelled to the rest in the steerage compartment, "He lives!" Johann heard the many cheers to his health but did not fully understand them, and he still could not make out the voice.

"What is happening?" he asked. His head throbbed terribly, and he was unable to open his wounded right eye.

Marianna explained, "After you closed the hatch, a trunk came loose and hit you in the head, and it knocked you out. You fell hard onto the floor, but the rocking boat threw you into the water that had already washed in. Then Christoph saved you! He pulled you from it before you drowned and held you safely above the slosh until the storm passed this morning. You would have died for sure if he did not take hold of you."

The words were tough for Johann to hear and even harder to comprehend. He pried open his left eye to see it was true as Christoph stood in the dim candlelight. Anton and John stood close behind him. Christoph slapped Johann hard on the leg, "I knew you was tough! No wonder you bested me!" He chuckled deeply, which drew a similar laugh from Anton and John.

Johann closed his eye and fell back asleep. The boat slowly rocked in the storm's calmer waters and put many passengers into a slumber. Though several people in the lowest level drowned in the deluge, those that survived joined the rest in steerage. Several others passed in the wreckage, just as Johann almost did. All mourned the dead before they were buried at sea. It was a tough thing to do, but to keep the dead on the boat would only further invite more of the already present disease.

Through the stench that never diminished, through the rolling sea and storms that threatened to tear apart the little boat, and through the deaths that happened almost daily for one reason or another, the Tschohls, Schmits, Niggs, and Kaufmanns survived the trip. Whether turned by the storm or a fortuitous piece of loosened luggage to his head, Christoph became a friend to many on the ship. He helped by moving the large boxes of cargo the storm dislodged, and he saved many during the dark days and nights, of which Johann was only one. In gratitude for his help, Christoph received many meals from the other passengers, including the Tschohls.

Johann, for the first time in almost ten days, climbed the ladder to the top deck. Josef and Ignaz went with him. As they reached through the hatch, they quickly felt the temperature change as the boat traveled farther to the south. A great wind ushered them on their way. It was a reward for their survival of the mighty storm.

"I think we are turning," Josef said. "This is the calmest the ocean has been on the trip so far."

"Yes, we are turning away from the rising sun. We must be rounding the bottom of Florida, so we will soon be in New Orleans." Johann replied as he and his sons shared a smile, for they were quite eager to get off the boat. Louis also brought the others up as the captain invited the surviving passengers to take turns on the deck.

The captain heard of Johann's heroics. "The boat would have sunk for certain had you not been able to close the hatch. All of us owe our lives to you, Herr Tschohl."

"You are welcome, Captain," Johann replied. He did not like the attention. It was not lost on him, or the other passengers who heard it, that the captain called him Herr Tschohl. It was a far higher term than 'German.'

As the rest climbed to the upper deck, Johnnie jumped off the ladder and squealed in delight, "It is so warm!" He held out his arms and let the breeze wash over him. Marianna's family, the Niggs and Kaufmanns, and many others came out also. They brought food and ate a morning meal as they shared prayers of thanks to God for seeing them through the storm.

Johnnie saw a sailor staring off over the waters, and so he went over and asked, "What are you looking for?"

The man saw Johann was listening, so he bent lower and replied, "I am looking for the Burla Negra and the Morning Star. Have you heard or seen of them?"

"No, what are they?" Johnnie asked.

"Why, the Burla Negra is a pirate ship! She be guided by the ruthless pirate Benito De Soto, one of the most dangerous bastard scoundrels of them all. De Soto chased the Morning Star and killed every last one of them. Their blood soaked into the boat before it sunk, and it is said the blood made the boat rise in the night, and it sailed away. Anyone who boards her goes crazy. That is what they say."

"Oh my! Father, did you hear that?" Johnnie asked.

"Every word, son. What do you think of it?" Johann asked.

Johnnie stood tall and scanned the ocean in all directions. "I do not see anything, but I will watch for them. What should I do if I see one?" he asked the sailor.

"Well, you come and get me, of course," the sailor replied with a smile.

Johnnie turned back to the sailor, "What happened to the pirate De Soto?"

"They say he was hanged, but I am not sure. I think he is still out there, chasing the Morning Star. It is the one boat that still defies him," the sailor replied. He then saw the worry growing on Johnnie. "Son, do not worry. This ship is faster than any ship around, and we have the best men! We carry no fear of pirates!"

Johnnie smiled and went and sat close to his father, but not before he took another look at the ocean to check for pirate ships.

Ignaz and Elizabeth were the last to climb to the deck. Ignaz sat down and invited Elizabeth to join him. He sat for a moment as he basked in the sun and drank in the fresh air.

"The worst is over," he said as he took her hand.

Elizabeth smiled, but it soon left her. "I am fearful of what I did back in Le Havre. They will eventually find us and take me back." She rubbed the deep cut on her hand from when she stabbed the man.

"No! That is far behind us. No one is looking for the person who did that, and the Surete would certainly never track us here. My father even said so. That man deserved what happened for what he did to you," Ignaz consoled her.

"But what if they do come? What if they find me?" Elizabeth's lip trembled at the thought.

Ignaz reached for her and lifted her chin, "I will not let them hurt you, never. They will not find us. Even if they did, they have no proof. No one saw it. Please, do not worry over it."

"But you will be going north and leave me," Elizabeth stated.

"No. I intend to stay with you," Ignaz pledged. "If you will have me, that is."

Elizabeth smiled broadly, "Yes, I will have you." Ignaz leaned in and kissed her. As she pulled away, she added, "Please, let us wait until we reach Prairie Du Rocher to tell them. There is so much to be concerned about between here and there."

"We can wait. My father will not take it well, but we will be close enough to visit them. Thank you for having me. I promise to do everything I can to make you happy for the rest of your life!"

On the morning of the eighth day since turning west, and on the 21st day since leaving Le Havre, the ship Serampore entered the harbor of New Orleans. Many of the passengers sat on the deck and warmed themselves as the boat waited to be ferried into the dock.

"There are so many boats!" Johnnie chittered.

"Look at that one," Louis whispered in awe to his father.

Johann looked where his son indicated, and on the large boat stood many men of dark color, tied together. "Those are slaves. The southern states allow slaves for the working of their fields. They bring them over from Africa."

"What is a slave?" Johnnie asked.

"It is someone who works for someone else and does all the work they do not want to do," Josef explained.

Johnnie thought for a moment, "So are we slaves, too, father? Were you a slave to the people on the boat?"

"No, Johnnie. The men on the boat took them from their homes, and they whip them if they do not do what they are supposed to. They kill the slaves if they try to leave. You boys help me, and we helped the people on the boat. It is different." Johann tried to explain, but Johnnie's furrowed brow told Johann his youngest still did not understand. At the least, Johnnie did not ask any more questions.

The city of New Orleans was one of the largest ports in the United States, and it rivaled New York in every way. Many businesses and houses lined the shores, which were busy with boats that traded this and that. "We need to be careful of the men who walk the docks," Anton informed the others. "From what Alois Buchel said, they are just like the men in Le Havre. They look to steal and swindle at every turn and hope to take advantage of the newly-arrived immigrants. This is no place for the meek."

"How long will we be here, father?" Josef asked.

Johann read his son's eagerness to see the city, and he wanted none of it. "As short as possible. Anton will lead us to a steamer paddleboat that is headed upstream, and we will hopefully depart tomorrow." Johann did not want his children to walk around the port.

Ignaz walked toward his father. "Father, we need to get off the boat soon. I fear Elizabeth is not well."

Johann saw his son's concern and looked toward Elizabeth. She was pale and coughing, as were many of the passengers. "I am sure it will pass, son. We will be off soon."

"May we travel with you up the river?" Marianna asked Johann. "I fear to attempt the trip with my family by myself."

"Of course, we will see you to your town in Illinois," Johann offered. "I would want the same for my family if I had passed." He enjoyed Marianna's company, and she helped greatly with Johnnie and his family's needs. Without Mariana,

Thomasia, and Maria, the trip would have been far more difficult.

A steamer ferry came out to pull them to dock, and soon men tied the Serampore up, and the passengers unloaded. As each of them took their first steps on the solid land, they became dizzy. "What is going on?" Louis asked as he tried to catch his balance.

"Ya need to get yer land legs back!" one of the ship's crew barked with a laugh. "I love watchin' the first steps after a long trip!"

Though it took longer for some than others, eventually, their land legs returned. Before they could go further, they needed to go through the immigration station. This included a quick look over by a doctor, and he delayed many of the sick from moving on.

"To the showers!" a lady ordered them. The guards filed the passengers into rows, with the men and women separated. After quick showers in freezing water, Johann and his sons stood in a line. Several men doused them with powder to kill any lice that lingered. After a final check, another guard ordered, "You are free to go!"

Though it took longer, the doctor finally released Ignaz and Elizabeth. "She needs to rest and drink plenty of water," Ignaz told Marianna. Elizabeth looked weak and even paler than before.

He then went to his father, "The only reason they let her go was the large number who could not walk that they had to keep. She is quite sick, father. Is there something we can do?"

"Yes, we can set up a camp this evening and get her a good night's sleep. That should help," Johann replied.

After they made sure everything was off the boat, Johann told John and Anton, "John, please stay here while Anton and I go to find a boat to take us upriver." He then reached into his pocket and pulled out several gold coins. "Josef, go find a place to exchange this for money. Then find us some fresh food to eat, most of what we have is spoiled. And be careful who you show those coins to. You will attract attention that you do not want." Josef did as he was ordered, and he took Jacob with him.

Johann and Anton walked through the town and headed straight toward the docks at the river, where they secured travel up the Mississippi. "We will need to do this several times, as the steamers each work a certain portion of the river," Anton said.

The women picked over their food and only kept the best of what was left. "It is hard to throw this much food away," Marianna said as she dumped a load of rotten potatoes.

"I am just thankful we had enough to last us the trip so far," Thomasia offered.

"Do we have any extra we could offer those men?" Johnnie asked as he pointed to the slaves.

"I think we do. Please help me find some," Marianna replied. Johnnie helped Marianna as the two picked a basket of good food, and together they took it over to the man with the whip.

"Pardon, but we would like to offer your slaves some food. May we do that?" Marianna asked.

"Why ma'am, these slaves got to eat just this mornin'?" he grunted. Then he yelled at his slaves, who stared at the food with hungry eyes. "You's don't need more food, does you?" he challenged with a raised whip. The slaves all looked down, as they feared the whip over their hunger pains.

"Ha!" the man yelled and cracked his whip in the air. The slaves winced at the stark sound and then marched off. They left the food behind.

"You are a kind boy, Johnnie," Marianna said as she led them back. He dejectedly walked away as they left their extra food for whoever needed it. A crowd of people from the dock area quickly grew around it, and soon it was gone.

Johann paid a man with a wagon to move their things for them. "Josef, Ignaz, and Jacob, you will go with the wagon to watch our things until we get there. You better take Elizabeth too," Johann told his boys, and they helped Elizabeth climb into the wagon. She was far too weak to make the long walk.

"I will go with them," John said as he climbed up.

"Take care to mind your own business and stay away from the ruffians along the shore!" Johann sternly stated.

"Yes, father," all three answered, and Jacob risked a smile. They jumped on the wagon and rode off with the luggage.

"I hope Elizabeth gets better soon," Marianna said to Johann as she held her youngest. "It is a miracle more of us are not ill. She looks like many who did not survive our journey. I fear she has typhoid."

"She needs clean water and a warm, cooked meal. Tonight, we will have both," Johann reassured. In his mind, nothing could make a person feel better than a well-cooked meal, and he knew Marianna, Thomasia, and Maria were excellent cooks.

Just before they departed on their walk, Johann saw Christoph as he meandered around the dock. Johann walked over to the man who saved him, "I never thanked you for helping me. I know you saved a lot of people on that boat. Thank you."

"It was the least I could do. Besides, I needed to do something to get some food. You would have beat me silly if I tried to steal some more," Christoph laughed. "You have a nice family, Johann, and you are a good man. I hope you reach your destination."

"Thank you again. I greatly fear for what my family would be doing now without your help, and I would have drowned for sure," Johann replied.

Christoph smiled and extended his hand to shake Johann's. "You saved all of us by closing the hatch. My thanks go to you, Johann. You know, I ate a lot better after helping you than I ever did by just taking food from people. You showed me a new way."

"I am glad you have changed. What are you going to do now?" Johann asked.

A look of dread spread over Christoph's face, "I am not sure. I never really thought we would make it this far. I have no money, no food, and no place to go."

Johann reached into his pocket and pulled several coins from within. He gave them to Christoph, "This is for helping me. You are a good man also, and very strong. Find a job, and you will be fine. This is Amerika! You can be whatever you want."

The men shook hands again, and Johann returned to his family. "We have a long walk," Johann said as he took Johnnie's hand and led the rest of them through the busy streets of New Orleans.

"How long will it take to get to Prairie Du Rocher from here?" Mariana asked.

"Several more weeks I should think. We will be going upstream, and we have a long way to travel," Anton answered. As they walked through the town, they came upon a sale. They stopped for a drink from the well as the heat of the day picked up. Behind them, on an erected stage, several men brought families of black slaves up for presentation.

"A family of slaves here! One man, Tom Coleman, age thirty. He is a great field hand and an excellent blacksmith. His wife Mary, age 37, is also a great field hand, though she is known to have a failing of health from time to time. Their son, Tucker, a sprightly boy, is said to be a nimble dancer. They are sold as a family to the highest bidder. Bidding starts now!" the man yelled over the crowd.

The four families watched in amazement as voices in the crowd yelled their bid, with the answers coming in flurries. It was quick and furious, and then it was over as the winning bid was attained and the Coleman family was sold.

Johnnie could not help but stare into the eyes of the boy Tucker, who was just a little older than he.

Johann felt Johnnie squeezing his hand. "What is it, son?"

"That boy looks so sad, father. Why?" Johnnie innocently asked.

"He is probably worried about where he is going and what his life is going to be like once he gets there. Do you have the same worries about where we are going?" Johann asked.

"Maybe. Can you buy them, father so that they can come with us?" Johnnie's big eyes looked into Johann's.

Johann watched as the owners took the Coleman family, who were chained together, and led them off. The guard carried a large whip in hand. "I do not think they have a choice, son. They are already sold, and I do not have the money. I am sorry." At his words, Johnnie buried his face into Johann's coat to hide his sad tears.

"Let us go," Anton said as he pulled them away from the scene. Then they heard a loud crack, followed by a scream of pain. All in the square looked when one of the men who ran the sale whipped a slave who had tried to take food from a table. The man cursed his slave, who lay curled up on the ground to protect himself as the man continually whipped him. Johann could not make out the words the man screamed. He hurried away, as he did not want anymore to do with this dreadful place. The family walked in silence for several blocks as Anton led the way.

"Is this part of France?" Louis asked as they walked down the street, the sale of the slaves left far behind.

"No. There are just a lot of people from France who live here. They founded the city of New Orleans. We are still a long way from Gutenberg. There we will be with a lot of German-speaking people."

"I hope our first glimpse of Amerika is not what the rest will be like," Anton uttered to Johann as they led the families toward the river port. "Agreed," Johann replied.

Though it took about an hour, they finally arrived at the docks where the steamboat Natchez ported. It would take them on the first leg of their journey up the river, and it would leave directly in the morning. They said their prayers and ate their dinner, and then they readied for their first night on land in over a month.

Ignaz sat by Elizabeth, who was too sick to eat. He fanned her along the bank and occasionally soaked a rag in the cool water of the river to place on her forehead.

"How is she?" Marianna asked as she sat next to him.

"She is so hot and sweating terribly. I cannot get her to eat or drink anything," Ignaz replied. He tried again to get her to sip some water, but she only turned her head away from him.

"You are a good boy, Ignaz. Thank you for watching over her," Marianna said as she hugged Ignaz. "Now, you need to go to eat and rest. Hopefully, she will feel better in the morning."

Ignaz did as she told him and left Elizabeth with her mother.

✝

After eating, the women and children lay down to sleep. Johann saw Josef, Louis, Jacob, and Alois milling around. He suspected their intentions. "What are your plans, boys?"

Josef stepped toward his father, "We wanted to go look around, to see the city."

Johann understood the young interest in adventure, though it greatly feared him what they might encounter. "You are responsible for them," he said to Josef. "Stay together and be back before midnight. Be careful!"

Josef could not believe his father allowed them to go. "Ignaz, we are going into town. Do you want to go?"

"No, I am staying with Elizabeth," Ignaz replied.

"You boys be careful," Anton warned.

"Stay together and do not get mixed up with any of those men or women from the docks," John added. After the boys left, Maria looked to her husband, "You have never been that good about staying away from such people."

"Dear, where we come from, we *are* those people," John laughed.

The four boys quickly walked off to see the city before Johann could change his mind. As they hurried toward the downtown section, back toward the docks, Jacob gasped, "He let us go. My father would not have!"

Josef smiled, "They were young once. I think part of him wishes he could go with us."

It was not long before they reached the busy streets of New Orleans. "Look at the dresses those women have on," Josef said. "I have never seen women dress like that!"

"What about the suits the men are wearing? They must all be made and fitted here," Jacob added.

"We need to be careful of the crowds hugging the dark edges," Louis said as he motioned to the alleys. "Let us stay away from there. I do not like the look of them," Louis said as he urged Jacob forward. Josef turned to listen to Louis, and when he turned back to where he was going, he bumped into a burly man. The man pretended to get hit harder than he did. Then he abruptly turned on Josef.

"Say, boy! You better watch where you are going!" the man shouted.

"My pardon, I did not see you," Josef responded. Three rest of the large man's friends stepped out of the shadows to join him.

The man stared down at Josef and the others. "Germans! Boys, we have a few Germans here! You walk around like you own the place!"

"Herr..." Josef started again, but this time the man interrupted him. "How about you join us for a game of cards? We can show you the *finer* side of New Orleans, and maybe even introduce you to some ladies?" The man flared his eyes to entice Josef to go with him.

"We must be going," Josef said as the four rushed past the man and his friends.

"We will see you around!" the man yelled as they ran away.

"I do not like that man! Maybe we should head back," Louis said as they slowed their run.

"We are going back, but not straight away. I do not want them following us." Josef led Jacob and Louis as they hurried through the busy streets. They constantly looked back over their shoulders to see if the men followed them. They made a large swath around several city blocks before they headed back to their camp. As they crossed the last street before their families, four shadowy figures stepped before them, cutting them off.

"Look who it is! The ungrateful Germans! We try to show you a good time, and you run off like little boys!" The ruffians laughed at their leader's remarks, but the sound of them sent chills up and down Josef's spine.

Jacob, without warning, lunged at the large man. "No!" Josef yelled, but it was too late as Jacob punched the man hard on the side of the head. He knocked the fat man to the ground, but the other three quickly grabbed him and started to beat him. Louis jumped in, and they punched and dragged him to the ground also. Each of them had axe handles that they swung at Louis. He groaned with each blow that thudded off his back.

"Leave him alone!" Josef yelled as he tried to pull the men off his brother. Then the men turned their attention to Josef. The largest man hit Josef over the head with a board, and he fell hard to the dirt, his senses reeling.

The dark men laughed at the boys who lay beaten on the ground, and Josef rolled over to see the fat man as he stood again. He stepped into the light, and Josef noticed the sparkle of a blade in his hand. Worry took Josef as he tried to stand. He had nothing to defend himself. As the man took another step toward Josef, a board swung out of the darkness across the large man's head and took him to the ground.

Josef didn't wait. He turned and punched one of the men who held an axe handle. Josef then dodged the swing of another and heard another board smash into the man's head. Jacob tackled the man closest to him. Josef went over to help, but a large hand moved him aside. Josef was sure it was his father who had come, but instead, it was Christoph, the man from the boat.

"Move on, lads, I will take this from here. Get back to your father and stay there. You must be gone in the morning, for they will come looking for you!" Christoph slammed his large fist into the man wrestling with Jacob, and the fight was finished. Josef and Louis helped Jacob from the ground.

"Thank you, Christoph," Josef offered.

"Go on, boys, get to your destination and stay there. The rest of the world is too messy for the likes of you." Christoph kicked another one of the ruffians who began to stir.

"You should come with us. We can always use a good man," Josef stated.

Christoph stared back for a moment before he responded, "Josef, there are two worlds. One for good people like yourselves, and one for the rest of us." He looked down and gave a final kick to the man who wriggled on the ground. "I wish I could fit in with people like you, but my bad habits are always gettin' in the way!"

"We are leaving from the docks in the morning. We would love to have you join us."

Josef, Louis, and Jacob hurried back to camp. The rest were already asleep when they arrived, so they laid down next to the fire and tried to rest. Each one took turns to watch for the ruffians the rest of the night. Josef feared they might come looking for trouble again. Thanks to Christoph, they did not.

CHAPTER ELEVEN

THE OLD MAN

The brilliant sun rose over the mouth of the mighty Mississippi River. The red streams of light expanded across the sky and harkened a new day and a blessing on those who started the final stretch of their journey. The waterway opened the middle of the United States to the immigrants hungering for a fresh start. Though both trips were long and dangerous, many preferred the steamboat ride up the river over the long trek through the settled territory from New York to Cincinnati and then further into Illinois and Iowa.

Johann greeted the day with a smile in his heart, and then he woke up the others. Jacob's black eye was swollen shut. "Some lessons need to be learned, and a little harsh experience goes a long way," Johann muttered.

"Yes, sir," Jacob responded. Johann walked over to check on Elizabeth, where he saw Marianna and Ignaz as they hovered over her.

"It is time to board, Elizabeth," Marianna whispered. The concern in her voice told Johann that Elizabeth was still very ill.

"I will carry her. She cannot walk that far," Ignaz interceded. He carefully lifted Elizabeth, and they walked to board the boat. The Niggs and Kaufmanns went first. Johann, Jacob, and Louis then loaded their things as Marianna walked the littlest of them to board the boat.

The man on the dock accepted Johann's payment for the ride up the river and counted each passenger as they walked past. He stopped Ignaz as he approached, "Son, that girl cannot come aboard this ship."

"She is coming with us," Ignaz protested. Johann heard their argument and quickly came back to help.

"What is wrong?" Johann intervened.

"This girl is sick, and we cannot run the risk of her getting our passengers sick. It will ruin our business. She does not ride this boat!" the man sternly stated again.

Johann saw Ignaz shake as a wrathful look raged in his normally peaceful eyes. His anger quickly rose to the point of desperation. Johann worried about what might happen next. "Sir, please, let us talk." Johann led him a short distance away. "Are you sure there is no way you can let the girl board? We are taking care of her, and yes, she is very ill. But we cannot leave her here, and we have to keep going, or we will never reach our destination. We will set up wherever you wish and keep her hidden from the others. We have traveled with her for over a month, and she has yet to infect any of us."

The man took another look at Ignaz and Elizabeth. He then looked back to Johann, "You must take her onto the second level. She cannot come down, and you must keep her out of sight or else I will get fired."

"Yes, sir, and we thank you. Is there anything else we can do to help you? I have several strong men who can help," Johann asked. He was very appreciative of the man helping them.

"You and your sons will make sure the fires on the boat do not go low. Shoveling coal is hard work! Do you think you and your men are up for it?" the man challenged.

"It is a deal," Johann replied as he reached for the man's reluctant hand.

✝

The four families boarded a steamboat called the *Natchez* and prepared to ride it from New Orleans to Vicksburg, Tennessee, with a night stop in Natchez, Mississippi.

The captain of the steamboat carried a load of cargo and animals. Also on board was a slave owner who had just purchased several of them from the auction. The people who were already on board stepped aside as the sweaty slaves drearily trudged aboard, each chained to one another. The owner marched them over where the animals were kept.

Johnnie hung his arms over the top railing and watched the rest board below. "Father, those are the men we saw sold, the family!" he blurted. "Do you remember?"

Johann saw them too. He felt sorry for their predicament. "Yes, Johnnie, I remember them. I am not sure how an otherwise good man can make owning another man right in his mind."

Johnnie turned to Johann and tugged at his suspenders. Johann bent low to listen. "Will we have slaves?"

The terrified look in Johnnie's eyes hurt Johann. "No, son, we will not. There are no slaves where we are going, at least not that I know of."

A look of relief covered Johnnie's face, but it disappeared as another question rushed to his lips, "Will we be slaves? It seems a lot of people do not like us Germans much."

Johann smiled, "I think not. We will soon have land and go to minding our own business."

Johnnie was again relieved, but the look of the slaves, especially the ones his age, burned into his mind. Several of the black men carried the last slave onto the boat. He was the one that received the whipping in town, and blood stained what was left of his ripped-up shirt. The scars on his back spoke of the many whippings he received in his life. Most of the women turned at the horrible sight. The owner sneered with delight as the onlookers gasped. "Do you ladies like my handiwork?" the man asked.

After the slaves boarded, Johann had his family and the rest settle down in their area. It was close to the little tent Ignaz had made for Elizabeth on the boat's second deck. They hid Elizabeth the best they could.

Johann met another family, one from Amerika. They spoke German and English. "Would you be willing to teach us English?" Johann asked.

"Of course, it will help pass our time on the boat. We are going to Davenport, so we will be together quite a while," the man replied. The group quickly made friends with each other, and the four families from Liechtenstein worked hard to develop their English speaking skills.

The well-to-do took the upper cabins and had their things carried for them. The many complaints of the other passengers surprised the Tschohls, Niggs, Kaufmanns, and Schmits.

"It is so hot! How are we going to survive this?" one lady said as she fanned herself. "We should have ridden in the cabins, not down here by the stinky animals!" At her last sentence, she looked sideways at the Tschohls and their friends.

"She thinks she is better than us," Marianna said as she adjusted her dress.

Johann stopped her. "Marianna, you look very nice. Do not let that lady make you question yourself." Then he looked to his sons. "I was wondering earlier how people can get to the point where they can make owning another man right in their mind. Hearing that lady makes it pretty clear to me." He paused as his sons looked at the people, the slaves, the other immigrants, and the rest of the Southerners. Johann continued, "There are good and bad people in all of the groups. Each person can even be good and bad at the same time. But we need to remember that God put us here for a reason, as He also did them. We are better than no one, remember that."

Johnnie thought for a moment and then asked, "There is bad in us, too?" His furrowed brow hung precariously over his curious eyes.

"Yes. I know there is in me. I get angry too often and desire revenge when what I should do is forgive. I am also quick to judge. We all have things we need to work on, and I am sure if you think about it, and if you are honest, you will find things you need to work on too." Johann thought about what it must have been like to be a slave, through no fault of his own, other than being born in a disadvantaged place and time.

"Louis, Josef, and Jacob, come with me. We have some coal to shovel." Johann led them down to the furnaces, and they began the hard work of fueling the boilers, which got the ship moving. The men usually assigned to the job greatly enjoyed the break. Anton, John, and Alois stood by and waited for their turn.

The Natchez was a fine steamer, one of the many that worked its section of the river. When they plowed upstream, it seemed as if they were barely moving.

"It is hot and sticky, but it is far better on here than what we experienced on the Serampore," Anton said to the others.

"You are right, Anton. How can these people complain? Even what we are doing here, shoveling coal, this is first-class compared to life on the Serampore," Josef replied as he threw another load in the hot furnace.

"They have not been through what we have, and to be honest, I am happy for them. I would not wish to do it again either," Johann answered with a grin. His sons agreed and continued to shovel. "A breeze, even a hot one like today, is far better than that disease-infested carriage on the Serampore."

"Why are we not below the deck now?" Louis asked as he leaned on his shovel.

"There is no below deck, son," a steamer hand heard the questions and laughed his reply as he strode past. "The water is only fifteen feet deep, and far less in some places." Having dropped his tidbit, he moved on.

As they sat down on the deck above, Marianna, Thomasia, and Maria made the rest a small lunch, which consisted of meat, cheese, and apples, of course. They had plenty, and many of the white people did the same.

"Johnnie, you should take some food down for your father and brothers. They will be getting quite hungry," Marianna asked.

"Yes, ma'am!" Johnnie agreed as he eagerly helped.

Johnnie took a load of food in a sack and rushed through the people to his father down below. "Thank you," Johann said as he accepted the food, and they took a break. Johann noticed the slaves who watched his son. The hungry look in their eyes called to him. He also saw many others who did their best to ignore the slave's destitute stares.

The owners of the slaves paid them no heed and ate directly in front of them. Though they took the time to feed their animals, they gave neither food nor drink to the slaves.

Johann felt sorry for them and wished there was something he could do. Much to his surprise, he noticed Johnnie as he spoke with one of the slave owners. "Oh no," he said as he jumped up and rushed to his son.

As he approached the owner, he heard the man say, "Son, they do not need to eat but once a day. They is fine. But, it's your food, and if you want to share it with Negroes, go ahead. I won't stop you."

Johnnie did not stop to ask his father's permission, but he rushed up to their barrel of apples. He piled them into his shirt. Several squirted out and rolled across the deck. Johnnie picked them up and then rushed back down to the slaves in their chains and handed each an apple.

"Thank you, son," the black man said as he and his family gratefully took the apple. Without waiting, they devoured them. "This is the first bite we had all day, and I does not expect to get any until late tonight!"

Johnnie went back and stood by his father. "Does that make you feel good, Johnnie?" Johann asked.

"Yes, father. I wish I could give them more." Then Johnnie noticed there was still one more slave that needed to eat. He picked out a perfect apple and rushed back over. It was the slave who had been whipped. As the owner saw the boy's intentions, he sternly put his hand before him, and Johnnie stopped.

"Son, this one is not getting anything to eat. He is bad to the core. But worry not," the man said as he bent low. "He will not be hungry tomorrow or ever again." The grin on his face brought tears to Johnnie's eyes. He turned to see his father standing behind him. Johann put his arm around his son and led him off.

The black man lay face down from the whipping he received. He heard the man's words, which foretold of what awaited him the next day. His unblinking eyes stared at Johnnie, who tried his best to hide from them. Johann saw and knelt low to Johnnie, "Do not let that man bother you. You did what you could for the slave."

"What is going to happen to him?" Johnnie asked, his eyes big and wide. He waited for his father's response.

"I do not know," Johann answered, but he knew full well the man's destiny. "The boilers are burning hot," John interrupted. "You should go check on Elizabeth and the others. We will take our turn down here."

Johann and his sons handed over the shovels and marched up the steps to the second floor. "Dear Lord, please help that man," Johnnie whispered as he clenched his father's hand tightly.

They watched Elizabeth as her health continued to fade throughout the day, despite the constant attention Ignaz showered on her. The families stood vigil over Elizabeth as they slowly passed the moss-covered cypress trees that lined the river.

Some of the passengers sat with their legs hung out over the side as they fished. One of the men working the boat gave Josef and Louis a pole to fish with, out of thanks for his work reprieve. To their surprise, they caught several catfish.

"We are going to have a fish feast tonight!" Josef gushed.

Johann saw that Johnnie's face was red and that he was gnashing his teeth. "What is wrong?" he asked the boy.

Johnnie did not look up. He stared into nothingness and said, "The look on the whipped slave's face will not leave my mind, no matter what I try to look at."

"I am sorry, son. I wish we could help him," Johann consoled.

In the late afternoon, they arrived in Natchez, Mississippi. The city bustled with people moving about, though it was far smaller than New Orleans. "We leave at first light!" the captain warned as the plank to shore was set in place. "Be on time, or you will be left!"

Before long, many of the riders from the deck area settled on the banks and cooked their day's catch. "Interested in going into the city?" Johann asked Josef and Louis. "No!" they replied in unison.

Johann saw Johnnie, who already made for his bed. He went to talk with his youngest son. "Are you all right?"

Johnnie looked to his father, and his tears flowed. "We should have helped that man."

"As I said earlier, there is nothing we can do for him. I am sorry, son," Johann replied.

Johnnie kept his resolve and said, "We should help him escape. They are going to kill him!"

"They will kill us if we do. We cannot help him," Johann said and left his son to cry himself to sleep. After their dinner, all laid down, and most of them fell fast asleep under the starry sky.

Ignaz stayed awake with Elizabeth. She no longer sweated, for her body had already delivered all the water it carried. Her shallow breaths told Marianna all she needed to know. Tears filled her eyes as she looked at Ignaz. "I have buried enough to know the end is near. I thank the dear Lord for bringing you into her life. She loves you so much."

"Did you know we were going to get married?" Ignaz asked. He took Elizabeth's cool hand.

"I did not, but it does not surprise me. You are a good boy, Ignaz, and I am so glad she was able to find love before her end."

The words consoled Ignaz little. "God, please," he prayed, "If it must be done, take me, and not my dear Elizabeth." He prayed it over and over again as the night went on.

Shortly after midnight, Ignaz woke to see Elizabeth as she looked at him. It was the first time in over two days that she was awake. His hopes soared for her survival. Even in her deep sickness, she looked so beautiful to him.

"Ignaz," Elizabeth said with the slightest squeeze of his hand, "My time is near..."

Ignaz watched every small moment pass as he tried to draw them out longer. Before he could answer, her breath stopped. He expected a dramatic moment when she died, but there was none. Elizabeth passed as Ignaz held her on the bank of the Mississippi. He lay his head into her neck and cried his hardest cry in years. He begged one last time for God to save her, but he knew the time for that had passed.

Ignaz stood. He went into the woods, alone, to dig a grave for Elizabeth.

Johnnie woke in the night as he heard a stick break in the forest. He peered into the darkness, with the dying fire next to him. Then a man, the slave who the man whipped a few days prior, slowly stepped out from the shadows. He quietly crept into their camp.

"Do you want some food?" Johnnie asked quietly. The slight sound startled the scared slave, and he turned on Johnnie out of fear. Then Johnnie saw the bloodied blade the slave held.

"Boy, you best go to sleep!" the man said in a hushed voice. He then reached for the pot Marianna had cooked the fish in earlier that night.

"It is not there!" Johnnie said. He jumped from his roll and rushed to the pan in which Marianna kept the leftovers. The slave frantically looked around the camp and waited to see who else would wake. Johnnie quickly took the pieces of fish to the man, as well as a bucket of drinking water.

"Thank you," the man said as he smashed the fish into his mouth.

"You must be hungry!" Johnnie muttered as he watched the man devour the fish. He then noticed the man's bloodied wrists, "What happened?"

The man stopped eating and looked at Johnnie. "The boss man chained me. They was gonna kill me in the morning, so I decides not to be here for that. I pulled those chains off and am running away. I had to kill a man to escape, but better him than me!"

Dogs barked not far away and woke Johann. Ignaz ran back into the camp with his shovel raised. "Who are you?" he yelled.

"Johnnie! Get away from him!" Johann shouted.

"Father!" Johnnie protested as Johann reached for him. He quickly pulled his son away from the slave.

The man stood between Johann and Ignaz with his knife brazened at them, "He just give me some fish, sir. He did not mean no harm. They is gonna kill me for sure, boss!" The man breathed heavily and stared Johann in the eye as the dogs closed in. Ignaz saw the torches through the dark woods along the bank as the voices of the searchers interrupted the night.

"Get into the river and swim downstream for a while and then get out on the other side. They will not expect it," Johann said quietly. The slave gave a last look of a smile to

Johnnie and did as Johann said. He ran to the edge of the water and silently slipped in as the first men, and their dogs entered the camp.

"Where is my slave? He is a killer!" the man barked. His eyes searched the people in the camp. He laid his eyes on Ignaz, who still held the shovel. Johann also noticed the shovel and guessed at its need.

"He went that way! He just ran through here and stole some of our things!" Johann yelled. He hoped to convince the slaveowners that their slave ran off.

The man gave a sideways look to Johann and then to Johnnie. "You are the one who fed that..." the man started, but his impatient hounds pulled him hard and forward. The group followed the slave's trail to the river, just where he slipped in. The man yelled, "Go north along the bank. He will be heading that-a-way!" The sound of the group heading north slowly drifted off.

Johann and Johnnie returned to the center of the camp and found Ignaz standing in the near darkness. "What is it, son? Is she passed?" Johann asked Ignaz.

"She is gone," Ignaz said as he sat down by the dwindling fire, his head covered by his dirty hands.

Marianna woke as the dogs had approached moments before and heard Ignaz's words. She slowly stood and went to see her daughter's body. Thomasia and Maria went with her.

Johann turned on Johnnie. He harshly grabbed his son's shirt tight with a fist and lifted the frightened little boy off his feet. "You cannot save everyone! If you try to help that man or any other of them, you are going to get us all killed!" Johann's angered voice filled their camp and woke everyone who was not already awake.

Johnnie never saw his father so angry. Tears again rolled down his cheeks. "What if we were the ones who needed help, father?" Johnnie sniffled. The words slowly sunk into Johann and past his immediate wrath. He turned to see Johnnie's brothers and the other families who watched the two. Johann set Johnnie down, though both still shook from the interaction.

"I just want to make it to Gutenberg. Nothing and no one else matters, especially the slaves!" Johann yelled as he stomped off. He picked a spot against a tree, several paces outside the camp, and sat down to calm himself.

"Come sleep by me," Anna, Elizabeth's sister, said as she led Johnnie away.

"Father hates me!" Johnnie cried as he lay down.

"No, he does not," Anna comforted. "He just wants to keep us safe. Those men are dangerous. If they hate black men, they probably do not like us much either."

The three women prepared Elizabeth's body for burial. When they were ready, Marianna brought Ignaz over, and Josef went to wake up everyone to say their goodbyes. As they all walked over in the darkness, with only a small fire nearby to provide light, Johann stood before them and helped his son bury his love.

Johann prayed for Elizabeth, "Dear God, we wish to thank you for the life you gave Elizabeth and the many others who passed before we deemed they should. We also pray in thanks for the love that You gave her and Ignaz. I pray the souls of my two wives and Richard welcome Elizabeth's kind soul to Heaven and that all of them look over us as we head to our new homes."

"Thank you. That was beautiful," Marianna said as Jacob led her back to camp to prepare to depart on their trip up the river. Ignaz did not speak as he went back to the camp. Johann left him alone to give him time to reflect.

CHAPTER TWELVE

VICKSBURG

Before dawn, the passengers loaded the Natchez again. The four families did so with heavy hearts for the one they left behind. Sadness gripped them as they boarded.

Josef sat next to Johnnie, who stared over the railing as the sun's first light filled the sky. "What are you thinking about?"

"I wonder what will happen to that slave," Johnnie asked.

"I do not know, but I hope he got far away," Josef replied. "You are kind, Johnnie, do not ever lose that." Johnnie lay his weary head on Josef's leg and quickly fell asleep.

Ignaz led Marianna onto the boat after both said their final goodbye's to Elizabeth. "It is so hard to leave her behind," Ignaz whimpered as he clutched Marianna's hand.

"I know," Marianna replied. "But it is what we must do. It is what she would want us to do."

The man who took their tickets the day before noticed the sad look. As Ignaz passed him, the man reached out, "I am sorry for your loss." Ignaz accepted the kind gesture and found his spot on the boat. He sat in quiet sorrow. Marianna consoled him as Anna, with the help of Thomasia and Maria, watched her young children.

"Get them loaded!" the captain ordered. "We need to go if we are to reach Vicksburg and return before nightfall!" It was a daily chore to travel to Vicksburg and back, but they had no chance of completing the task without a keen focus. Josef and Jacob went down to stoke the coal fires and did their part to get the boat moving.

A passenger woman, one who did not enjoy being hurried, scowled at the ticket man, "Is that not what we have lamps for, to finish our daily business in the dark if needed?"

The captain heard her coarse words. He quickly turned and addressed the woman very curtly. "Madam, many an accident befell a *brave* captain who was certain where the main channel lay. Sand bars and snags pop up overnight from every storm on this terrible river. Hazards such as those easily spell doom for a steamboat and its *brave* captain." He fully dressed the lady down and said no more. Her husband stood dutifully by her, but his grin was undeniable.

Another passenger, a man quite worried about the scene which played out before him, risked another question, "Captain, are their other hazards?"

The captain saw the nervous passengers and ran with the offer. "Other hazards? How about blowing the boiler? Those explosions blow half the passengers off the boat!"

"And the other half?" the man asked with a gulp.

"They burn!" the captain gleamed as he leaned toward the trembling man.

The man looked to his fellow passengers and yelled, "Board the boat! If you are not on in three minutes, we are leaving you behind!" The captain and his crew smiled as the passengers dictated who was, and who was not, getting on.

Johann watched. His understanding of the local language was growing, thanks to Anton and the other passengers. He read the faces of the people involved and guessed the rest. Then he saw Ignaz, who sat alone in the corner of the boat.

"How are you, Ignaz?" Johann asked as he slunk down next to his son.

"I will be fine," Ignaz answered sorrowfully. "Father, I cannot remember the last time you called me by my name?"

"After you have gone through what you have, you are a man. I wish you and Josef were still my boys, but you grew up. Louis is not far behind you. I know you loved her, and I am sorry you have to go through this."

Ignaz did not answer but just stared ahead. Johann said no more, and he sat quietly with his son.

✝

After the people loaded, Johann rose to make certain his and Marianna's things were back in their place. Johnnie, who Josef woke up as he went to load the furnace, did not speak or look at his father. He was unable to stand his gaze and fearful of his anger.

"Go tell father you are sorry," Louis urged Johnnie as he sat next to his little brother.

"No. I am not sorry! God tells us to help people, but we only want to help certain people. That man was hungry and hurt, and father wanted me to pretend I did not see it," Johnnie answered.

"You are so stubborn!" Louis scolded.

"We both are," a voice uttered that raised the hair on their necks like no other. Louis stood and quickly walked away as Johann took Johnnie's hand, and he took his youngest son for a walk. They left the middle of the deck and went to the outer deck isle. They stood next to a railing. Johann took a box and placed it so Johnnie could stand on it and look out over the water. He then reached for two fishing poles and got one ready for Johnnie.

"I get to fish?" Johnnie gasped excitedly.

"Yes. Today, at least for this morning, we get to fish," Johann answered. "Anton and John will take care of the furnace for us. Fishing is best done in the morning, my son."

"So why are the others not fishing yet?" Johnnie asked. Only a few of the men fished. Far less than the day before.

121

"Because they are lazy, and they only want to fish when they want to. You are never going to accomplish anything if you only do it when you feel like it. You need to do it when it needs doing. And to get ahead, you need to do it when everyone else is resting!"

Johnnie listened to his father's wizened words. "You never talk to me like this, not like you do to Josef and Ignaz," Johnnie responded. He soaked up every word.

"You are getting older now, and perhaps I am getting a little wiser." Johann flitted both hooks out into the water. The two sat there and watched their lines as the sun rose in the early morning. "What do you think of the slaves on this boat?" Johann asked.

Johnnie's head bowed. "I feel sorry for them. I want to help them, but I do not think the fat man will let them go. But I bet you could make him," Johnnie wistfully replied with big eyes to his father.

Johann saw the hopefulness in Johnnie's rising eyes. "No, son, I do not think I could. He has several men with him, and I do not think I could take them without all of you getting hurt. Someone may even get killed. I made a promise to your mother to get this family back together, and that is what I am going to do." Johann turned back to the river and watched the lines. "Do you understand that?"

"I do, I guess. Do you want to help them?" Johnnie asked. His little voice innocently challenged Johann unlike anyone had before.

"Truthfully, at first, I did not. They were them, and we were us, and they were not my problem. My problem is getting us to Iowa, not freeing the slaves."

"But we helped Marianna? She was not your problem, was she?" Johnnie asked.

"Well, there is the problem, is it not? I suppose I will need to answer to God for that," Johann replied. In no way was he brushing his son off. In truth, Johnnie touched on a point Johann wrestled with since he first saw the slaves. Johann looked back to his son, "It is not a decision of whether to help them or not. It is a decision of whether to risk our welfare for theirs. It tears at me hard, son, trying to do what is right or what is best. Maybe even what is easiest? It is too much for me to understand right now, and the answer to all the questions might be the same. I just do not know."

Johann was surprised when Johnnie dropped his pole on the rail and threw his tiny arms around Johann's neck. Johann put his arm around Johnnie, worried he might topple over the rail.

Then Johnnie's pole lurched downward. "Oh my, you have a fish!" Johann exclaimed as he saw the pole pulled to the side. Johnnie quickly let go of his father and reached for it. He held on tight with both hands as the pole pulled taught.

"Help!" Johnnie said, even though Johann was already reaching for the line.

"God almighty, this is a big fish!" Johann yelled. The passengers on the boat, the rich and the poor, rushed to watch the fight. Johann pulled with two hands on the tight line. Josef took the fishing pole from Johnnie and wound the line around the stick to keep it tight in case Johann lost his grip.

"Holy moly!" Johnnie gasped. The beast of a fish showed itself on the surface with a huge splash. The audience applauded the battle before them. As the struggle continued, the Natchez pulled alongside another steamer. The people from both boats watched as Johann reeled in the mighty catfish. Johnnie jumped up and down with excitement and cheered for his father to land his fish.

Dried bales of cotton lined the entire lower row of the other boat, the Annie. Only the people on the higher deck could admire the struggle as they roared and cheered with each large splash.

"Pull my fish in!" Johnnie ordered as he repeatedly slammed his hand down on his father.

"I am trying!" Johann barked back at his son. Johnnie reached for the line and almost tumbled over the side. Johann caught the britches of his son with his left hand and pulled him back in. The crowd cheered for that also, with each onlooker caught up in the struggle to land the big fish.

Johann wrestled to pull it from the water to the rail. He finally did so and landed it over the edge. The wide fish was over half Johnnie's height. The little boy beamed with delight at the fish he caught. He eagerly offered advice to the other fishermen who hoped to match him for the rest of the trip.

Johann pulled his knife and cleaned it as another show began. The captains of the two boats traded barbs back and forth. At first, it had to do with the fishing capabilities of the passengers, and then it went to which boat could hold the most people, then to which boat had the highest and most ornate stacks, and finally on the topic that ended every argument, which boat was the fastest.

"The Natchez is the finest boat on this or any part of the Mississippi river!" their captain barked.

"Twas not true last week, when we bested you on this very stretch! It will not be true this'n week, nor next'n week neither!" the Annie's captain retorted.

"Last week was a fluke, and you cheated to boot!" their captain snarled. "I am quite eager to right that wrong!"

"So, a race to Vicksburg, you say?" the other captain challenged.

"Yes, if you call it that! At least you can pick up any that fall off the Natchez, as you will certainly be behind us wallowing in our wake!" The captain of the Natchez retorted. He then turned back below, "Fire up the boilers! The hotter, the better!"

"The race begins!" the other captain replied. Both men slammed the doors shut to their Pilot Houses. Both stacks responded as the boilers were put on high. The deep bellowing horns of the boats tooted as each Captain prepared to show off his boat. The ship's men walked to and fro and asked passengers to balance the vessel for faster sailing. Everyone believed they were part of the race, and they took their role seriously. The two steamboats were neck and neck most of the morning. But the captain of the Natchez had one more trick. He ordered several of the slaves to sit on the safety valves of the boiler. For this tough and dangerous task, he fed and watered them to their content. The added weight on the valves increased the pressure in the boiler, and its engine roared even louder as the Natchez pulled ahead.

A man went to sit with the slaves to help his boat win the race. "I, too, should like some food and water," he said. One of the ship's men stopped him short, "Just what do you think you are doing?"

"I want to help win the race!" the excited man blurted.

The shipman pulled him away, "We have the slaves for that!"

"Why them? I am hungry too!" the man finally stated.

"'Cause if the boilers blow, they are dead for sure! With them sitting on the valves, the likelihood of them blowing is much higher," the shipman whispered. "It is a risk we are willing to take, but only with them!"

The man gave back an uneasy look and silently worked his way to the outer railing to a safer place.

The port of Vicksburg was within sight, and the passengers of both boats cheered for the furious finish. "Father, they are catching back up to us!" Ignaz yelled. The merriment of the race was a welcome diversion for the sadness that gripped him. "I am going down to help Josef!" he yelled to Johann as he raced below.

The Annie pulled ahead. Then a fateful spark, one of many that came from the smokestacks high above, landed on the dreadfully dry bales of cotton. It immediately burst into flame, along with the bales next to it, as the breeze from the rushing boat fanned the fire. The boat slowed as the men on it turned their attention to the quickly raging fire. "The fire will take us down!" the captain yelled. "Act quickly!"

The men discarded the bales by shoving them over the side and into the river. Others rushed to dump buckets of water from the river onto the slower burning wood. Their quick action saved the boat, but the distraction cost them the race.

The people of Vicksburg saw the race from far off. They were quite used to the contests in which the hot-headed captains often partook. They gathered to welcome the winner as the Natchez pulled close to the dock, and many cheered the victors.

A doctor boarded the boat first to look over the passengers. "Breakouts of Cholera have arrived from the many immigrants traveling upstream," the doctor informed. "More towns are inspecting those arriving at their shores before we allow them to enter." The doctor did not allow several of the sick to step off the boat. The captain would need to let them off elsewhere.

As they took their things off the Natchez, Johann told the others, "We need to get a new boat. The Natchez is turning around for its trip south." Several other steamers were there as they waited for passengers. The Imperial was the name of one, and the other the Amulet. Johann, Anton, and John went to speak with the men who sold tickets for each packet. They returned with purchased tickets for all. "Both boats are going to Cairo, but the Amulet is going up the Ohio first. We will take the Imperial.

A man approached them as they gathered their belongings and prepared to lug them to the next boat launch. The man could have been one of them, and then he spoke, "May I help you with your luggage?" The man's strong Irish accent was clear.

Johann stared at the man for a moment, and then he replied, "Of course."

"Which boat, sir?" the man asked. An unmistakable twinkle in his eye caught Johann's attention.

"The Imperial," Johann replied. The man smiled and hurriedly reached for the women's bags and swiftly carried them to the Imperial. Johann saw the man's wife and two young children standing off to the side. They looked more meager than most and in need of a solid meal.

"Father," Josef interrupted, "We can carry our things. I have never seen you pay a man to do something you could have done yourself."

"Son," Johann said as he pulled Josef close. He pretended to straighten Josef's shirt to make sure he had his son's attention. "I made a promise to a man that I would help others if I could, and that is what I aim to do." Johnnie overheard his father's words, and he smiled proudly.

"This is how he is paying for his family to get wherever they are going, and we are going to help them. If we do not, who will? When we start our own business in Gutenberg, we will need others to do the same." Johann patted Josef on the back and took the bags he held. He set them on the ground, and the others did the same. Then they followed Johann to the trees and stood close to the other families.

"Ladies, what would you think of making lunch for all of us? We have time before we board the next boat," Johann asked.

"That is a splendid idea. We will be back shortly, and then we will cook up Johnnie's fish," Mariana answered as she hurried off to get her things. "Josef, make us a fire for the cooking. We are going to have that fish!"

The man eagerly carried all their things to the boat. He set them down and then helped Marianna get her things for cooking. The four families waited anxiously for their lunch. The man carried the last of the bags and set them down next to the others not far away. Johann, Anton, and John paid the man handsomely for his work. The man teared up, "I made more in that one load than I had all day. Thank you! I hope you and your families have a blessed day! May the love and affection of the angels be to you!"

"What is your name?" Johann asked.

"George McSwain. My family and I have newly arrived from Ireland, perhaps you noticed our language!" the man laughed nervously.

"Well, Mr. McSwain, I assume you noticed my speech. We are from Liechtenstein, and we are working our way up the Mississippi. Is this your lovely family standing over here?" Johann asked.

"Why yes, it is! And your name?" George asked.

"Johann Tschohl. This is Anton Nigg and John Kaufmann," Johann introduced.

"Please, George, have your family come and share our meal. We have plenty," Anton offered.

George looked confusedly at the three kind men as tears rushed to his eyes, "Not once, sir, on the voyage have we been shown favor by anyone. And twice in an afternoon, you have paid me handsomely and now extend an offer to break bread with you and yours. You are kind men, and I thank you."

"You would thank us more by accepting our invitation. Please, bring your family and come and eat with us," Anton insisted. "We've had our share of mistreatment on our journey, but we'll not show that to another."

George called his family over, and together with the Tschohls, Niggs, Kaufmanns, and Schmits, they had their lunch. The ladies happily prepared the meal for the McSwains, and each family told of their adventures and destinations. "It is a good thing Johnnie here caught that huge fish, or we would all be hungry right now," Johann said, and everyone congratulated the little boy on his big catch.

"We caught some fish too," Josef added.

"Yeah, but they were not very big!" Johnnie said as he set the record straight. When they finished eating, the children played, and Johnnie made quick friends with the McSwain children. Johann promised George, "After we get settled in Iowa, we will return to your city of Ethel to see you and check on your progress."

As they broke from their meal, everyone wished the McSwains well on their journey. Marianna stepped close to Johann. "You are a good man for helping that family."

Johann smiled at Marianna as she began to cry, "My heart breaks for the loss of my daughter, but I thank you for taking care of us. I hope Ignaz is making it through this."

"Ignaz will recover in time, as will you and yours. It is a sad thing to bury a child, but they are with God now. I have buried three of my own," Johann consoled Marianna.

"I know you are right. God bless you and your family, Johann." Marianna took his strong arm for support as they walked the rest of the way to the Imperial.

Marianna reached for Johann's hand and turned toward him, "Thank you for treating us like yours. I hate explaining our situation to others."

"I know. It is just easier to say we are together. You will soon be with the rest of your people in Illinois, and we will continue onto ours in Iowa." Johann said it very plainly, as he never had any other intention.

"Johann, your words pain me, though I must say it even surprises me. My husband was lost so quickly, and I never had time to consider things fully. You stepped right in during my largest moment of need and saved us. I will miss you greatly when we part," Mariana said as she kissed Johann on his cheek before she moved on. Johann looked down and walked several paces behind her. He was glad his sons did not witness the innocent gesture.

Little more occurred on the steamboat ride north to Prairie Du Rocher, Illinois. The farther they went, the more Germans they encountered. They spent their days fishing and telling stories and the nights sitting by fires along the banks of the Mississippi.

The day finally came when they reached Prairie Du Rocher, which was just below St. Louis. They switched to a new steamboat in Cairo, called the Horizon. It was a smaller boat, and the slaves were long left behind. A wet spring meant the waters were high on the river. This allowed the captains to travel without any worry of bottoming out, but they had to fight the strong current. They did have to keep a vigilant eye out for large log snags that would puncture and sink an unsuspecting boat, but those were mostly on the sides of the swollen river. They easily and safely traversed the main channel.

As Josef and his brothers unloaded Marianna and her family's things, Marianna approached Johann. "I know it is too forward to say such a thing, but I would ask that you consider staying here." The hopeful look in her eyes caught Johann unexpectantly. "You are a good man, and I have grown quite fond of your sons." She paused as she looked down and blushed, and then looked up and continued, "I have grown fond of you too. We could make a good family, yes?"

Johann took her hand and led her farther away from their children, who watched the scene. He then turned to her. "Marianna, I am sorry..."

Marianna could not bear to hear the words, and she placed her hand on his mouth and quieted him. "I understand. Please, do not say the words." She turned to walk away, but Johann stopped her and turned her back.

"Marianna, you are a wonderful woman. Any man would be lucky to marry you and help raise your amazing children. But I have been married twice, and with each passing, my heart is more torn. As you know, I have committed to getting my family together again, and I can consider nothing else until that task is completed."

"You are an even better man than I gave you credit for, Johann Tschohl." She embraced him, and then together, they walked back to the rest. Goodbyes were said, and hugs and handshakes were given as they parted ways.

Johann paid a man to take the Schmits the short distance to Prairie Du Rocher, and the three families watched as the horse and wagon carried the Schmits off. They waved until the wagon passed into the thick forest that lined both sides of the river. The parting was especially sorrowful for Ignaz, and he promised when they were settled, he would return to visit them.

"You should have stayed," Josef said with an elbow to his father.

Johann looked back at Josef, more as a friend than a son. "You should be quiet." He then put his arms around Josef and Ignaz as Louis raced Johnnie back to the boat. The Niggs and Kaufmanns walked with them. "We are getting closer every day!" John announced. "I, for one, am very excited to arrive and start our new life."

"It will be good. I hope to see some of our old friends who should be there to welcome us," Anton added. "So many people are looking forward to our arrival."

The captain sounded the whistle that announced its intention to depart. With every passing hour and day, they crept closer to the end of their long journey, Gutenberg, Iowa.

CHAPTER THIRTEEN

GUTENBERG

As evening set on May 15th, the steamboat Die Vernon approached the landing in Dubuque, Iowa. The sun had already disappeared over the steep bluffs that stood as guardians on both sides of the swollen river. Dubuque was the last large city before Gutenberg and the destination for many passengers traveling the river. As the men tied the steamer up on the dock, a man shouted to Johann, "Hello German! Where are you from?"

Johann and his sons were quite pleased to hear the sound of their common language, spoken as if they were still back home. "Liechtenstein," Johann responded. A crowd of onlookers waited for the passengers to get off the boat.

"What news have you from downriver?" one of the men asked.

The captain replied, "The spring flooding is almost over, but I have no other news for you today."

"That is it?" the man asked, his disappointment was obvious.

"Well," the captain continued as he thought back over the past few days and weeks. "I suppose you would have heard of the train by now? The one that crossed in Davenport?"

The crowd stopped their idle chat as they fixated on the captain. "A train crossed the river, my Lord?" the man answered as his disappointment turned into disbelief.

"As sure as the sun rises in the east and sets in the west! It was the first train to cross the Mississippi, from Rock Island to Davenport. Quite a sight it was... from what I am told," the captain ended his story. "How many steamers landed here today?"

"You are the thirteenth today, and we had twelve yesterday!" the man proudly replied. All the while, the crew members loaded new passengers, packages, and dried goods for the next leg of their journey. Johann excitedly went to meet the pleasant man he had spoken with, who heartily shook his hand.

"Liechtenstein? You have made quite a trip. Will you be staying here or going on to Gutenberg?"

"One hour, and we depart north!" the captain informed the passengers going ashore of his strict timeline.

"We go to Gutenberg. My daughters are there," Johann answered. "How did you know where we were going?"

"You said you were from Liechtenstein, and many of your people reside there. I am hoping to change your mind!" the man stated his plans.

Johann's boys took up similar conversations with others on the banks, as did the Niggs and Kaufmanns. The friendly locals invited the family to come into town with them. Anton and John encouraged Johann to go. "We will stay behind to watch our things," John assured.

"Yes, we will go to see your city," Johann accepted. "We have not been welcomed so on any port on their trip. This is a nice change."

"I am David Wilson," the man said as they sat down for a fine meal of kraut and sausage. "I am a leader of the city, and I would ask that you consider staying here with us. We are filling houses faster than we can build them, and we need strong men like yourselves if we are to continue growing. Iowa is just beginning, and we intend to be a major part of the politics of the state."

Johann sat back in his chair. He took a quick look at his sons. "Mr. Wilson, I have traveled around the world to see my daughters again. I also did so to leave oppression from a government that cared little for the people. I do not wish to be part of ruling others. I only hope to live my life and earn what is mine. You have a fine city, and I appreciate your asking us ashore, but we will be moving on shortly."

Mr. Wilson saw the look on Josef's face. "Young man, you are old enough to make your own decisions. Are you thinking of staying? There are many young women here looking for husbands, and hard workers will never need to fear of running short of things to do here."

Josef thought for a moment, "How far is it from here to Gutenberg?"

"A half a day's horse or boat ride," Mr. Wilson answered. "Have I just snagged a new member of our growing Berg?"

Josef thought for another moment, "No, Mr. Wilson, I shall have to pass, for now. I am going with my father to see my sisters and Gutenberg. But should that not go well, I will come back here. I believe you may see me again, Mr. Wilson." Johann was proud of his son's answer.

"I hope to see all of you again!" Mr. Wilson exuberantly stated. They ate their meal and talked of the Tschohls', Niggs', and Kaufmanns' journey to Amerika and the part of Liechtenstein from where they came. After they finished, Mr. Wilson stood and shook each of their hands again, including Johnnie's, who finished the last of his sausages. "Good luck on your journey, and may you find your sisters still reside in Gutenberg. It is a quaint little town, too small for my liking, but many do enjoy it. Until we meet again!"

Johann and his family walked back to the boat. They took their time as they wandered through the orderly streets of Dubuque. The people of the town built many homes made of wood logs from the plentiful timber they cleared. They also built homes from the stone cut directly from the bluff. Johann took a moment to feel one of the stone walls. "This is good building stone. My hands are ready to work again as we start our new life! I also want to see Theresia, Juliana, Franziska, and Scholastika. We are very close to them!" His sons smiled as they boarded the steamer that would take them on the last leg of their journey.

The Die Vernon left Dubuque and made a short trip north to a portage at Potosi, Wisconsin, where they stopped for the night. The Tschohls slept on the deck of the Die Vernon on a clear, early summer evening. Johann dreamt of the next day and seeing his daughters.

Early it was when the sun gloriously announced itself over the bluff to the east. The steamer chugged away from the port and took on several new passengers going to Gutenberg, and others going on farther to the north.

Josef and Ignaz marveled at the bluffs that hugged the river on both sides. The main channel bounced back and forth from one side to the other, as a ribbon strung recklessly on the floor. Trees overhung the low banks and climbed high above on the bluffs. They also covered the endless islands of varying sizes that dotted the lazy river. Occasionally they saw a home on a lonely island and even a home that floated by on a raft. The rafting people seemed a rough sort.

"Do not speak with the drifters, sons. It will only lead to trouble," Johann counseled. "It seems to me as though they are hiding something."

One of the ship workers hailed a raft close, and he quickly exchanged some coins for a bottle. And just like that, the exchange was over, and both went on their way. Johann asked the man, "Pardon me, sir, just what did you purchase?"

"Whiskey!" the worker boasted, and then he offered Johann a swig. Johann tried it, and he spat it right out.

"That tastes horrible!" Johann sputtered as his sons laughed at their father. "If that is the level of whiskey in these parts, I think I might have an idea for new business for the Tschohl family!" Josef laughed, but an idea sprouted in Johann's mind that did not soon depart.

Several men on the steamer fished and did quite well. The older boys took no notice of them as they pondered the day ahead.

Johnnie, however, had other thoughts. "Sir, how do you expect to catch the big ones fishing like that?" he scolded. Johann saw his son irritated the passengers, and he led Johnnie off. "Father, I was just trying to help them. They do not even know what they are doing!"

"Johnnie, these men did not get to see you catch that big fish, so they do not know you are an expert. Some men are slow to take advice from a child. Anyway, a good fisherman keeps his secrets to himself. We do not want these men to catch all the big fish by our new home, do we?" Johann asked the last question and hoped his son would quiet down.

"Oh, yes, father! Let them keep fishing that way!" Johnnie answered. He sat behind the fishermen and giggled as they pulled in the smallest of fish.

"The people of Gutenberg are so nice, a perfect little town it is! It sits on a flat plain that leads out to the river. Prairie La Porte is what they used to call it, but no one has for a while now. You will like it there," a woman told Johann as the steamer chugged along. He continued asking questions as they went. Several other small towns passed them by, the first of which was Cassville, which sat on the Wisconsin side. Then they went on and landed near a town called Buena Vista, where several passengers got off, and two others boarded. The two getting on brought several barrels of cargo with them. The men seemed quite boisterous, and each paid the captain in several bottles of liquor instead of money.

Johann knew a thing or two of the making of wine and liquor, and after he introduced the men of his group, he took up a discussion with the men. The liquor transaction back on the river piqued his interest. He also noticed a healthy interest from the locals in the making and selling of alcohol. One of the men offered him and his older sons a drink. "I am Josef Heinrich, and this is Mathias Hammas. We work together!" Mr. Heinrich stated.

"And together we work," Mr. Hammas repeated as he clinked his glass with Mr. Heinrich.

"And drink!" stated Mr. Heinrich.

"And drink!" Mr. Hammas agreed.

"Yes, we do, sir! Yes, we do!" Mr. Heinrich also tipped his hat to Mr. Hammas as though they were just meeting. After the two drank their glasses completely, Mr. Hammas asked, "And to where, Mr. Tschohl, will you be going?"

"Gutenberg," Johann replied.

Both men's eyes lit up, "Gutenberg, you say? We love Gutenberg, do we not, Mr. Hammas?"

"Yes. Yes, we *love* Gutenberg! The people there might even like us more than we like them. As fine a place as I have ever done business, if I say so myself, which of course, I just did." Mr. Hammas said as he took another pleasurable drink.

"These are the thirstiest men I have ever seen," Johnnie said to Louis. Mr. Heinrich heard Johnnie's words. He leaned over toward the lad and answered him directly, "Indeed sir, indeed!" He raised his glass to Johnnie, who, of course, had none. Mr. Heinrich took another drink anyway.

"No town lines the banks like Gutenberg. A most welcoming and pleasant place as I have ever been to," Mr. Hammas said. "To Gutenberg!" he toasted.

"To Gutenberg!" Mr. Heinrich answered as both drank.

They continued to talk as the steamer rounded the last corner to their destination. At each possible moment, and even when it made no sense, the two toasted each other and took more drinks.

The steamer wound through the maze of small islands of trees that covered the river bottom. It raced across the channel and up to the town's sandy bank in a final triumphant burst. The locals had built several large stone buildings into the bank, with the steamer landing at a dock just behind the first of them.

Unlike the many towns before, and in surprise to the woman and Mr. Hammas who professed differently, not one single person from the city of Gutenberg was there to welcome the vessel. There were many small boats tied up and barely room for the steamboat to reach the dock.

"My word, they must all be dead," Mr. Hammas slurred in dismay as he took another drink. He tipped his cup in honor of the souls departed.

"Here, here! To the dead!" Mr. Heinrich replied as both took another drink, this time with sad intent.

As they ported the bank, Johann heard a raucous from within the town. A man ran to the bank above. He saw the new arrivals, and he harkened to them, "There is a fight! Come!" He waved them on but did not wait. The passengers from the Die Vernon rushed up the bank, unsure of what awaited them. Mr. Hammas and Mr. Heinrich came also, but not without their barrels, which they paid one of the shipmen to roll up the steep bank.

As Johann reached the top, a large crowd stood before him and his sons. It was far larger than the number that lived in the town for sure. A scant number of homes and businesses, some made of wood and others of stone, spread across the town's broad plain. The bluff lay to the west of the town as if it were a sleeping giant that could arise at any moment. It lowered almost to the plain level at its southern tip and rose ever higher as it went north.

The two well-liquored men quickly set up shop. "I may be afflicted by my drink this spry morning, and heck, maybe even by the spirits I imbibed the evening last, but I will not let this opportunity for a few sales pass me by. Do you not agree, Mr. Heinrich?"

"You are quite right, Mr. Hammas! Quite right!" Mr. Heinrich, of course, lifted his glass to his wizened partner. And, of course, the same salute was offered back and accepted. Twice.

Many of the locals rushed to purchase the fine drink offered by the salesmen, as they were frequent customers of Mr. Heinrich and Mr. Hammas. With drinks in hand, the crowd surrounded two quarreling men, who circled one another slowly.

Johann noticed the influence of alcohol on the two fighters, who stammered circles around each other. "They must have been drinking all day," Johann said with a grin as he watched the stumbling men. His immediate interest in the fight was far higher than it should have been, much to his surprise. He even accepted a drink from Mr. Hammas. Anton and John were quick to follow suit.

"Here, here!" Mr. Hammas responded in a whisper. Then he offered a cheer to no one before emptying his glass again.

"I say it is Coon Creek, and that is what it will be!" the first burley man yelled. A particular section of the crowd erupted in cheer. "That is right, or your name is not John Murray!" an ardent supporter yelled.

Then his combatant answered, as surely as could be, "Miner's Creek it is, and this fight settles it!" One of his supporters, not to be outdone, chimed in, "Daniel Justice will win the day!"

The entire scene entranced Johann and his sons. A little old man took bets from the frenzied crowd. Mr. Hammas and Mr. Heinrich sold their drinks at an alarming rate. "Mr. Hammas, be careful not to sell too much," Mr. Heinrich warned.

"Too much?" the well-liquored Mr. Hammas asked. "I am not sure I follow?"

"If we sell it all, we will not have enough to last us the day, my friend," Mr. Heirich said.

"Here, here!" the enlightened Mr. Hammas cheered, with his newly filled glass raised.

Mr. Heinrich responded in kind as the two drank.

The two fighting men continued their saunter around each other. "It seems as though this is all they plan to do," Anton said to John.

Before John could answer, John Murray pounced like a cat and slung his fist toward Daniel Justice. The punch rocked Daniel back towards Johann, who kept the man from falling to the ground. "Thank you, kind sir," Daniel slurred as he caught his senses.

"You are most welcome. But please, watch for that right fist," Johann coached.

"Which side are you on?" a Coon Creek fanatic bellowed at Johann. In reaction, Johann let go of the man, who fell to the ground. One of his supporters then barked, "Hey fellow, you are not in this fight!"

"Do not talk to my father that-a-way!" Johnnie yelled back in his growing excitement. Johann covered his young son's mouth, and the fight continued.

The two men exchanged repeated blows, but each seemed unable to block the other's weakest and slowest punches. Back and forth, they slung their fists as each tried to knock the head off the other. For over an hour, the deliberate brawl continued, right through the time the boat had been completely unloaded as Ignaz and Louis finished carrying their things to the top of the bank.

Eventually, Daniel managed to block a punch from John. He followed it up with an uppercut that lifted John off the street. The man landed hard on his back, beaten. The old man who took the bets walked over and inspected the combatant. "What will it be, son? Do you wish for this fight to continue?"

John turned his head and spat out a mouthful of blood. "Minor's Creek it is!" The crowd cheered at the end of the fight and the effort of both entrants. Daniel helped John to his feet and shook his worthy hand. They each took a drink from Mr. Heinrich, whom they knew quite well. John looked to the victor, "But, there is sure a lot of coon in Minor's Creek!"

Daniel agreed, "Yes, but not quite as many coons as there are Minors!"

Johann looked to Josef, "What day is it?"

"Saturday," Josef answered.

"As tomorrow is Sunday. Let us make sure to pray this is the right place for us. Right now, I have my doubts," Johann stated. "So far, I am unimpressed by this town and its level of whiskey." Josef laughed as they turned, and before them stood three ladies. One with three little kids, one with two, and one with none.

"Father!" the oldest blurted. She set down her children and threw her arms around Johann. The other two did the same, as they handed their littlest to their husbands who stood behind. For the first time in ten years, Johann embraced his daughters.

CHAPTER FOURTEEN

A NEW HOME

"I cannot believe I am holding you," Johann whispered through his tears as he held three of his daughters, Maria, Juliana, and Scholastika. "Are these all of your children? I have missed so much."

"Yes. Where is Katharina?" Maria asked.

"She passed less than a year ago. Her death is what drove us to come here, and her dying wish was for us to be together again, and that is what God has allowed." Johann bowed his head as he thought of his two wives he left in Liechtenstein.

"We are sorry we were not there for you," Maria replied as she hugged her father again.

Juliana and Scholastika cried as they embraced their father. "We have missed a lot too! My brothers have turned into men!" Scholastika said as she reached for Josef, Ignatius, and Louis.

"What about me?" Johnnie asked as his chest huffed in sadness.

"Daughters, this is your youngest brother, Johnnie," Johann informed. His three daughters rushed to Johnnie. Each took turns as they hugged him tightly.

"Johnnie, you look just like your mother. She is no doubt in Heaven with our mother. Father, she will be quite proud of you for bringing us back together here in Gutenberg. It is an amazing act of God for us to be here just when you arrived. We so hoped that Mr. Buchel would bring you back with him. He told us last week when he arrived that you were planning to come. What a glorious day," Juliana said as she

143

hugged Johnnie again. The girls all spent extra time with Johnnie before letting him play with their own children.

"Father, I know you remember my husband, Franz," Maria said. "Our oldest son, Franz Michael, passed away at the age of three, shortly after we arrived." Maria wiped a tear from her eye as Johann reached for her hand.

"Both of us have missed some events we should not have. I am sorry for his passing," Johann consoled.

"Our next son is named after you, Johann Baptist," Maria added.

"I am pleased to meet you," Johann said as he bent low to shake the little boy's hand. The boy smiled back and shook his grandfather's hand for the first time.

"And this is Katharina and Franz, my two youngest," Maria introduced. Johann hugged each, ages 8 and 4. "And I will let Juliana and Scholastika introduce their husbands."

"Father, this is my husband, Frank Fischler," Juliana said as she handed her baby to her father.

Johann shook Frank's hand, "It is a pleasure to meet you." Frank responded with a smile, "I thought we might meet one day. The pleasure is all mine."

"Father, this is my husband, John Steffen. And my young sons, Jacob and Peter, ages 4 and 1," Scholastika said. Johann again shook John's sturdy hand.

"How come you do not name any of your kids after us?" Johnnie asked.

"We are having more. I promise to name my next boys after you," Scholastika answered as she picked him up and saved him from Katharina, who chased him. "You boys are so handsome. You will not have a hard time finding girls here!" Maria said as she smiled at her brothers.

Josef accepted the compliment, but Ignaz and Louis turned away. "I am sorry. What has happened?" Scholastika asked.

"It has been a long trip, and often it was not easy. There were several dear friends we left along the way. God has seen us all through to here and now, and we will start over," Johann answered. He placed his hands on his two hurting sons. "Where is Franziska?"

"She lives in St. Louis. You passed her on your way here. She met a wonderful man the day we arrived there, and the two were married shortly after. His name is Edward Flukes, and they have two children last we heard."

"It is very good to see you again, Johann. We hoped you would make the trip," Franz, Maria's husband, said.

"Johann, look who we have found!" Anton exclaimed as a small crowd approached them. "Alois and Theresia Buchel!"

Alois marched toward Johann. "Johann, so glad to see you made it. We arrived less than a week ago. I want to introduce you to the leaders of our new home." Alois's wife, Theresia, took the ladies to meet the other women of the community at the same time. Alois took Johann, Anton, and John, to meet the men.

"Gentlemen, these are families from Liechtenstein. This is Johann Tschohl, Maria Vogt's father. This is John Kaufmann and Anton Nigg."

"Gentlemen, welcome to our city of Gutenberg. We welcome you and thank you for growing our number yet again," one of the men commended.

"Friends, this is our mayor, Christian Weiss," Alois introduced. Then he continued, "And now for some other men of Gutenberg: Mr. Overbeck, Mr. Heitman, Mr. Krephane, Mr. Block, Mr. Wolter, Mr. Bierman, and Mr. Erdhardt."

"Welcome to our city," Mr. Weiss extolled. "Here, you will find everything you need to make your start. Good land is for sale, both for farming and for lumber. The forests teem with game for food and pelts. I have no doubt you will like the German feel of our town also."

"But you do not sound German?" John asked awkwardly.

"You are right. I do not. I was here already and lived in Cincinnati when the government opened the land after they

145

moved the Indians out. But I have come to love these great families and their hard work ethic. I have no doubt yours is the same. Together we are building a great community, and soon we shall be the county seat again, or my name is not Christian Weiss!"

"To Christian Weiss!" Mr. Hammas's voice came from several feet away. Mr. Heinrich's expected reply followed right behind, "Yes, to Christian Weiss!"

"Mr. Weiss, thank you for your kind welcome. We are happy to be here. We will be making our way onward now, as it has been a long trip, and we are tired. You will see much of us, and we look forward to becoming good members of your community," Johann replied as he shook Christian's hand and most of the other men's also. John and Anton did the same, and then they returned to their families, who waited nearby.

"You should come with us, father. We live just across the river. A new ferry has started, and it will take us there in no time," Maria urged. "Yes, we would love to have you, Johann," Franz added as he took Maria's hand.

"Not another boat ride," Johnnie wailed. The others laughed at the remark.

"You should go on. We will stay here at one of the inns. Tomorrow we will start figuring out our next move," Anton said.

"We will do that. Anton and John, despite many hardships, have made it to Amerika," Johann congratulated. The Tschohls retrieved their things and loaded up the wagons his three daughters' families brought. Each was loaded heavily as they made their way north. The street lay on the bank, which ran alongside the river.

Johann rode with Franz, Maria's husband. "There are a lot of buildings going up. Several very tall ones," Johann admired. "Yes, the limestone is readily available and great for building. There are many masons here in Gutenberg, and across the river and in the small towns we live by. They are all quite busy," Franz replied.

They came upon a large stone structure that was half-way to completion. Franz rolled to a stop. "Charles Albertus, how are you this fine day?"

"I am well, Mr. Vogt. More Liechtensteiners, I see?" Mr. Albertus replied. His wife did not stop working as the discussion continued.

"I would dearly love to help you complete your building, which would keep your wife from having to do such things," Franz said.

"No, Mr. Vogt, that will not do. I am not paying anyone to do something I can do myself, with my good wife Crystal's help, of course," Mr. Albertus interjected as his wife shot him a stark look. "And we will not get done anytime soon if you keep stopping to talk to every passerby either!" she scolded.

Franz smirked, "I think you should go back to work, Charles. God's blessings on you *and* your beautiful wife. Good day!" Charles tipped his cap, snapped his suspenders, and went back to work.

"They have built that entire structure themselves, and they have every intention of finishing it by themselves also," Franz said to Johann as they rode on. "It will still be another year if they do not take anyone's help."

"I admire that. We do most everything ourselves also," Johann replied.

"That is true," Franz answered. "But they are trying to build a four-story stone home with just a man and his wife."

"I believe you do have a point there, Franz," Johann said as they rode on. Several homes dotted the laid-out streets, with more under construction as they rode north along the river. Some were log cabins, while others were made of limestone. Various farm animals also roamed the many open areas between the homes as kids played in the early summer day.

"Is this not beautiful?" Maria asked as she reached up to take her father's hand.

"Yes. Your mother would have loved this," Johann replied. Straight ahead and rising above several trees rose a steeple.

"That is an impressive church," Johann said. "Is it Catholic?"

"Of course!" Franz answered. "It is only a few years old, but already it seems to be too small. We are thinking of building another. Maria, you should tell them about the *event*."

"What event?" Josef asked as his interest peaked.

"Oh my, where to begin!" Maria started as Franz pulled to a stop in front of the church on the north end of town. All three wagons listened as Maria continued. "It is the most amazing thing and a true sign of God watching over us in the new world. This happened about two years ago, Father Weniger, a missionary, arrived here. His boat broke down, and we asked him to do a mission for a week while his boat was getting fixed. He agreed to do so, and the crowds grew each day. On the final day, this very cross," Maria motioned to the large wooden cross that was placed in the ground, "made by our own Mr. Kamphaus, was erected. During the blessing by Father Weniger, a cross of light appeared in the sky. It was a cloudless day and nothing but blue for the backdrop, and the cross appeared. Mrs. Eilers saw it first, though her husband is loath to speak of it. Everyone who was here, Catholic or not, saw the cross. No one denies it."

"How long was it there?" Louis asked.

"A quarter of an hour, at the least. Then it slowly began to disappear," Maria answered. Johann stood from his seat and jumped down. He walked over to the cross and knelt to pray. The rest followed him. Johann prayed, "Dear Lord, thank You for delivering us to this place and for bringing my family back together. We pray for Franziska, who we hope is well, and for those who have passed before us. Please watch over our endeavors and keep our hearts pure as we make our way in this new world. Amen."

"This is where we should be. It is a blessed place. I know it in my heart," Johann said to the rest. They then jumped back in the wagon that carried them to the ferry, which was just a short distance away.

As they rode the ferry slowly across the river, the families watched as the sun descended over the rim of the bluffs to the west. "This is truly amazing," Johann uttered. He then looked to his daughters, "How far do you live from here?"

"Not far at all," Franz answered. "We live in Bloomington, which is a short ride after we cross. We will be there before it gets dark."

"We live in Patch Grove, which is just a little bit farther," Juliana added. "I would like to have Louis and Johnnie come and stay with us for a few days." Her husband Frank added, "Yes, the help would be appreciated as I have some haying to do."

"Can we, father?" Johnnie asked excitedly.

"Of course, you may," Johann answered.

"We live south of Patch Grove, in the country," Scholastika's husband John said. "Josef and Ignatius, would you like to stay with us for a few days?"

"Yes, that would be just fine," Josef accepted for both of them.

"Well, father, it looks like you get to stay with us," Maria said. "Then that is what we shall do," Johann replied. "I am so glad we are all here. There are great things in store for us. I just have one thing to figure out."

"What is that?" Maria asked.

Johann looked back and forth from one bluff to the other. "I need to decide which side of this magnificent river to live on!"

Brian Spielbauer

THE LEGACY of FAITH:

THE JOURNEY

Of

Mathias John Rohner

Date: 1865
Origin: Hard, Vorarlberg, Austria
Route: Le Havre, France
New York, New York, USA
Guttenberg, Iowa, USA

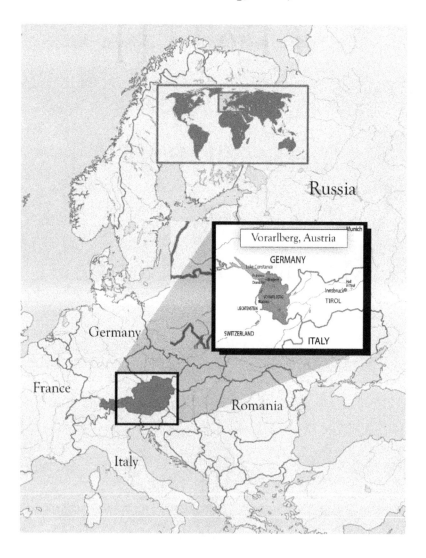

TIMELINE

Mathias Rohner	Year	World
	1861	Civil War Begins.
	1862	Steuben Guard of Guttenberg, an all-German regiment, joins the war as Company D of the Iowa 27th Regiment.
Mathias Rohner swims Lake Constance to escape war in Austria.	1865	
	1865	Civil War Ends.
	1867	A rift occurs in St. Mary's Church about the location for a new church, with close to half the families leaving.
Mathias Rohner works for and lives with George Weist, according to the Census.	1870	
	1871	The first train reaches Guttenberg after the town voted to raise $30,000 to entice the railroad.

CHAPTER FIFTEEN

HARD, VORARLBERG

Mathias trembled at the sight. Hans and Adolph, his friends since his earliest memories, shuddered next to him. Their two nervous looks continued to pelt Mathias, but he refused to look back to them. Captain John Rohner, known far and wide for his toughness and bravery, marched three young men who were charged with evading the draft in for interrogation. Mathias and his friends dared not say a word as they watched the events from a safe distance, hidden in the ever-thickening crowd.

"Your charge is evasion! For that, how do you respond?" Captain Rohner, Mathias's father, asked. His voice shot through the crowd like a clap of thunder, which signaled impending doom to the charged.

Two of the three men dropped their heads in disgrace, while the other defiantly answered, "Guilty! I am not ashamed of my actions," he dared to challenge the captain.

"And the rest?" the captain demanded as he angrily stepped toward the insolent youth.

The other two frightened boys did not answer. They shook their heads in agreement with the answer already offered.

"As punishment for your offense, you will work the lines for our soldiers and carry food and ammunition to them. You will..." the captain barked, but the brave dissenter refused to stay silent.

"I will not! I am leaving for Amerika to start a new life! I will not endure another day of this unrighteous rule!" the dissenter yelled for all to hear.

Brian Spielbauer

"There will be no discord!" Captain Rohner admonished as he brought his short club hard across the boy's determined face. The lad dropped to the ground as the awful crunch sound caused many in the crowd to shudder. Having arrived to witness how his captain dealt with dissenters, the general of the local army fully studied the captain's reaction.

"Silence until I am finished!" the captain demanded to the felled boy. He then eyed the other two, "You will endure this punishment for six months, at which time you will enter the army of Austria with honor!" Captain Rohner stared at the other two. His strong hand gripped his club tightly. He was fully prepared to answer more defiance from the youth.

He then turned back to the bleeding boy, who attempted to stand. He smacked the boy again with every bit of power he could muster. Blood flew from the force of the club to the skull of the boy. "As a sign to all of what happens to those evading the draft, you will be executed!" Mathias's mouth stood agape.

The crowd quieted. Much to Mathias's surprise, the captain ordered, "Death is his sentence!" Four soldiers rushed the boy. Two held him high and tight as they led him away from the crowd. The other two soldiers waited for the captain's order and aimed their shots.

"Fire!" the captain bellowed. Without pause, the soldiers pulled the triggers, and the boy's life was forfeit. The captain then turned the crowd, "A lesson to all! Should we call you to serve, you must answer! Should you know of anyone who evades the call, and you do not bring him forward, you will have the same penalty as he!"

Mathias reached for each of his two shuddering friends, and he tried to hold them still. Adolph whimpered, "We knew him! We have known him our whole lives!"

The crowd hurried away from the wicked scene. Mathias led his two friends out to a quiet alley, where he quickly shoved them around the corner and into the shadows.

Hans yelled, "We cannot go! Not now! They will kill us!"

156

"How could your father shoot him?" Adolph questioned. "How many meals have you eaten with his parents, and how many has he eaten with you and your parents?"

"This changes nothing! It only solidifies the importance of us not getting caught. There is no doubt we will be killed if they catch us!" Mathias assured his friends, but their frantic looks worried him. "In two days, we will be forced to enter the army against our will. If we do that, the war will kill us anyway. It is not for me." In a quieter voice, he repeated, "It is not for me."

"You are right. I am going with you," Adolph committed.

Mathias looked to Hans, "And you?"

Hans looked around the corner at the boy's dead body as his sad family took him for burial. "I am going. Midnight it is." Hans brushed past the two and ran back to his home. Adolph shook Mathias's hand and went back to his family also.

Mathias took the long walk home as many thoughts raced through his troubled mind. He worried his father would read his face and learn of his intentions should the two meet at their home. If he did so, Mathias was not sure what his father would do. He feared to let his mother know and the penalty to her for knowing. He also dreaded saying nothing to them, for he knew how heartbroken they would be after he left. "I cannot risk staying. I must go," he swore to himself as he drew closer to his home.

Mathias rushed back and hurried through his chores in half the time he normally would. "I need to be gone before my father and mother expect me back for dinner," he thought to himself. He had placed everything where he needed it before he departed his home earlier that day. As darkness seeped into the low lying areas of Vorarlberg and the fog grew from the dampness that announced the coming of an eerie night, Mathias snuck quietly into the back door of his somber home. There he stored a small sack of food, along with the gulden he saved up for the trip. He slowly closed the door in silence and reached for the sack that he knew to be on the table across the small room.

A small candle was lit in the darkness. Mathias stopped. Standing before him was his mother, Lucia. Tears welled up in her eyes as the small light hit her son's face. "My son! Please be safe!" she said as she handed him the sack. "I have already placed bread and cheese in here for you to eat." She wrapped her arms around Mathias and felt her son for the last time.

"How did you know?" Mathias whispered. He felt her tears as they ran down his neck.

"A mother always knows," she whimpered.

"And father?" Mathias asked, but he dreaded the answer.

"He prays I am wrong and is determined to stop you should you go." Lucia's words resounded in his head.

"But I must go! I will die should I stay here. I am certain of it!" Mathias replied as he stepped back and looked down at his mother. He never planned to see her again, and dearly wanted to remember her face for the rest of his life.

"Mathias, go! Go and do not look back! I pray you will make it to where your heart desires and that your dreams come true!"

"And what of my father?" Mathias's voice cracked, and his jaw quivered. He loved his father and dearly wanted his approval, but that could not happen.

"Your father wants great things for you. He has ever since you were born. You are just like him in so many ways and completely different in others. God oversees both of your hearts, and though He places desires in each of them that are different, neither is wrong. Let God guide you in thought and deed, and no missteps will you make!" She hugged her son and then quickly opened the back door to the house and ushered him out. Mathias disappeared into the darkness.

The thud of the closing door echoed unendingly in Lucia's mind. Then the urgent creak of the opening front door demanded her attention.

"Mathias!" John bellowed as he stomped in. He angrily searched the home. He said once more, "Mathias! Come forward!"

"He is not here," Lucia's meek voice struggled to fill the dark void. "Do not ask me where he is. I will not tell you."

John grabbed her by the shoulders and violently shook her, "Tell me where he is! Where is my son?"

"I will not!" Lucia fiercely defied her husband. John dropped to his knees, "Where is my only son going? What will I be forced to do because of this?"

Lucia draped her loving arms around John. "I love you and my son. I cannot choose between the two of you. Please do not make me."

The tree branches flashed by as Mathias rode hard on the dark trail. He repeatedly whipped the flanks of his loyal horse's hide on their frantic run to the lake.

"The guards are on high alert for us deserters. I dare not waste time!" Mathias thought to himself. He rushed for the abandoned shed, where he and his friends agreed to leave their steeds. Mathias pulled hard on the reins as he tied up his horse. The other two had already left their steeds behind and were off toward the lake. Mathias finished tying up his horse and gave it a last pat on the back before he turned toward the forest.

He hurriedly dashed through the trees to catch up to his friends. On a clear day, the walk would take him several minutes. On this night, it was far longer. After covering half the distance, a familiar whisper came from the darkness ahead, "What took you so long?" Hans asked, his voice full of irritation.

"I came as soon as I could!" Mathias defended as his two friends stepped out from the shadows.

"What is that?" Adolph asked as several sounds came to them in the darkness. "I hear something from where we left our horses."

"This way!" a soldier's voice echoed through the forest. The horses the three left behind neighed at the soldiers' rough handling of them. Other soldiers answered the first as they rushed through the trees as torches lit their way.

"Run!" Mathias urged as he led his friends toward the water ahead of them. The three stumbled through the brush as they stove to reach the lake before the soldiers caught up to them.

"What about the border guards? They will be waiting for us by the beach!" Hans frantically stated.

"They went to town after capturing the others. I do not think they have returned yet," Mathias said as he approached the beach to Lake Constance.

"What if they are waiting?" Adolph asked.

"Then we are going to die!" Mathias knew his words were true. He hoped his father would not be the one to do it.

They crashed through the last of the branches and burst forward onto the beach. They turned to see the torches that approached through the trees as the soldiers closed in. Mathias looked up and down the beach quickly. He saw neither torches nor soldiers. "A stroke of luck," Mathias whispered to the others as they resumed their race toward the lake.

"I hope our canoe is still there," Hans asked as they plunged into the cold water. They wasted no time being quiet as their chasers came on them hard from the forest. They swung their bags on their shoulders to keep the contents dry.

"Just swim!" Mathias barked as they left the shore. The soldiers burst onto the sand as the three were merely a stone's throw away. They could not make out the deserters in the dark, but they heard their splashes as they frantically swam away from the shore.

"Fire!" a man yelled. His voice boiled with rage. Though he swam for his life, Mathias easily knew the stark sound of his father's voice.

"Dive!" Mathias gulped. He took a half breath and dove under the water. He bumped into Hans but refused the urge to come back up for air. He heard the muffled shots, and the bullets sped through the water around them. Though he was out of breath, Mathias dared not resurface until the bullets ceased. When he could not hold out any longer, he slowly rose to the top and stole a brief gasp of air. He was on the edge of the range of the soldiers' weapons and far off course of the swimming platform where they hid their raft. He still heard the voices onshore. One, in particular, stood out, "They are dead! We will come back for their bodies when the sun rises!"

Mathias quietly swam for the platform, but he heard no sign of his friends. He hurried to the other side and hoped they survived the shooting.

"You made it!" an exasperated Adolph said. "We thought you were hit!"

"We need to go. They will be looking for us the moment the sun comes up!" Mathias said as he reached for the canoe. He pulled it from under the platform, and they placed their packs on the one-person canoe and held with one hand as they began their long swim. The three pushed hard as they swam the lake under cover of night. In doing so, they crossed into Switzerland and out of the Austrian Army's reach, but Mathias did not feel safe. "We are going to walk all night, and we will not rest until tomorrow evening. My father will come for us. Be assured of that!"

"Are you sure we cannot rest a bit? We are in Switzerland now. He cannot reach us," Hans argued.

"No!" Adolph retorted. "We know John Rohner all too well! He will find a way to get us. If he does, we will die. We must go!"

In the early morning hours, the three caught a break from a man taking his furniture to Paris to sell. "So you need a ride?" the man asked.

"Yes," Mathias confirmed.

"Well, I need help from you to protect my things on the way. Will you do that in exchange for the ride?" the man asked.

"Of course!" Hans responded. "I want a ride even more than I want a fire." All three eagerly jumped in the wagon. They rode throughout the day and put a lot of ground between them and John Rohner before the following night fell.

The door creaked open in that late and desolate hour. Lucia did not stir. "John?" she asked at the sound of his familiar heavy footsteps. The door closed with the same slow creak and finally clicked shut. Even the slow noise of the shutting door sounded defeated. There were no other footsteps as she heard John sit down heavily on his chair at the table. Lucia silently slid out of bed and stepped into the dull lamplight that John carried in. Even in the darkness, she made out her husband's wet cheeks. She cried with her husband as she knelt before him at the table. Lucia dared to ask, "I do not know if I have the strength, but I must ask, where is Mathias?"

John reached to her trembling hands and locked eyes with his wife, "He is gone." John sobbed as his lip and chin quivered with fright.

"Is he dead?" Lucia's last bit of courage dissipated in the final desperate question.

"I do not know." John pulled his wife in tight as he whispered. "They went into the lake to escape. I ordered the soldiers to shoot, as the general watched me closely. I stepped in and knocked my best shooter to the ground, and scolded him for missing. I started shooting, but I missed high every time. My men just kept shooting! I do not know if Mathias or the other boys were hit or if they got away!" John frantically told the story as his words sputtered from his immense sadness. "I finally called off the shooting. We will go back in the morning to see if they are dead or alive. Either way, our Mathias is gone. We will never see him again!"

Brian Spielbauer

CHAPTER SIXTEEN

PARIS

Mathias, Hans, and Adolph sat quietly by the fire. None of them risked the slightest word. The three young men laid out their wet things from their still soaked bags for the first time since they swam Lake Constance. Thoughts of the bullets as they whizzed past them in the dark water rushed through Mathias's mind.

The Swiss man who gave them the ride asked, "You boys seem to be running from something, or to something. I know not which." He was a nice man, and Mathias appreciated him giving them a ride.

"We are going to Amerika for a new start," Mathias answered resolutely. His friends let Mathias do the talking.

"Amerika!" the old man replied with an unmistakable glint in his eyes. "You are brave men indeed! If I were younger, I would go with you! Hell, I might go anyway!"

"You would go with us?" Adolph asked sheepishly.

"But of course, or I am not Faegin Caflisch!" the old man boisterously replied.

"Faegin, it is nice to meet you. My friends here are Hans and Adolph, and my name is Mathias."

"Well, boys, it is very nice to meet you. I can tell you a thing or two of travel!" He then went on about the marvelous new world and the fun of young men seeking his fortune there.

Hans and Adolph continued listening to the man about what lay ahead on their journey to Le Havre and what the man knew about traveling across the ocean. Mathias ignored him and concentrated on the contents of his pack. He counted the gulden he saved for the trip and carefully tracked every thaler he had. He threw out some ruined food, which was wet from the swim in the lake. Then he saw a folded yellow parchment, one he did not recognize. It was far heavier than it should have been. He slowly opened it and found more coins within. It doubled the amount he had already saved. He set them aside as he saw writing on the paper. He slid closer to the fire so he could read it. Though the paper was wet, and the ink smeared, Mathias recognized his father's handwriting immediately.

Dear Mathias,

I know not when you will read this, but I pray you live to get the chance. I have known of your intentions for some time, though I have told no one. I fear for your safety on the journey to Amerika, but if any should have the strength and determination to withstand the test, it is you!

I have dreamed a thousand dreams of what I wanted for your life. All of them pale when compared to the dream you have for your own. Wherever you go, and whatever you do, keep God in the center. Make a difference to those you meet every day. Lastly, remember the sacrifices your mother and I have made to help you. Use the ducats wisely for your new start.

I pray for your safety, but no matter what happens or what you hear, you must never return to Austria. It will not be safe for you. I love you, as does your mother. We will pray for you in our hearts throughout our remaining days.

Love, your father, John Rohner.

Mathias laid the paper out carefully as he fought off the feelings that were determined to shake him. He tried to keep busy as the others spoke, as he did not want to get drawn into their discussion.

Mathias and his friends were safely out of the grasp of the Austrian Army and slept well that evening. In the morning, the old man shook him, "Wake up! I want to be in Paris in a few days. That will not happen by you three sleeping all day!"

Mathias woke up and sat with Faegin. "Would you like some coffee, Mathias?"

"Very much, thank you," Mathias answered as he accepted the cup from Faegin.

"You seemed very troubled last night, even more than the others. Is it something I could help you with?" Faegin asked. Mathias only remembered seeing his grandfather one time before his death, but Faegin resembled him.

"I do not think I should tell you. We are in quite a dangerous position. I do not want to draw you into it," Mathias replied as he took a drink of the hot coffee. He looked at his friends, for he did not want to wake them quite yet.

Faegin looked around the empty woods, "Mathias, whether you tell me your problems are not is your business. But I feel quite certain that your secret will be safe here in the clearing, especially to a man likely to die before the year is up!"

Mathias looked to Faegin, who grinned ear to ear. Mathias smiled and thought his reservations silly. "We are from Liechtenstein and are escaping to Amerika to avoid joining the army. My father is the local captain, and up until last night, I thought he was chasing us."

Faegin's look changed. "Son, I have known soldiers to cross into other nations in search of deserters. We are still not that far from..." Faegin began as his worry quickly rose.

Mathias interrupted him, "But then I found a note last evening, just before bed. It is from my father, telling me I have his blessing. You need to understand that if the army back home found out that he knew we were leaving and perhaps even helped us, he and my mother would both be killed."

Faegin raised his hand, "Son, I understand your position. Please, say no more! Your secret will go with me to the grave! But let me say this; the note your father left for you, at great risk to himself, is a tremendous gift to you. Guard it and keep it safe. I do not doubt that he cares for you deeply!"

Mathias then woke his two tired friends, and they quickly gathered their few things and prepared to board the wagon again. With the coins his father left him, Mathias had more than enough currency for the journey. As he rode on the back of the wagon, a smile grew on his face that he had no interest in hiding.

"What is it with you, Mathias? You seem very happy today," Adolph asked. "I am still very nervous about this. I will not rest until we reach Amerika."

"I know in my heart that we are doing what we are meant to. Our journey has just begun, and fortune has already shined on us. God is on our side, so who can be against us?" Mathias answered. He carried with him his parents' blessing, which was worth more than gold to him.

"I wish I felt as good as you. I keep waiting for soldiers to show up and take us back to our country," Hans replied as he suspiciously eyed the sides of the road.

"You are wrong about the soldiers," Mathias replied as he leaned back against a wooden chair.

"What do you mean?" Adolph asked.

"They will not take us back to Liechtenstein. They will kill us on the spot if they find us and only take our heads back to show the others what happens to deserters." Mathias laughed as he said the words, but his two friends rubbed their necks.

"I would like to avoid that," Hans replied.

Mathias felt more at ease since reading his father's note. He knew his father would not come looking for them, and he hoped his father and mother were safe. Other perils of the journey still lay ahead, but he left the dangers of Austria far behind.

THE LEGACY of FAITH:

THE JOURNEY

Of

George Spielbauer

Date: 1865
Origin: Hohenschwangau, Bavaria
Route: Le Havre, France
New York, New York, USA
Guttenberg, Iowa, USA

TIMELINE

George Spielbauer, Mary Pankraz	Year	World
Joseph, their son, is born.	1868	
	1870	November, Bavaria joins the North German Federation.
	1871	Jan. 18th, Ludwig refuses to attend an event, his brother Otto and uncle Luipold attend to represent Bavaria.
Mary and Joseph arrive in Iowa.	1872	
	1874	The foundation of the new St. Mary's church was laid, at its current block of location.

CHAPTER SEVENTEEN

HOHENSCHWANGAU

"Everything is planned perfectly. Surely she will take me as her husband," George mumbled to himself as he placed the bouquet under a blanket in the back of the wagon. He climbed into his seat, happy to sit again as his knees continued to shake. Nervousness gripped him about the upcoming evening and his proposal to his love. He urged the horses forward as he slowly made his way through the town and eventually up the familiar brick path leading to Hohenschwangau Castle, the summer home of the royal king of Bavaria and his family.

As he did every day, he picked up Mary Pankraz from her job as the librarian in the palace. "You are crazy, George. She will never say yes to you. She could have any man she desired," George argued with himself as he pulled the wagon to a stop. He was so consumed by his thoughts he did not notice his lady as she stood there, waiting impatiently for him.

"George, you need to watch where you are going! You almost ran me over. And just who were you talking to?" Mary scolded as she climbed into the wagon before George could get off to help her. "People will think you are crazy!"

"I am sorry, Mary. I was just thinking over the things my mother asked me to get for her tomorrow. So sorry!" George was embarrassed. It was a poor start to what he hoped was a magical evening. "I hope *you* do not think I am crazy."

"Of course not, George. It is all right. You are a good man to pick me up every day. You will make some lucky lady a good husband one day," Mary answered. "You have always been so kind to me, and I do not know why. I can be quite difficult, as you know."

"Not at all, Mary. Not at all," George answered. Her kind words melted George's heart, which began to beat excitedly. He said little as he took her back down the hill toward her home. Then he did something he had never done before and took a right instead of a left at the bottom of the hill. The turn took them toward Lake Alpsee.

"What are you doing, George? This is not the way home?" Mary asked.

"I want to show you something I noticed earlier. Do you have time?" George asked. He needed to get her to the edge of the lake for his proposal, which he wanted to be just right.

"Yes, I have a little time. My mother will not be worried for a while still. It is such a pleasant evening for a ride, and I love the lake. It is the most beautiful place in the world."

Once again, her words tickled him. "I could not agree more."

George pulled the wagon to a stop next to the lake. The sun lowered past the rim of the mountains, but its last rays of the day created purple, red, and orange waves against the clouds. The amazing view reflected on the mirrored surface of the lake. "What do you think of this?" George asked as he stared at Mary.

"It is amazing, George! I love being here." Mary gasped as she took in every detail of the clouds and lake, and the amazing mountain caught in between.

"I have something else for you!" George said excitedly. He reached into the wagon and pulled the bouquet and handed them to Mary. They were the same colors as the sky. "I picked them just today, for you and this moment. Do you like them?"

Mary took the flowers. They were beautiful, but Mary replied with unease, "George, you should not have. You must have spent all day looking for these."

George ignored her words. He ramped up his courage and was determined to see his plan through. "Do you see that house, Mary? I have saved up over the past two years, and I am going to buy that house," George paused as he read the confusion on Mary's face. "For us."

"George," Mary began. She carefully chose her words. "Please, help me down." She reached her hand out for George to take. He quickly jumped down and rushed around the wagon to her waiting hand. Each petite hand was a miracle to George.

Mary got to the ground and looked at George as he leaned in for a kiss. She allowed a quick kiss but then pulled away. "George, I am so sorry. I do not know how I feel about this."

"Do you not like the view? Would you not enjoy spending the rest of your days living in the cottage and watching the sunrises and sunsets?" George asked. He then finished, hesitantly, "Or is it that the part of this you do not like is me?"

"George, I do not wish to hurt you! Please do not make me do so. I like you, George, and you are my best friend. But I do not think of you in that way." Mary lifted his dropped chin. Tears pooled in George's eyes, with more than a few racing down his cheeks. He did not bother to wipe them away.

"Could you not? In time, would you be able to love me? I will provide for you, and there is nothing you could ever do to make me feel otherwise! Please, take your time. Reconsider this, will you not?" George begged her.

"George, if I did not already feel the same for another as you feel for me right now, I would strongly consider you. I think so highly of you and your intentions. Another girl will..."

George cut off Mary as he turned away to hide his agony. He was unwilling to hear the most painful phrases come from her. "Your mother will be waiting. Let me help you back into the wagon," he said as he rushed to help Mary to her seat.

"George, please do not be mad," Mary protested as he hurriedly walked back to his side. He quickly climbed to his seat and sat down in a single motion, and whipped the horse into movement with a loud "Ha!"

Mary sat in silence as the horses quickly carried her to her home. George stared straight ahead, as he was unwilling to speak to Mary.

They came to a stop in front of Mary's home. George quickly dismounted the carriage and helped Mary to the ground. He tried once more, "How could I feel so strongly about you, and have you not feel the same way?"

Mary did not answer, so George turned to walk away. Mary's soft hand restrained him. He turned to Mary as she spoke in a quivering voice, "George, I have hurt you, and I apologize for that. Do not hate me, I beg you, for that is something I cannot stand. I wish more than anything to tell you what you want to hear, but to do so would be to lie to you. Finding that out later would cause much more pain than finding out now."

"I know you are right, but that does not lessen my pain," George answered, his voice weak. "If by some chance you should ever change your mind, you will find me in a place called Gutenberg, Iowa. It is in Amerika, and I am leaving in the morning. I knew there was a chance you would rebuke me, so that is where I have planned to go."

"No, please do not!" Mary protested.

"Mary, I understand your feelings and believe your words. If they are true, then the man you desire will take your hand. Believe me when I say I cannot watch that and pretend to be happy for you. My only chance at happiness is to leave here. I can stay by you no longer."

Mary pulled George in close, and the two embraced. She kissed him on the cheek once more and wished him well on his journey. Neither of them got what they wanted that day, but both set themselves squarely in a new direction.

CHAPTER EIGHTEEN

NEW FRIENDS

George pushed through the side country between him and Le Havre, France. He dared routes and dangers a more careful man would not deem prudent. He purchased his ticket to Amerika at the border of France and never looked back. Time flew by as he rode each day on his horse, and he left all his worldly possessions behind. He was far from the first in his family to go, with many before him going to Wisconsin and a few to the growing city of Dubuque, Iowa.

Day after day, George rode in silence. He stopped only for his weary horse to eat and drink, and he worked for farmers as he went in exchange for a night's stay and feed for his horse. The sight of a farmer with his family depressed him, as his thoughts went back to Mary and what he left behind. He departed early each morning, as he was eager to push onward toward his destination.

Eventually, he arrived in Paris, which was far too large of a city to avoid. Unlike smaller towns, he could travel through Paris without drawing attention to himself when he did not speak to others.

As evening closed in at the end of another lonely day, George found a small inn within the magnificent city. For the first time since departing Schwangau, he paid for a night's stay. After boarding his horse, he went to a local tavern and ordered a hot meal and several drinks. He spoke to no one except the bartender, and then only to order another drink.

A pretty girl came to sit by him, "So, German, are you going to Amerika?" The French girl tried to speak German, but most of her words came out wrong. George turned to her, "Please, I do not want to talk. Go find another."

The girl leaned closer, "I do not want to talk either. Would you like to have one last good time before you depart?" Her warm breath huffed past his ear. She then placed her hand on his, which indicated her intentions. He thought for a moment of taking her up on her offer.

"I have heard of girls like you," George replied.

"Oh yeah?" she asked. "And just what have you heard?"

George thought for the smallest moment, but the thoughts of what Mary would say erased the temptation. He pulled his hand away from hers, "You should leave."

"You have plenty of money. You paid to stay here and board your horse! What is wrong with you, stinky German?" the upset girl said as she raised her voice. She stood up quickly and slapped him on the arm.

Others in the tavern took notice. Three large men came over to handle the situation. "Greta, is this man bothering you?" the largest one asked. George saw the men had eyed him since he walked in, and he searched for a quick way out.

"He promised to buy me a drink, but now he will not!" she scorned George.

"I did not!" George defended. A club slammed down on the bar next to his hand. It quickly drew their attention.

"I will not have trouble here tonight! Leave this man alone. Greta propositioned him, and he declined. Nothing more. Go away, Arman!" the barkeeper shouted to the man and his followers as he held the club high.

"Maybe we will see you later. You might reconsider that drink!" the man stated to George as he leaned close. Then the three took Greta and walked out, bumping into several others on their way through the door.

"They will be waiting for you when you leave. Go out the back door and do not stop until you are safely in your room. Do you hear me, boy?" the barkeeper whispered over the bar as the low din of the tavern returned.

George nodded. "I only want others to leave me alone. I should not have come here," he uttered to himself as he hastily got up to leave. The barkeeper quickly led him out the back of the tavern. George slid into the darkness and stumbled down the filthy alley. He realized how much he drank as he bounced from wall to wall, unable to walk straight. When he turned the corner, the three men from the tavern stood before him with their lady in tow.

"German, you are going to pay the lady whether you spend time with her or not. Give us your money, or we will beat it out of you!" The three stepped toward George as he backed against the brick wall of the building behind him. He clenched his ticket to Amerika in his hand.

"I will not pay! I did nothing with her!" George defied as he tried to stand tall and ready for the fight.

"Have it your way!" Arman laughed as he shoved George farther down the alley. The three pounded on George as each took his turn and repeatedly punched him. They finally knocked George down, and he sputtered senselessly on the ground. "No, I need that to get to Amerika!"

George tried to stop them from taking his money, of which only a small portion of his total was in his pocket. The prized possession was his ticket, which he regretfully forgot to leave in his room. The largest man pried it from his hands. He then kicked George in the face as he parted, "Stupid German! You should have stayed home! Do not bring more of your filth to Paris!"

Mathias, Hans, and Adolph sat like little children as they marveled at the buildings and people of Paris. Faegin drove the wagon through the bustling streets. They rode deep into the heart of the city and saw the many finely dressed men and women.

"The well-to-do walk past the paupers that litter the streets, picking up the scraps of higher society. Mingled within them are thousands of people who fall somewhere in between. Some hope to dress to the hilts one day, while others are comfortable with where they are. All hope never to fall so low that they will be looking for the scraps," Faegin lectured. "And you, my friends, where do you hope to land one day?"

Mathias spoke up, "I just want to earn a good living and raise a family. I do not need to be rich, and if I am poor, I want it to be of my own doing."

"Boys, I present to you Port St. Denis, Paris!" Faegin proudly stated as he raised his free hand to the massive brick archway that covered the road's width. The archway sat on building-like pillars that stood at both sides of the street. Mathias sat, mouth agape, in wonder at the sight. The old man smiled as he watched the boys. "I love to show people Paris for the first time. It is the most beautiful city in the world!"

He pulled the wagon to a stop as the sea of people milled around them and the other businessmen who hoped to sell their goods. "Here is where we set up our business," Faegin ordered as he stepped down from the wagon.

"And how long is the business open?" Hans asked.

"Until the furniture is sold, Hans. Then I will take a few orders for more and be on my way back to have my son make it. Most of this load already has orders for it from my last stop here. It will be gone quickly, while the rest may take a little longer."

Hans looked to Adolph, "The old man knows how to run a business. I hope one day..." A tug on Han's pant leg stopped him. He saw the old man staring at him. "Hans, that is your name, yes?"

"Yes," Hans answered.

"And yours is Adolph, and yours is Mathias." The old man said to each of them.

"Yes," the two answered in turn.

"Mine is Faegin, and I hope you will be calling me that from now on instead of *old man*. You, too, will attain my age someday, God willing. Trust me; you will want people calling you your name!" Faegin sternly stated. He had a hint of a twinkle in his eye, but he seemed far from amused.

"Yes, Faegin, we can do that. Many pardons!" Mathias replied as he jumped down from the wagon. He shook Faegin's hand while the other two bent down to do the same.

"Thank you. Now, let us get that furniture down and set out for purchase. The sooner it is gone, the sooner you can be on your way to Amerika!" Faegin went about his business as if the misstep of only the moment earlier had dissipated away.

"Furniture! From the Swiss Alps to Paris, the finest you will find! I am taking orders for more, of course!" Faegin began his usual chants, as word of his arrival traveled fast to those who already made their order. He sold several pieces already ordered to a different buyer as the person who ordered it arrived late to pick it up.

"Why did you sell those chairs if someone already ordered them?" Hans asked.

"A bird in the hand is better than one, or even two, in the bush, so they say!" Faegin gleamed. "I will not get stuck with unsold pieces. Perhaps they will come more quickly next time!"

Hans learned a lot from Faegin quickly and learned to appreciate the wisdom of the old man.

Mathias watched with amazement as the people hurried to see the furniture. "This is very well-made furniture. The people are so anxious to attain it. You will be busy for months!"

"We have more demand than we can satisfy, with no end in sight. There are times when several pieces do not make it, though, as I cannot stop the thieves on the way. They dared not try us this trip, thanks to the three of you!" Faegin stated.

As Faegin said, several large table sets were already spoken for, and those who ordered it arrived that afternoon to pick them up. The people paid him handsomely for the furniture. Before the first day's nightfall, Faegin sold the remaining furniture and had another full order for two trips.

Faegin paid the boys nicely and thanked them, "If not for your help, I would not have arrived as quickly. Usually, I also have several pieces stolen before I am able to unpack them. It is well worth it to have you gentlemen help me. Would even one of you consider staying on, to learn the trade?"

"Faegin, thank you for your offer and ride to Paris, but I must go to Amerika. My heart is set on it," Mathias answered as he shook Faegin's hand again.

"Thank you, but no. I am going to Amerika also," Adolph answered.

Hans looked around the city, "These people and this city mesmerize me. I am staying here to work for Faegin. If your offer still stands?"

Faegin's eyes lit up, "Yes, of course! Thank you, Hans. I did not believe any of you would take me up on my offer!"

"Neither did I," Mathias added. "Hans, are you sure? I thought we had this all planned out?" Mathias was hurt that his friend was leaving him.

"We did. But this journey has been long already, and I do not trust the trip across the ocean," Hans replied.

"We have just started! We have not even reached Le Havre, and you are leaving us? We bought you a ticket!" Adolph protested.

Hans placed a hand on each of his friend's shoulders and took the time to look them in the eye. "God has a plan for each of us, but I think they are different. I wish you the best, but I am not going on from here."

"You cannot go home. Ever. They will kill you on sight," Mathias informed. "We are traitors to their cause."

"I know. I will not go back. I am going to stay here with Faegin and seek my fortune," Hans promised.

"I never really thought any of you three would take me up," Faegin repeated to Hans as they walked back to the wagon. "I am very appreciative that you are staying. The journey from my home in the country to Paris is far more dangerous than I let on. There is no doubt that many know of my repeated trips and plan their thievish intentions accordingly. Having you with me will certainly make them think twice!"

Hans looked to the others as he climbed into the wagon, "I am glad to be gone from Vorarlberg, but Amerika is too far away. Paris is the city for me. God bless each of you." The two saw the determination in Hans's face and knew they could not convince him.

"I wish you the best," Adolph said as he reached up to shake hands with his dear friend Hans.

"May God bless both of you," Mathias said. He and Adolph watched as Faegin's wagon rolled away. They then turned and walked through the city of Paris to see what fortune would deliver them next.

They strolled along the Seine River and watched the sunset at the end of the remarkable day. "I cannot believe he left us," Adolph said of Hans.

"Of the three of us, he was the least interested in leaving. I am not surprised. Besides, Faegin needs his help. I am glad for them," Mathias replied. "I need a drink, though, follow me!"

"I am thirsty too," Adolph replied. They followed a windy brick-paved street and walked into a tavern as three husky men brushed past them on their way out. Mathias saw the first knock hard into Adolph, and he was almost pushed to the floor. Mathias, larger than most men, was not above using his girth when needed. He leaned into the first man, who didn't expect the blow. Mathias knocked the man back and to the ground.

"Sir, I am sorry for my clumsiness!" Mathias said as he extended his hand to the fallen man.

His friends quickly picked their leader up, who did not accept Mathias's offer. The man steamed at Mathias, "Watch where you're going!" Mathias stared at him, eye to eye. Then to his friends, he said, "Just another stinky German! Come, we have business to deal with!" They stormed past Mathias and walked hurriedly down the street. Mathias was courteous enough to wait until they departed to smirk at the three and the lady who followed them.

"Why do people hate us so?" Adolph wondered.

"I guess they hate sauerkraut," Mathias answered, which made them both laugh. The two sat at the bar to have a drink. The bar was busy, and it took the bartender a few minutes to get to them.

"A lot of Germans in here tonight!" the barkeep said as he wiped the bar down in front of Mathias and Adolph.

"Would you prefer we were not here?" Mathias asked. He was getting irritated with the loathing of his kind.

"No! I like Germans and their manners. I prefer it to the French ruffians who frequent here. The mix just brings trouble, and I do not want it," the barkeep replied as he poured them a drink. "That, my friends, is on the house. I might suggest you go soon, though, before the three you bumped into on your way in return. It did not go well for the last German lad who sat there before you." He then walked away and prepared to make a drink for the next patron.

"Do you think it was Hans?" Adolph asked.

"I do not see how, but let us go look," Mathias replied. "I am concerned about whoever it is."

They left the tavern and walked up the street to look for the three French men they bumped into. It was not long before Mathias saw the three emerge from an alley. "It appears they just finished their deed," Mathias said.

They rushed to the dark alley and searched the dingy corners. Adolph found a man moaning in pain, "My ticket... They stole my ticket."

"Get up, friend," Adolph answered as he helped the man to sit up.

"Are you all right?" Mathias asked as he knelt next to the man.

"No!" the man grunted. "They took my ticket to Amerika and my money! I need to get them back!"

"Friend, wait," Mathias urged as the man rose to his feet. "What is your name?"

"George Spielbauer," he mumbled. "Are you going to help me get my ticket back or not?"

"No," Adolph answered as Mathias said, "Yes."

"What are you saying?" Adolph questioned. "This is not our business."

"They do this to German travelers every day. It most certainly is our business!" Mathias countered. "I am tired of the French who repeatedly take advantage of my brethren," Mathias replied. He turned and walked after the stumbling George as Adolph dutifully followed behind. The three trounced out of the dark alley, which hid most of George's worst injuries. He carried a large cut over his eye, which still bled.

"I cannot believe he can stand," Adolph whispered to Mathias.

"Me neither. He's a tough one! I would like to have such a man be on my side in a fight." George impressed Mathias, and he was eager to help his new friend. They searched the streets and looked for the three ruffians.

They eventually arrived back to the tavern, and without pause or thought, George burst through the doors as he looked for the man who stole his ticket. The girl from earlier was already working on her next victim as the other men waited for her to signal them to step in. They also enjoyed a new round of drinks, most probably on George's money.

"Well, look who has returned!" one of the followers said to their leader. He looked up just in time to see George's fist smash down on his temple. It was a tough blow, but the man took it well and rose quickly from his seat.

"I am going to kill me a German tonight!" Arman growled. Then he realized there were not one but three foes who stood before them.

"You should think twice," Mathias's barreled voice flooded the suddenly quiet room. He and Adolph stood behind the huffing and angry George.

"I want my ticket back!" George shouted.

"You will not get it, but you can try," Arman calmly sneered as he grit his teeth and clenched his fists.

George rushed Arman, who easily corralled him. The large man then flung George toward one of his friends, but Mathias was right behind the throw and smashed the large man to the ground with both of his hands clenched together. The patrons of the tavern hurriedly rushed away, and many quickly left the establishment. The barkeep reached for his club but was not sure at all whom he would use it on or whom he wanted to win.

Adolph rushed the remaining ruffian, and all three engaged the three men who preyed on traveling Germans. Each man threw punches that landed hard on their foe's face. A large area emptied around Mathias and the largest man, as those watching formed a ring to enclose the two mighty fighters. They continued to slug it out in the center of the tavern, as each fell and smashed tables and chairs before they rose to fight again.

George worked his way out of the hold his man had him in. He then wheeled around to the back of his man. He lifted a stool and smashed it down on his enemy and knocked the man out cold. He then dropped the broken pieces of the stool and rushed toward the back of the largest man. At the same moment, Mathias powered his right fist across the man's chin and spun him hard, but not down. The man spun right into George's reckless charge. He lowered his head and shoulder and slammed into the man's fat belly. George's bull rush lifted his foe off his feet. He then crushed the man onto the remains of a shattered table and into the unforgiving stone floor.

The man's air burst out of his body as a blue color took over his face and neck. He gasped for air as he held his hands up to give in. Adolph punched the remaining man and knocked him to the floor also. The fat man reached into his pocket and pulled out the ducats he had left from earlier. He handed it to George.

"Where is the ticket?" George demanded as he took his money back.

"It is already gone. I lost it on a bet," the fat man huffed.

George kicked him again as the three triumphantly walked out. George could not be consoled as he sat hard against the wall of the tavern.

"What is the problem, friend? You got your money back," Mathias asked.

"I need a ticket to Amerika! It is gone!" George lamented. He buried his head in his filthy hands.

Mathias looked to Adolph, who nodded back to him. "George, it just so happens we have another ticket. Would you care to earn it?"

The words were like the sun breaking through stormy weather unexpectedly. "What do I have to do?" George asked. "I would do almost anything to get that ticket!"

"You must travel with us, that is all. You are a tough man, and we would feel better traveling with three than two," Mathias replied. "My name is Mathias, and this is Adolph."

"I am George. George Spielbauer."

Mathias helped George to his feet and handed him Hans's ticket.

"I cannot believe God has helped me so. I was certain He had all but forgotten me. I cannot thank you..." George began as his lip trembled and tears flooded his eyes. "I cannot believe I still get to go." He took several steps as he gathered himself. "Thank you. It has been a very tough several weeks for me, and you are the first one to show me any help. Please, I have a room at the inn. There is plenty of space for us."

"That sounds good," Mathias answered with a smile.

"I could not be more grateful," George uttered as they took the short walk to his hotel.

Brian Spielbauer

CHAPTER NINETEEN

AMERIKA

George led the two to his room. He took special care to stay clear of any others that looked suspicious to him. After entering the inn, they went all the way to the third floor and into his room. "I am sorry, but there is only one bed."

"A floor with a roof over it and some clean water are far better than what we have had for a while. We thank you, George." Mathias's grateful words reassured George that he had made two good friends. They excitedly talked late into the evening of their grand plans.

"Our boat will leave within the next week," Adolph told George.

"Where will the boat let us off?" George asked.

"New York City," Mathias answered. George smiled as he thought about the famed city in Amerika.

"I cannot wait to see it," George replied. He laid on the bed and tried to go to sleep.

"I do not know where I will go from there or if I shall leave at all," Adolph said as he and Mathias lay on the floor.

"I am going to Gutenberg, Iowa," George said. "Many from my area have already gone there. It is in the far west of the great country, up the Mississippi River. It is a place where a man can make his way without the troubles we face here," George repeated what he had heard many times before. "I want a piece of land and the health to work it. I will do the rest on my own."

"A civil war between the northern and southern states is waging there, and it divides the nation. I am leaving here to stay out of such things, and I hope to avoid it altogether. This place,

Gutenberg, seems to be about as far from everything as can be, and hopefully at the far end of this war. It is a place I would like to go to. Tell me more about it."

George told them everything he knew of the area, with just a little embellishment to impress his new friends. "I should think that all three of us would do quite well there. Do you want to go there with me?" George peered over the edge of the bed at his two friends on the floor.

Mathias looked to Adolph and then answered, "Yes, it is settled! We will make our way to Gutenberg after we land in New York. But for now, I must go to sleep," Mathias suggested. "The lodging is a blessing, but I am quite weary from the day. My destiny is laid out before me, but first, I must sleep."

George and the others woke early. As it was Sunday, they made their way to the closest church, which happened to be the Cathedral of Notre Dame. Each bowed deeply in reverence as they entered the majestic church. "Let us stay to the rear. We are not dressed well enough to get too close to the front," George advised.

Mathias finished praying. He noticed George still knelt. He had a strained look on his face as he offered his prayers to God. "May I ask, what are you praying for?" Mathias asked George as he finally sat back in the wooden pew.

"My family and the others that I leave behind. I pray God will watch over them and keep them safe. I also thanked God for bringing us together. I feel that we can make it to our destination if we stick together."

Mathias agreed, "I believe you are right, George. I also pray for my parents, who will go on without my help. I am glad we ran into you. God meant for that to happen; I have no doubt."

As they walked out after church, Adolph confessed, "Throughout the rest of my days, I shall never forget this magnificent church. It is the most beautiful building that I have ever been inside."

They left Paris that day and made their way to Le Havre. There they waited just a few days before their boat, a large iron steam-powered ship, departed for Amerika. The trip was less perilous than many endured, though they greatly aided themselves by their willingness to help others and to work as needed on the boat. It also was a shorter trip, and it lasted just eight days.

On a warm spring day in late April 1865, the ship carrying George, Mathias, and Adolph pulled into the harbor, which led to Castle Garden, the great immigration center in New York. The endless lines of homes and buildings in the city of New York captured their imagination.

"Amerika," Adolph uttered in complete wonder. "This city intrigues me."

"Be careful, young men," one of the shipmen said as he overheard Adolph. "It is not a place for the meek or dumb. Many an immigrant is taken advantage of and never heard from again."

"We are hoping to have left that in Paris and Le Havre, but it is not so?" Mathias asked.

"No, sir. Sadly, it is not," the man answered. "That day has passed."

Mathias nodded his appreciation for the advice, and the three readied to depart the boat. The lines through Castle Garden were long, but the guards quickly ushered the three healthy young men through. Several travelers on the ship became sick on the journey, and the guards quarantined them upon arrival.

"Where to from here?" George asked. "This city is far too big for me. I have no idea how to get where we need to go."

"I asked some passengers as we went through the lines. Many Catholics are going to Cincinnati by way of trains. We will start that way." Mathias replied. "George's path is a gift to me, and I am determined to make it happen."

After they heard the warnings of the man on the boat, the three men stayed clear of the inner part of the city. They took a ferry to the train station and then stuck close to the station until their train was ready to depart for Cincinnati. Each earned their trip as they helped at the station, and they did all sorts of necessary jobs. The train workers reserved certain jobs for German and Italian immigrants. They were the dirtiest, hottest, and most dangerous work, as those were the jobs the people in Amerika refused to do.

Mathias, George, and Adolph found work shoveling coal into the furnace of the train they were to take the next morning. "This work is hard and dirty! Are you young Germans up for it?" The man who did the hiring sneered at them.

"Yes, sir!" Mathias answered. "You will not regret hiring us. We will keep that furnace stoked!"

"All right then. Now this here is an immigrant train, which is full of your types going west. Do not get mixed up in there. If you got confused for the passengers and sent into one of the cars, no one will be able to get you out! When we check for tickets, they will throw you off. They will not wait for the train to stop either!" The man barked his orders with a mouth that overflowed with chew. Each word he spoke spit more of it out at their feet.

They followed the grotesque man as he walked toward the front of the train, which in the early morning light was quiet and calm. "These are your quarters and workplace. The passengers will be here soon. Again, when they arrive, it ain't time to go findin' your relatives! Do that, and you will be gone, with hundreds of them begging for your spot!"

"If the job is so dirty, why would they want it?" Adolph asked. Mathias jabbed him with his elbow to get him to shut up.

"Well, you wanted the job, did you not?" the man challenged as he spun on Adolph.

"Of course, we did! We signed up for it!" Mathias stated.

"Germans, these cars are built to hold fifty passengers each, and I have never seen one that did not have upwards of three times that many stuffed in there. For hours on end, they are in there, standings tight, sweating, and stinking all over. Pigs smell better by the time we let them off!" The man proudly stated with a disgusting smile. "So, remember, if you get tired, sick, or injured, you will be replaced, just like that," the man professed with a snap of his blackened fingers.

"Now, get ready. They are coming!" The man said as he stalked away. He barked to his guards, "Open the damn doors for the immigrants!"

"Oh, my," Mathias wisped as he watched the people. Each shoved, pushed, and pulled their way to the car. Loading was a sheer matter of survival, as each man made a valiant attempt to keep his family together with no regard for anyone else. Every family rushed into the cars and searched for their personal one-foot space. The cars were standing room only.

Mathias watched as the car just behind them filled first, with the creaky doors slammed shut after it was well past full. He saw the sad people crammed inside, with those on the outside pressed up against the barred windows. The vision haunted him. "Look at all the room the three of us have and how little they have. We have clean air and as much heat as we want! We are living like kings, boys! I would pay him to let us do this job over having to ride in that filthy car!"

A harsh voice snapped them from their talk, "Stoke the fires, boys, or I will replace you!" The train engineer slurred at them from above. The whiskey from the empty bottle in his hand deeply affected his speech.

"Shovel hard! I do not want to ride in there!" Mathias urged as he quickly shoveled two heaping loads of coal into the furnace. The thoughts of the engineer moving them to the train cars drove Mathias hard. The burning coal boiled the water in the engine, with the steam building all the while. When he was ready, or more so after he opened his next bottle of whiskey, the engineer pulled the lever that released the steam. The train inched forward. Slowly at first, the train roared to life as it picked up speed.

"Now more than ever, boys!" The engineer growled as he lit the thickest cigar that George had ever seen. He then gleefully jammed it into his coal soiled face.

"This is hard!" Adolph gruffed, and he shoveled more coal into the raging furnace. "My back is getting sore already!"

"Keep at it, or you will get kicked off the train!" George grumbled back as the engine roared the train forward through the Appalachian mountain range.

"There is only room for two of us to shovel into the furnace at a time. The other needs to go back and shovel coal forward. We can rotate places, so we do not tire as fast," Mathias told them, with no complaint offered back. George went farther back and shoveled the pile forward.

When it came time for their first rotation, Mathias took a quick break to take in the beautiful scenery as the train hurried through the lush spring forests in the valleys. Then, in an instant, it barreled into another of the seemingly endless darkened tunnels dug through the base of the mountains. "So this is Amerika!" he bellowed at the top of his lungs. Though it was a scream, the engineer who was less than twenty feet from the three barely heard it. George and Adolph laughed. They worked hard the remainder of the day, and the train worked westward.

"No more coal. Not until after the next town!" the engineer ordered. Then he took his cigar out and cracked a grin. "We have never made that trip so fast, my boys! You are going to be good at this job someday!"

"I am not sure this is a job I want to get good at," Adolph uttered to his friends under his breath. Coal dust, smoke, and sweat coated all three men as they finally rested, and the train coasted into the next town.

"When we stop, you need to refill the waters for the engine and shovel the coal from the back to the front of the train car," the engineer requested of them, his grin from a short time ago a distant memory of the past. "After that, I suggest you go wash up and rest for the evening. We depart early in the morning!"

The train workers went up and down the cars and opened the doors for the many passengers to exit. They flooded out of the crammed cars and were eager for clean air, food, and a space to sit down.

After they completed their shoveling work and topped off the engine waters, Mathias led them down to the river nearby. "My Lord, two rivers converge here!"

Each of the dirty men washed in the cold water and readied to enter the town. "Where are we?" George asked.

"Pittsburgh, Pennsylvania," Mathias answered as they walked to the edge of the bustling town. "I heard a man say that name as the people unloaded the train. The man also said to be careful of mixing it up with the people who live here, as they do not like the immigrants from the trains. I want no part of such things. Let us get our food and get out."

"I learned my lesson all too well in Paris. It is best to stay away from the people in these large towns," George agreed. The city, even from a distance, amazed the men. It lay along the two rivers, and it was built on the hill between them. The lights from Pittsburgh and from the many riverboats and bridges that spanned the rivers caught their eyes and fascination as they found their place to eat for the evening. After a solid meal, the three weary coal men laid down by the fire for the evening. "I prefer the crisp, but clean, night air to what they must be enduring in those dingy immigrant hotels," George said.

"I second that. It is a bit colder, but this fire will do us just fine," Mathias replied as he nodded off to sleep.

CHAPTER TWENTY

DUBUQUE

The early morning whistle from the train rudely woke the three. "I have not been this sore in quite a while!" Mathias confessed as he stood and stretched. "My back is tight, but we have got work to do."

"But you are probably not as sore and tired as you will be tonight," George chided as he pulled Adolph to his feet. The three trudged back to their post, and they began heating the furnace for the next leg of their trip.

The engineer sounded his horn that announced the departure of the train. The passengers responded and boarded again, with less getting back on from the day before. Some had already reached their destination, or the local authorities detained them for unbecoming conduct.

"Where will we end our trip today, boss?" Adolph questioned the engineer.

"Galena, Illinois," the engineer responded with a ruthless spit of the chew toward Adolph's feet. "And you's ain't leaving me there, are you? If so, you can just get off right now! It costs me a lot of money to find good coal shovelers for the way back to New York!"

"No, sir. We plan on getting back to New York at least. We will stay longer if you will have us. The pay is good, and we have never been treated so well," George interrupted. Mathias and Adolph stood by, stunned.

"Well, that is good! That is good indeed! You are smart lads. This is a pretty good job, and you get to see the country and earn your living. Keep up the good work, and I will see if I can hire you back. *After* we get to New York, that is." The engineer snarled again as he climbed back to his perch. In no time, he opened his first bottle of whiskey for the day.

"We are leaving the train at Galena. You know that, right?" Mathias asked in a hushed voice.

"Of course, but he does not need to know that! It will take us weeks to get there on foot if we get off now, and a pretty dangerous walk that would be. The train is fast and protected. We will just have to jump off as we get close to Galena." The others agreed, and they each picked up their shovels and went to work.

Just as they started, the same man who hired them walked up with a new man, "Gents, this is Dubuque. He is going to help you, so show him the way." Adolph helped the man into the coal pit and handed him a shovel. The extra person meant they would be able to have a break as they rotated through their system.

"Dubuque? That is a strange name?" George asked as he shook the man's hand. "Is that not the name of a town?"

"It is my nickname," he proudly stated. "On the last train I worked on, everyone had one. My real name is Bert. Bert Finney. But I like Dubuque better," he explained. Dubuque reached into his upper pocket. He took out a massive pinch of tobacco and placed it into one side of his cheek. He then followed that amazing feat up with a large cigar, which he masterfully placed in the other cheek.

"That is a lot of tobacco!" Adolph laughed. The mouthful prevented Dubuque from answering right off, so he just happily, but dumbly, nodded his head and smiled.

"Well, Dubuque," Mathias started, "Then my name is Hardy, as I am from Hard, and he is Aussy, as he is from Austria." Mathias referred to Adolph.

"I was hoping for a better name," Adolph admitted with a jab to Mathias, who ignored it. Mathias continued, "And this fine man," referring to George, "his name is Paris, as that is where we found him fighting three of the most dastardly

198

Frenchmen ever assembled, all by himself at that! So do not quarrel with us, but certainly not with Paris!" Mathias cajoled.

"Where are you going?" George asked Dubuque.

"I am going west. I am originally from Dubuque, Iowa. I was told to go west for health reasons, so that is what I have done," Dubuque said as he started his shoveling. Several chunks of his chaw fell out of his stuffed mouth. The largest of which Dubuque picked up off the coal pile and shoved back in.

"Why did you go east first?" Mathias asked. The puzzled look in the other's face added to his question.

"I went the wrong way, I guess," Dubuque explained. "Everyone told me to go west, but I did not know the direction." Dubuque stopped shoveling for a moment. He looked quite concerned as he asked, "Am I going west now?"

"Of course," Adolph answered, which brought a quick sigh of relief to Dubuque. "What is your health issue?"

Dubuque withdrew his cigar and stood tall to answer. He was not a large man and seemed old for his age as the soot from the coal began to cover him. He took a deep drag from his cigar, while at the same time he spat an unusually large amount of chew spit on the ground and answered, "I have asthma. They believe the dry air out west will cure me. So, I goes west!" Without delay, Dubuque stuffed the cigar back in and went back to shoveling as each of the other three considered his answer.

George opened his mouth to ask another question, but Mathias waived him off. Throughout the rest of the day, they did their usual deed, which consisted of shoveling the coal and filling the boilers at each quick stop. Finally, they closed in on Galena, Illinois. Mathias filled Dubuque in on their plan, which he was immediately excited about.

"I like the way you think! I will show you how to get to Dubuque from here. I know this land like the back of my hand," he eagerly stated. "Even though I have been gone less than a week, I cannot wait to see my hometown and family again. They threw me such a nice party when I left. Heck, they might throw me another one when I show back up!" Dubuque spouted.

"I am glad you know the land. Have you been to Gutenberg?" George asked.

"Of course I have. It is a short ride north from Dubuque, but you better have a horse, 'cause it ain't flat. There ain't much there, a dinky little town it is. It is beautiful, though! But I will warn you; the girls are quite tough. I cannot understand why none of them were interested in me," Dubuque stated as he sucked another deep draught of his cigar and spat his chew again, seemingly at the same time.

"That does not make sense to me, either," George offered as he chided his new friend.

"Let us load the furnace one last time. That will get the train into Galena," Mathias informed the others.

"No, we should just leave. This is not our problem anymore," Adolph grumbled. "My back is sore the way it is!"

"I do not want the people on this train to suffer because of us. We are going to make sure they get to Galena," Mathias scowled. Adolph quickly fell in line.

The four shoveled hard to fill the furnace. Then Adolph and Dubuque headed to the back of the coal cart first.

"Where are you going?" the engineer sneered at George, who was the last one to shovel his final load. He then reached for his pack.

"We need to shovel some more coal up to the front so we can be ready for tomorrow. We decided to go into town tonight, and we may sleep in a bit," George answered. The four stood still and waited for the engineer to react.

"That is good thinkin', boys. I might keep you on after New York yet," the engineer sneered. "But you best not be late in the morning!"

Mathias led them over the shaking coal. The footsteps were hard to hold as they slid into the shifting black rock. Mathias and George pretended to shovel as the other two scampered over the back of the cart and down to the connector to the next cart. They waited for just the right moment, and then they jumped into the passing trees and rolled to the bottom of the track, clear of the rolling train. The people in the car behind them cheered, but Mathias quickly placed his finger to his mouth and urged them to keep quiet about their early departure.

"It is your turn!" Mathias said as he waved George forward. George climbed over the back as Mathias shoveled harder to keep up the image. As George jumped off, the engineer saw him in the mirror as he rolled to the side of the track. He jerked his head around in time to see Mathias as he climbed over the back of the cart. For a moment, the two locked eyes, and the engineer offered Mathias the most wicked scowl ever delivered. Seconds passed as the engineer's glare told Mathias that he better not abandon his post.

"You unappreciative immigrants! Get back here!" he yelled over the roaring train. Mathias merely smiled back and winked as he jumped off the side, rolled down the grassy incline, and he finally came to a stop at the bottom. The first three ran to pick up Mathias, and together the four laughed as the train rolled on. The engineer fumed just as much as the boiling water within the engine.

Brian Spielbauer

CHAPTER TWENTY-ONE

THE LONG RIDE

Dubuque led them through the woods, and he was careful to steer clear of the railroad and the Galena Depot. The engineer cursed the four up and down, but it was far from the first time, or last, he needed to fill those positions.

"Follow me. I know this place like the back of my hand," Dubuque urged as he rushed through the thick forest that lined the tracks.

"You keep saying that. Are you trying to convince yourself or us?" George asked.

Dubuque ignored the barb and darted excitedly through the underbrush. He led the other three as he sought the best path. Mathias followed tight on his tracks, so much that when Dubuque stopped suddenly, Mathias, then Adolph, and finally George ran into the person in front of them. All four then plunged over the steep bank of a stream and rolled down into the gully. Each screamed as the bottom of the rocky gully raced up to meet them.

"I thought you knew where you were going!" George lamented as he stood up, covered in mud. He landed only several feet from several jagged rocks. Adolph cursed Dubuque as he washed the mud off his pants. The water was little more than a stream, but the fall was quite far.

"Like the back of your hand, you said!" George scowled.

"And twice you said it!" Mathias added as he knocked water from his ear. Adolph was too angry to say anything more but instead sat on the creekside and dumped water from his boots. His agitated look burned into Dubuque's side.

"This must be a new stream," Dubuque offered. He stood there and scratched his head as he looked up and down the creek as he searched for an explanation.

"A new stream? Are you serious?" George scorned again.

"There is the town. Let us go have a look," Mathias interrupted. He was ready to move on and see what the town had to offer. The four men, wet and muddy, wandered into the town of Galena as the sun went down on another day.

They climbed the small hill from the creek, and they were eager to enter the town. As they closed in on the outer buildings, a man stepped in front of them and barred their way. He carried a gun and yelled, "What are you doing in these parts?"

The four stopped abruptly. Mathias held up both of his hands. "We ask to enter the town. We wish to have a drink and something to eat."

"We do not like vagrants, and vagrants are what you appear to be! Even worse, you look like succesh trash from down south," the man barked in Mathias's face. Mathias held his calm as he slowly reached into his bag.

"What are you reaching for?" the man yelled louder as he raised his gun.

"Please, friend, do not yell in my face again. We have money," Mathias answered as he showed the man several of his coins. He then quickly put it back in his bag, which he then tucked under his arm.

"Why are you wandering up from the creek soaking wet if you have so much money? Why did you not ride the train in?" the man questioned.

"Because we just jumped off it! We needed to get off before we arrived so we could ditch our jobs. Our friend here, Dubuque—" Mathias started.

Dubuque quickly reached for Mathias, but he could not stop him in time. "Do not say that name!" Dubuque urged in a hushed voice, but it was far too late.

"Dubuque? Why do you say that damn name!" the man demanded. He then notched his musket and pulled it tight to his shoulder, ready to fire.

Mathias was perplexed as the guard seemed angrier about the name than the apparent vagrants standing before him. "Why, that is my friend's nickname. He hails from there."

The man raised his musket directly toward Dubuque, who quickly raised his hands in defense, "No sir, you misunderstand. I am not from Dubuque. I am from... Menomonee! I *hate* Dubuque. I hope for a flood to ruin that Godforsaken place as soon as possible!"

Mathias and George stood still. Mathias gave George a quick look to make sure the two kept quiet.

"Then why do you call yourself that?" the man questioned again as his finger cradled the trigger.

"Sir, it is like a fat man called Skinny, or a bald man named Hairy! 'Tis a joke of my friends in Menominee, nothing more!" Dubuque frantically chattered his words, which were followed by a nervous giggle that allowed his chew to run down his chin.

The man relaxed the notch, which pleased George, Mathias, and Adolph plenty. "So, a man of Menominee? What is your real name?"

"Bert Finney, sir," Bert proudly answered. He reached his hand out to the man. The man lowered his gun and took Bert's hand. "Well, Mr. Finney, that was a close call for you. We shoot people from Dubuque before asking too many questions, so be careful of the words you throw around here. Believe me, I am one of the more sensible fellas. Welcome to the city of Galena, home of the war hero, General Ulysses S. Grant! Good evening gents!"

The four walked past the guard, and each offered untrusting looks toward him.

"What the heck are you doing? You do not say the word 'Dubuque' here, and before you make the mistake, do not utter the word 'Galena' in Dubuque either, if you know what is good for you, which none of you seems to," Bert scolded harshly as they marched into town.

"Why is it such a big issue?" George asked.

Bert stopped. He quickly sized up his three friends. "Because they hate each other! Listen, you all are from a different country, so let me teach you something. We just finished a civil war. We did not even fight another country. We fought ourselves!"

"I am sorry, Dub... I mean Bert. I still do not get what you are saying?" Mathias asked.

Bert, exasperated beyond measure, huffed, "I cannot believe you all could be so dumb! Listen, we do not need a reason to hate other people here. It comes very easy for us. White people in the south hate black people down south. The white people in the north hate the white people in the south. The white people in the north do not talk about how they feel about black people in the south or even black people in the north, for that matter. Everyone here hates you Germans, but not quite as much as we hate the Irish. You Germans hate the Irish..."

"I do not hate the Irish," Adolph interrupted.

"You will!" Bert continued as he brushed past the ignorant interruption. "Trust me. It happens to everyone. Lastly, and most importantly, the people of Dubuque hate the people of Galena, and in all listed cases, vice versa!" Bert was out of breath from his lengthy explanation. His words were gone, with a tiny dent made in the thoughts of the three before him. A huge spit from Bert ended his teaching.

"What does *vice versa* mean?" George asked. Bert stood still as he tried to think up an explanation. "I am not sure, but it has something to do with the opposite being true. In this case, the people of Galena hate the people of Dubuque too. Do you understand?"

His calm answer settled into the three, and for the first time, they understood what he was trying to say.

Mathias looked at George, "Well, at least we will be north of that. I sure hoped we had left things like this behind. I guess it is everywhere."

"At least you are going to Gutenberg," Bert added. "It's all German people there anyway, so there is no one to hate!"

"I need a drink," George stated as he walked away from the conversation and toward the tavern that was close by.

"The DeSoto House it shall be!" Mathias answered as he read the sign above the street. "I am always ready for my next drink." It was the first city they risked venturing into. As they left the train behind, they had little choice. The men sauntered into the tavern. It was thick with patrons, which allowed them to hide their wet garments. They finally found a table and had a seat in the back. A pretty barmaid came to them, "What will it be?"

"Four beers, please," George replied. The lady smiled at George, but her eyes quickly shifted to Adolph.

"I will be right back," she answered as she batted her eyes toward Adolph again. Her German accent was obvious, and Adolph was intrigued.

"She is the most beautiful woman I have ever seen," Adolph stammered, unable to take his eyes off her as she went to the bar to get the drinks.

Mathias and Bert laughed. Mathias then noticed George had his face down. He leaned into him, "George, there are many women in Amerika. You will certainly find one."

"My heart is spoken for. There are no other women for me," George answered.

As the night went on, Adolph became friendlier with the barmaid, while George sank lower into his depression. Towards midnight, Mathias made the call to leave.

"No, I am just getting to know Martha," Adolph protested. By this time, he was helping her get drinks for people and clearing tables.

"I am getting George out of here. You can stay if you wish," Mathias replied. He helped George from his stool.

"Dolpha, we gotsta get George home. But I will'st come back if'n you want?" Bert asked. His drinks greatly slurred his speech and he was barely able to stand on his own. He tried to help with George but stammered past him and bumped into another man.

"Hey, Kraut! Watch what yer doin'!" the man barked as his strong Italian accent carried across the tavern.

Bert looked up to the man, who stood several inches taller than he did. Bert went to speak, but instead, his body unleashed the massive amount of alcohol stored in his stomach. The refuse erupted onto the Italian man.

"Oh no!" Adolph uttered as he ran to help.

"Stronzo!" the man yelled as he punched Bert and knocked him to the floor. He then tried to kick Bert, but Mathias laid George on the floor and caught the man's leg. He then dropped the man next to Bert, who threw up on him again. The Italian's temper exploded. He shoved himself from the floor and readied to fight Mathias.

Adolph jumped between them with a club from behind the bar in his hand. "No more! Stop this!" he ordered. The Italian rushed him, but Adolph was ready and smacked him alongside the head. The man fell to the floor, once again into the mess left by Bert. Adolph yelled to everyone, "It is time to go! Get your things and leave!" It was close to closing time, and everyone departed without further issue. The club-wielding German ensured no more issues as the customers left.

"I am sorry," Mathias apologized. He picked up Bert and George the best he could.

"Do not worry about it. You did me a favor. Go wait outside. I will be out shortly," Adolph said with a wink. Mathias took George and Bert outside and sat them down on the boardwalk in the cool midnight breeze.

"I think I should buy dat man a drink," Bert slurred.

"Shut up," Mathias retorted. "I hate dealing with drunk people!"

It was not long before Adolph came out. "Mathias, go in that door and up to room 209. Here are the keys. Martha says we are welcome to use it. She was glad I hit that man, as he handled her in a poor way earlier. I am going to help her and her father clean up. They own the entire building. I would do anything to spend more time with Martha," Adolph said as he disappeared back into the tavern.

Mathias pulled the two drunken men up the stairs and opened room 209. Bert stammered for the bed. He fell during his attempt and missed badly. He hit the floor hard and did not move until morning. Mathias set George on the bed and lay him back.

George grabbed his arm, "Mary is the only girl for me. I will never love another." George whimpered several times before he fell asleep.

Mathias pitied George's broken heart, and his thoughts trailed to his own family left behind. He spent the night on the floor, but he made sure to stay clear of Bert.

Brian Spielbauer

CHAPTER TWENTY-TWO

IOWA

Mathias woke early the next morning, even though he knew his friends would not be quick to do so. "Time to rise, boys. We are going the rest of the way today!" Bert and George slowly rose from their sleeping positions as their hangovers quickly announced themselves.

"I feel horrible," George uttered as he held his head in his hands at the edge of the bed.

"George, you really cannot handle your alcohol," Bert replied.

"The only reason you are not sick right now is you threw up all over the tavern last night. If not for Adolph, a large Italian man would have split your head open!"

Bert scratched his head, "I do not remember any of that?"

"Where is Adolph?" George asked as he opened his eyes for the first time.

A knock at the door stopped the conversation as Mathias hurried to open it. Adolph burst through the doorway, "Here are some muffins, fellas!" Adolph's beaming smile filled the room. "Holy cow, you guys smell terrible." Adolph opened the window, and then he turned back. "Can you believe how nice this place is?"

"It is very nice. But we need to get going if we are going to reach Dubuque today. I am ready to get there and start my new life. Everything between now and then seems a waste of time to me."

George and Bert scarfed down the muffins Adolph brought, and Martha brought in a pot of coffee too. "Adolph, have you told them the good news?" Her words stopped the three. They looked directly at Adolph.

"Yes, Adolph, tell us the good news," Mathias said as he grew more irritated.

"Well, gentlemen, I am staying here." The dower looks from Mathias and George slowed Adolph, but they did not stop him. "I am the newest employee of the DeSoto House, and I plan to make my new start here in Galena. I can get you jobs here also if you want. This town is doing great things."

"That is great, Galena is a terrific town, and the people are smart and friendly," Bert overstated as he put in his first chew of the day. He gave a slight sarcastic grin to Martha, who smiled as she left the room.

Bert closed the door behind her and turned sharply to Adolph, "Are you crazy? This place is a hole in the wall. Hell, the Indians did not even want it. Anywhere but here, Adolph! Anywhere but here!"

Mathias stood. "Adolph, you are my best friend. Are you sure you want to do this? We planned to go to Gutenberg. I thought we were going to do that? It saddened me when Hans left us, but now you, too?"

"You are my best friend also, Mathias. You always have been and always will be. My heart is here, though, and I want to be with Martha. She is so amazing." Adolph turned away from Mathias and walked to the door. He turned back before he walked out, "I wish all of you the best, and I hope you like Gutenberg. It is only a two-day ride away. If you do not find what you desire there, please come back here. I will help you find work; I promise." He smiled at them and left the room.

Mathias turned to the others. "It is decided then. We are down to three again." George and Bert said little as they readied to go. They grabbed their sacks of clothes, their currency, and then they left the room.

"I am sorry about Adolph leaving us," George said to Mathias.

"Each of us needs to find his own way, and ours is in Gutenberg," Mathias replied.

George added, "The two of us, at least, will stick it out."

As they left the hotel, Bert asked, "You do not like Galena or the people, right?" Bert inquired.

"To be honest with you, this place seems fine to me. It certainly seems fine to Adolph. Too many people think their home is better than others, and for no other reason than that is where they were born. If I have not learned anything else on this long trip, it is that there are good and bad people everywhere." Mathias stared Bert in the eye as he gave his final answer on the topic.

"Huh," was all Bert said. He placed another dip in his already full mouth, and they walked into the street outside the DeSoto House.

"I am done with boats and trains. Let us get horses and ride the rest of the way," Mathias said as they walked to the stables. Each of the men purchased a horse and saddle, though Mathias needed to help Bert with his payment.

"I have no more money to repay you," Bert apologized.

"You can pay me back when you sell your horse in Dubuque," Mathias answered. "You are growing on me, Bert. I am not sure if that is good or not, but it is happening!"

"I wish I could go with you to Gutenberg, but as you know, I am quite ill," Bert stated as he shoved his large cigar into his chew-filled mouth. Bert led the way as the three rode off toward the city of Dubuque.

The country they rode through could not have been more beautiful. The rolling hills became ever steeper as they made their way to the northwest toward Dubuque. They reached the city of Menominee around noon. There they stopped, but only long enough to let their horses drink, and then they continued.

"I am surprised no one knew you," George said sarcastically to Bert. A huge spit of chew and another deep toke of his stub of a cigar, along with a whimsical smile, served as an answer from Bert.

From there on, the hills became rougher as rocky limestone outcroppings popped up. Cedar trees lined the rims of the bluffs. Oak, hickory, and walnut trees crowded the hills and valleys. In places, huge open areas of grass and wildflowers fought for supremacy.

"I think I am going to like this place," Mathias said to the rest. "It seems on the edge of the world, far away from the troubles most men deal with. My mother and father would have loved to see this. I am done with fighting and wars, and the only fighting I am going to do from now on is with the ground I am farming."

"You will have no trouble with that. This is great farm ground, the flat parts at least," Bert comforted with another large spit.

"Good God," George uttered. It was towards evening, they had just reached the last rim of bluff, and before them opened the mighty Mississippi River. "It is just like the Rhine."

"Only larger," Mathias agreed.

"No, gentlemen. It is home," Bert interjected. The three sat atop their horses and took in the magnificent sight before them. "We have arrived, boys!" A few homes dotted this side of the river, but a far larger town sat nestled in the bluffs on the other side.

"That is an amazing sky," George offered. An endless stream of red and orange colors waved across the horizon above the bluffs across the river. He wistfully added, "It reminds me of a view back home."

"Come on. Let us cross the river," Bert urged. He led them down the steep path for the ferry that sat below them. As they rode up, the man who operated it barked, "Hurry up, lads! This is the last ferry of the night!"

The three quickly dismounted and led their horses onto the wooden ferry. Several others were there also to catch the last ride. The small steam engine chugged as it pulled the ferry across the river. Several paddle boats had just come into town and docked for the night. The people of Dubuque lined the paths leading down to the landing and welcomed the newcomers.

"Now, be honest. Is this not far better than Galena?" Bert asked. The man they paid for the ride strode right at him.

"What is that you say, lad?" the man challenged. The dislike went both ways, as Bert suggested.

"I says to my friends here how much greater Dubuque is than Galena," Bert boasted. He continued to sing the many praises of his hometown. The man joined in as they degraded the village of Galena while they lifted Dubuque's name to the heavens. Mathias and George thought it best to stay out of it, but the exchange amused them greatly.

George was still recovering from the previous night's frivolity, and the three stayed the night at the Hotel Julien. "Why are you not going to see your family?" George asked Bert.

"Well, they already sent me off once. My mother made an awful teary goodbye, and I do not want to do that to her again. Also, I am not sure how I could explain to them that I went to Ohio on my way west. They already do not think I am too smart." Bert looked down as he said the words. "It is kind of embarrassing."

"We all make mistakes," Mathias comforted.

"Yes, but," George added, "that is a pretty big one."

They laughed at the thought, but none of them greater than Bert. "I suppose you are right!"

"Mathias, let us sleep on the floor and allow Bert to have the bed tonight," George offered.

"That is a great idea. Thank you for getting us here, Bert," Mathias added. Bert eagerly took the bed, and the three slept hard that evening.

They rose early the next morning. After selling Bert's horse, they took him to the train depot. As they approached the train, Bert turned to Mathias. "What do I owe you?" he asked.

Mathias thought for a moment. "Nothing," he said. You led us here, and a good guide you were. I wish you luck and Godspeed on your journey to the west. The train will take you for a while, but then you will need to purchase another horse and a saddle at some point."

Bert smiled but was sad at the parting. "You are a good man," George said as he took Bert's hand. "You are smarter than you give yourself credit for, and you will do fine wherever you end up."

"Do you think so?" Bert asked. "No one has told me that before!"

"Of course," Mathias answered. He shook Bert's hand, and the three parted ways. Mathias and George took a few steps, and Mathias stopped, turned, and yelled, "Bert!"

Bert stopped and turned back.

"The sun rises in the east, and it sets in the west," Mathias said as he pointed, first to the rising sun, and then to where it would set that evening.

Bert looked to the rising sun with confusion and then back to Mathias, "Every day?"

"Yes, Bert. Every day," George answered. Bert looked back to the sun for a moment and then, resolutely, turned the other way. He stuck his cigar back into his chew-filled mouth, smiled one last time at his two friends, and walked toward the train.

George and Mathias walked back to their horses. "Do you think he will make it out west?" George asked.

Mathias laughed and said, "No. He will make it somewhere, but probably not out west."

They mounted their horses and rode off on the trail that Bert told them would lead to Gutenberg. After climbing the bluff out of the valley, they stayed close to the Mississippi. The first town they reached was called Balltown. The hills were lush with trees and wildlife. Swift streams cut into the valleys, with each one even more powerful than the one before. After again climbing a steep hill, they rode across a long ridge that provided tremendous views in all directions.

"God must have stood in this very place as He directed the creation of the Earth," George gasped. "The sight is too much for me to take in all at once."

"I am sure this is the place for us," Mathias said as they rode past the small village. Several families lived in the town that looked over valleys. A restaurant operated there called Breitbach's.

"Should we stop?" Mathias asked. "I am hungry, and the smells from that place are making my stomach growl."

"Naw. Let us keep moving. I want to reach Gutenberg today if we can. It sure looks good, though," George replied as several men left the establishment. "Though I think I may need to come back and try it someday."

They rode on, and by early afternoon they reached a valley town called Buena Vista. As they rode down the hill into the town, George saw the small church nestled in the valley. A strong stream ran through it, and several businesses operated there. There were also several houses in the town. "This is the most beautiful place I have seen yet," George said.

"Even more beautiful than the ridge above?" Mathias asked.

"It is hard to say," George replied as he took another look around him. "I cannot say for sure which is lovelier, but surely God placed His hand on each of them."

Mathias could not disagree but changed the subject, "You already made me pass one place to eat, and I am not missing another." Mathias rode up to the saloon and tied his horse up to the rail. George did the same, and the two entered to find something to eat.

"What will it be?" the bartender barked. The new arrivals interrupted his business with four other men.

217

"We would like to eat and have a drink if it is not too much trouble?" Mathias asked. The bartender hurried to get them their drinks.

"All I have is ham and cheese sandwiches today until my wife returns. Will that do it?" the man asked as he set the sandwiches quickly on the bar.

"Why yes, I suppose so?" Mathias replied. The bartender hurried back to the other men, who seemed deep in discussion.

"We should have eaten at the other place," George uttered as he ate his sandwich. "I sure wish I had some of that pie."

"Let us eat and get out of here." Mathias agreed. They ate quickly, but as they finished, the oldest of the four men who spoke with the bartender rose and came toward Mathias and George.

"Gentlemen, from your speech, I would mark you from near my homeland. Would you be from Liechtenstein?" the man asked.

"Close," Mathias answered as he stood to take the man's hand. "I am from Vorarlberg, Austria. My name is Mathias Rohner."

George also stood. "I am from southern Bavaria, less than a day's ride from both of you. My name is George Spielbauer."

The man eagerly shook both of their hands. "I am Johann Tschohl, and my sons are back there delivering the whiskey we promised our friend here."

Just then, the bartender rushed back in, "That will be two dollars."

Mathias reached for his money, but Johann beat him to it. "Put it on my bill."

The bartender winced, "You never pay your bill!"

"Then take it off what you are going to pay me!" Johann barked back. The bartender smiled at the thought and did so at once.

"Some of the people here are not as smart as they should be. We are at the edge of the wild, but there are a lot of good folks," Johann said as his sons walked up, their load of whiskey handed off. "So, where are you going next?"

"Gutenberg, our final destination," Mathias answered.

"Well, that is close to where we live! We are going to one more stop in Balltown. Otherwise, you could ride with us. Just stay on the trail, and it will lead you there. You should reach it by nightfall if you keep riding. Welcome to Iowa," Johann answered.

"It was nice to meet you, and thank you for lunch." George shook Johann's hand again as they left the tavern. George and Mathias mounted their horses, while the Tschohls jumped in their two-horse wagon. Each hurried out of town in different directions.

Mathias and George rode through the valley as it wound and eventually came to another small town by a large river, much smaller than the Mississippi. The town was Millville, and it had a nice store that was busy servicing the local farmers. It also had a large hotel. The locals called the stream the Turkey River.

"As I have seen several turkeys already on this ride, I would say it is well named," George said. After crossing the stream and valley floor, the two rode up the steep trail. The hill seemed to rise right into the sky as they continued climbing for almost an hour. Then, just as they reached the top, they started down again. The view amazed them, as laid out before them in the valley was the Mississippi River, again. It wound north into the distance, as far as the hills allowed them to see.

Next to it, sitting alongside its natural partner, lay the town of Gutenberg. Mathias's heart leaped for joy as they hurried down the steep rocky path.

"Why, you seem more excited than I am to be here. But I am the one that planned to come from the start," George observed.

"Yes, that is true. But having the dream placed in my head by your description, I have never been so eager to be somewhere in my entire life. I am tired of traveling and knowing when I get somewhere that I am soon to leave. George, I am going to die in this town. Until that day, I will do everything I can to raise my family here and aid the town the best I can."

Mathias never told George about his father's letter, nor the wish his father had made for him.

"I am excited too, but without Mary, I am sure I will never truly enjoy anywhere on this Earth. I just wish she were here and that I knew she was in good health."

CHAPTER TWENTY-THREE

G. F. WEIST

George and Mathias carefully rode down the steep, rutted path into the lower valley. It was a hot and sticky day, and the horses breathed heavily from their exertion. "There will be a nice stream at the bottom of this hill, I would imagine. I could use a good wash in some cold water!"

"You and I both," Mathias added. "I want to see this town and just what is there." After watering themselves and their horses in the creek, they mounted again and rode into Gutenberg for the first time.

As they went, another valley opened to the left with a strong stream running through it, much stronger than the creek they had just passed. The hill in between rose steadily before them and separated the two valleys. "It is beautiful here, that is for sure," George admitted as they slowly rode across the stream. They passed several people on the path, with each saying, 'guten tag' as they passed.

"This is certainly a friendly place, and they speak our language!" George said excitedly. "Many of the people spoke some German on our way but only knew enough to do business with us. But the people here *are* German."

Some of the people they met walked, while others rode on horses as they passed. Soon George and Mathias reached the first buildings of the town of Gutenberg. Most of the more significant buildings were closer to the river.

"There will be no shortage of logs and stone for building, George. We will do quite well here!" Mathias said as he urged his horse forward ever faster. George kicked his horse to keep up. Large stone structures straddled the muddy road on both sides of the street as they approached the riverbank. The tallest was on the left as they came up, but the larger warehouse was built into the bank and down toward the river. Several docks were built off the back.

"Oh, my," George gasped again as he looked out over the river. "I have never seen anything like this in my entire life." A large wooden raft slowly came toward them. The raft was half as wide as the river and three times that in length. Many men watched along the edges for anything the raft might catch on and directed it away from the shallow parts of the slow-flowing river.

"Look at that steamer. It looks far too small to move that raft," Mathias offered as he took off his hat and scratched his head in disbelief.

"It does not have to move it. It only needs to steer it," a German voice from behind them remarked. Mathias and George turned to see a man twice their age who stood behind them, admiring the raft. "Logging men hewed those logs in the forests of Minnesota and Wisconsin, and this is how they send them down to mills far to the south. Several a week come by here, and this is not the biggest of them!"

"Pardon us, are we in your way?" George asked. The man answered, "Why no. I have seen many of these in my life. But it seems as though you are seeing it for the first time. You boys must be new here."

"Yes. We just arrived from our long trip from Bavaria," Mathias answered as he offered his hand to shake. "I'm Mathias Rohner, and this is George Spielbauer."

"Very nice to meet the both of you. I am George Weist, and I own these two buildings. I am looking for good help. Are the two of you interested?"

"We have just arrived, George. Thank you for the offer. We shall consider it," George answered.

"That is fine. You will not have a shortage of offers. Our town is quickly growing, you see. Farmers come here from many miles around to sell their crops since we have access to the river. While they are here, they spend a lot of money in our stores, and sometimes they stay in our hotels. As you can see, the forests are plentiful also, both with oak for building and game for hunting and trapping. Several veins of lead are also being found and mined in the hills around us. All of this just to say," Mr. Weist said as he put a hand on each of the young men's shoulders, "that you have landed in a good place, and we are glad you are here! I would say this to you, though, take a job while you can. There will be a great many men coming back from the war soon. Our own group from the immediate area, the Steuben Guard, entered the war to do our part. They have traveled many miles and fought in many battles to keep our country together. While many are farmers, the jobs in town will go fast, I fear."

"Well, Mr. Weist, we are happy to be here. I shall stop in your fine store soon to talk more about that position," Mathias answered enthusiastically. Mr. Weist smiled and walked into the front of his building that backed up to the dock below.

"We are in a great place for sure," Mathias said as he scanned the view in every direction. "Why did you not take the job he offered us? It was very nice of him to do so."

"I do not want to work in a store and have to talk with people all day. They will be watching everything I do, and I want nothing to do with it. I want a piece of land that is mine and mine alone. One that I can work in peace, where my success is based on my effort. I want to be my own boss," George said proudly.

"You are a good man, George, and I am glad to hear your plans. I do not mind farming, but I want to stay here for a while. When you need help, and you will, you let me know. I will help you anytime I can. But for right now, I think I should like to stay here. But first, I would like a drink."

"Well, look at that. The men are tying up the raft and coming into town. There must be at least thirty of them. I bet they will spend some money here tonight. We better get a room quickly, or there will be none be had!" George said as the two turned hurriedly and walked away from the shore.

A few more rock buildings stood tall along the river. Many log and wooden buildings filled in-between in the growing town.

"The Crawford House," Mathias announced as he read the sign. "This place looks nice enough." The two walked up with their horses and tied them upfront. After they entered, a man rushed out toward them. "I have one room left. Are you with the raft that just tied up?" the man asked harshly. "I do not want any raft men here. The last time I had some here I nearly had to condemn my building after they left!"

"No, we have just arrived from Bavaria," Mathias proudly answered. "We will take your room. Rest assured that we will take care of it."

The man's smile quickly grew. "That is good. Welcome to our great city! There is no nicer, or friendlier, place on Earth," the man announced as he reached for the key to the room. "My name is Moses Crawford, and this is my hotel."

Mathias gave a quick look to George, who smiled back. "Yes, quite friendly," George answered as he contained his laugh. "Except for to the raft people."

Moses took Mathias's money for the night. "Yes, except for them," Moses answered. "Follow me, gentlemen."

George and Mathias walked up the stairs to their room. Moses opened the door and showed them in. The room consisted of one bed and a large washing bowl on a stand. "I am sure you will be hungry and thirsty. I suggest you go to Buetel's Saloon. It is just down the street. My friend Gustav does a fine business there. Enjoy, and welcome to Guttenberg," Moses said as he left to go back downstairs.

"Several times now, you have said you were from Bavaria. Why not tell them you're from Austria?" George asked.

"You are from Bavaria, so it makes it easier. Plus, the fewer people who know I am from Austria, the better. Can you help me with that?" Mathias asked.

"Your secret is safe with me," George answered.

It was not long before Mathias and George found themselves at Buetel's Saloon. It was a wooden building with several horses tied up outside and a wooden boardwalk across the front. The double-doors to the saloon were both open, and the sound of the men inside met their ears. As they stood in the doorway, they saw the business was bustling as men from the raft had already filled the place. "This seems far from the quiet little town I had in mind," Mathias announced over the noisy business. Men lined the long wooden bar that spanned the room's width, with the backdrop of busy bartenders and shelves stocked with liquor and glasses on the wall. Most of the tables were also full of the raftsmen who ate and drank. "There is one table open. Let us take it before it is gone."

A man quickly came to them after they sat and took their order. In no time, the man came with their drinks and food. "That was very fast," Mathias complimented.

"It is quite busy, but very few of you seem to be eating," the man explained before he rushed off to serve a surly Norwegian.

"This is why I want to farm. This big city life is not for me," George replied as he took his food and drink from the waitress. Mathias replied, "I am not sure this qualifies as a big city." Several of the rough men bumped their chairs and table during their meal, with Mathias and George overlooking the mishaps.

After they ate and had a few more drinks, they prepared to leave. "These are rough and vulgar men. I do not care for the sort," an agitated George said as he stood.

"What did you say, German?" a large Norwegian man behind him grunted. George stood to see his angered look through his unkempt beard and mustache. "I know your dirty language enough to know it was not good!"

"I said we are leaving. That is all," George answered as he tried to step past the liquored man. Mathias was right behind him.

"Jaah! He says he was just leavin'. Just leavin', eh?" the man chuckled as he poked George hard in the chest. Close to twenty of the raftsmen stood behind him. "You locals are not very welcoming!" the man challenged as he stepped closer to George.

"That is not true. From what I have heard, this is the friendliest place on Earth," Mathias answered. He placed himself in front of George. "Is that not true, Mr. Tschohl?"

"Nothing truer could be stated, Mathias," Johann Tschohl's voice boomed over the now quiet saloon. The raftsmen turned quickly to see Johann, his four sons, and several other city men standing there. "Except, of course, when it comes to those who come here with no manners. Those who try to tear down our town as we try to build it up. We do not seem as friendly to that type of folk, do we, Gustav?"

"No, we do not!" Gustav snickered from the bar area. He lifted a board he used to dissuade fighting, and he and several of his barmen stepped out from behind the bar.

"Ha!" boomed the giant Norwegian. His friends joined him in laughter. The others stopped when he did. His eyes turned directly toward Mathias again. "So, you want a fight, ehh?"

"No, sir, we do not. Do you?" Mathias challenged.

"Why do we keep getting in these situations?" George asked Mathias under his breath.

"The last one was your fault, but I will take the blame for this one," Mathias replied without taking his sight off the Norwegian standing before him.

The man squinted his eyes as a slight grin emerged from his bearded face. "Yes," the man answered as he shoved Mathias. Calamity ensued and a brawl rapidly spread to every corner of the saloon. The Norwegian raftsmen from northern

Minnesota squared off against the Germans from Guttenberg, Iowa.

In every part of the saloon, fists flew, and men wrestled to the ground. Tables and chairs broke as the reckless brawl continued, and the sea of battle sloshed this way and that. Mathias and George both punched their gruff counterpart, the instigator of the fight, and knocked him to the ground. The Tschohls stood shoulder-to-shoulder and exchanged blows with the men from Minnesota, but their line did not falter. The Norwegians drug one of the barmen into the enemy area and beat him badly. Gustav defended his business fervently and wielded his board wickedly to curtail the brawlers from reaching the area behind the bar, where his largest investment lay.

A gunshot rang out, and everyone stopped. They turned quickly to see the youngest combatant, John Baptist Johll, standing tall with his pistol held high. He scanned the room harshly with angered eyes. "I did not travel this country under the order of General Sherman, fighting for the North every step of the way against our countrymen of the South, to come home and face more of this!" His voice shook with rage. "We are going to stop now, and the first thing we are going to do is pay Gustav for the damages done to his fine saloon. Then we are leaving for the night, lest another disturbance arise." He slowly lowered the pistol and aimed it around the room as Mathias and George helped the hefty Norwegian up from the floor. At last, John pointed the gun at the instigator and slowly stepped through the tangled mess of men and toward him. "Does anyone disagree?"

The Norwegian gulped and uttered, "No."

John lowered his pistol and shouted, "Good! Gustav, let these fine men know what we owe you for your damages. I will pay the first $5 for my part." John laid his $5 on the bar and walked out. The giant Norwegian and several of his comrades from Minnesota matched the offer. Mathias also laid down $5, and the raftsmen throng slowly trickled out.

Mathias, George, Johann, and his sons Josef, Ignaz, and Louis, along with Gustav, were the last in the saloon. "I have more than enough to cover the damages. What should I do with the rest?"

"Keep it for your trouble," Mathias suggested. "You would have sold quite a bit more tonight had the fight not occurred."

"Thank you for coming to help. How did you know of the fight?" George asked Johann.

"We supply the liquor to Gustav. He sent word for us when he heard the raftsmen arrived. This happens every time a raft pulls up. Now, my son John does not usually get involved, and this may be the last time we ask him," Johann replied. "He has just returned from the war. He was not in long before it ended. Less than a year, but it was long enough, I reckon."

"It was a pretty even fight until he stopped it. I am not sure we would have won," Mathias said. "We should be going. Our first day here has been quite long enough."

"We are glad you are here, Mathias and George. We need good but tough men like yourselves," Johann offered. "You will see us around. If you need anything, just let us know." He shook their hands. As Mathias and George turned to leave, Johann and his sons bellied up to the bar on several stools that remained unbroken and had a drink. Mathias stepped outside to see the large Norwegian who waited by the Tschohls' wagon.

"Do not get yer guard up. I want to do business," he said.

"Just what is that?" Mathias asked.

"My men and I want to buy some of this liquor. Is it for sale?" the Norwegian asked.

"It is always for sale," Johann's voice barked from the inside. "Come on in!"

Mathias and George stepped aside as the Norwegian politely stepped by them to do his business. They slowly strolled back toward the Crawford house. "This is quite a place," Mathias said as the kerosene lamps on posts lit the way.

"There can be no doubt, we have met some very good people in a short time. It is so much easier when they speak as we do. I am going to ride back toward Buena Vista tomorrow and see if there is land available. Will you come with me?"

Mathias thought for a moment as they walked. "No, I do not think I will. I am going to see Mr. Weist and ask if his offer still stands. It will allow me the chance to work and get to know the people here before I strike out on my own. We are off to a good start in our new lives, George. I cannot wait to see what the future holds for us!"

As they walked, they came upon the carpenter shop, which had several caskets sitting outside of it. George suddenly stopped. "What is that?" George asked frantically.

Mathias watched as the lid to one of the caskets slowly opened. He reached for a board which lay close on the ground and guarded against the specter that slowly sat up from death's resting place.

"Well, gentlemen, this must seem strange to you," the specter said.

"What are you doing?" Mathias asked as he still held the board ready.

A man quickly stepped from the casket in the dark of night with his hands held high. "So sorry, so sorry. I did not mean to scare anyone. My name is Clemens Kappen, and I make furniture and sometimes caskets. I heard of the fight, and when I walked by and saw the size of the men in it, I worried I would not have caskets big enough, should someone, you know..." Clemens trailed off.

"What? You know what?" George asked.

"Die," Mathias answered.

"Yes, yes. Die. It is an unfortunate thing, people dying. But it does happen, and it is good to be prepared. No one wants to see caskets ahead of time, but they sure want them right away when they need them," Clemens huffed, and he lit his lamp.

"So why were you in the casket?" a bewildered George asked.

"Measuring! I laid in it to see how much room there was and if I could fit one of those big Norwegians in one. It would not be the first time a raft man fell in a fight here in town, or that even one of our townspeople fell. It is my job to be ready when they do, or they will take their business elsewhere. I must be ready," Clemens quipped.

"Well, I guess I can appreciate that," Mathias offered as Clemens came near. The men formally introduced themselves and shook hands.

"Seeing no one has died, I suppose I shall go back to bed before my wife misses me. Good evening, gentlemen," Clemens said as he re-entered his store and locked the door.

Mathias and George walked back toward the hotel. "You were saying how nice this place was?" George asked.

"Yes, it is still very nice, but we left out another word," Mathias replied.

"What is that?" George asked.

"Interesting!" Mathias laughed as he put an arm on George's shoulder, and the two entered the Crawford House.

THE LEGACY of FAITH:

THE JOURNEY

Of

Mary Pankraz

Date: 1871
Origin: Hohenschwangau, Bavaria
Route: Le Havre, France
              New York, New York, USA
              Guttenberg, Iowa, USA

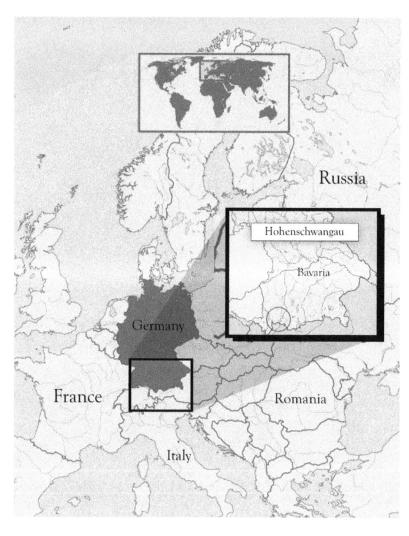

TIMELINE

Mary Pankraz	Year	World
Joseph, her son, is born.	**1868**	
	1870	November, Bavaria joins the North German Federation.
	1871	Jan. 18th, Ludwig refuses to attend an event, his brother Otto and uncle Luipold attend to represent Bavaria.
Mary and Joseph arrive in Iowa.	**1872**	
	1874	The foundation of the new St. Mary's church was laid, at its current block of location.

CHAPTER TWENTY-FOUR

THE BAVARIAN PRINCE

Mary woke with a start. Her feet hit the cold wooden floor quickly as she rushed to prepare for work. She hurried about the room as she dressed for the day. Mary paused only when she took the time to put up her hair just so. Her heart pounded for the excitement this day would bring her as the King of Bavaria, and more importantly, his brother Otto was set to return to Hohenschwangau for a short stay.

"Goodbye, mother," Mary yelled as she rushed out the door. She jumped into the carriage that took her to work before realizing that she had forgotten her lunch. "How can I eat on a day like today anyway?" she thought to herself as her jumbled feelings of elation and despair fought for supremacy. "My love returns, but his mother will never allow us to be together," she whispered.

"What is that you say?" her uncle, who was hard of hearing, asked over the clamor of the horses and the moving wagon.

"Oh, nothing. Please hurry. I must not be late," she begged of her uncle, who had transported her ever since George departed several years prior. She counted on him, but he was painfully slow at everything he did. Mary was also unsure of what smelled worse, her uncle or the horses that pulled them.

As the carriage slowly climbed the hill to the Hohenschwangau, the thoughts of a million moments between her and Otto rushed through her mind. Some of those moments were of the jubilation at seeing each other after a long separation, while others were of each painful parting. Finally, they reached the gate. For no reason at all, Mary leaned over and kissed her rickety old uncle on the cheek before she jumped to the ground and ran off.

"And a good day to you, Mary," her surprised uncle grumbled as he cracked the horses back into motion.

"Good day, Mary," Helga greeted as Mary rushed up to her at the gate. Helga was the only friend Mary had who knew her secret with Otto. "I am just as excited as you are for this day!"

"The wait has been so hard. How do I look?" Mary asked.

"You are beautiful! Otto will be so pleased to see you. You must wait, though, and do not let his mother see you, or it will all be for naught!" Helga urged as she stepped close to Mary so no others could hear. "You do realize it may be for naught anyway, do you not?"

The words pained Mary, for that same thought was never far from her mind. She bit her lip out of nervousness. "Why do you say such a thing?" Mary fretted.

"He is only eighteen, and you are twenty-two, for one! Plus, his mother detests you, as you have no royal bloodline," Helga replied. Mary teared up at the harsh words.

"Now, do not start biting that lip and worrying over this! Tears will not help you!" Helga scolded. "I am sorry to be so harsh, but it is true. You must find a way around it. Come, let us begin our work to keep busy before the king arrives." Together they hurried through their usual chores of rooms they tidied. What usually took them until noon the two accomplished in half that time, and then Mary was back in the library, where she awaited Otto's arrival. When word came that the king and his entourage were close, Mary and Helga went down to the main gate with the rest of the servants to greet them.

It was not long before the line of carriages slowly crawled up the hill. They seemed to take forever as Mary and other servants of the house waited patiently in the cool spring air. The head of the servants walked up and down before the line and uttered as he went, "We must put on a good face for the visit, for we risk that this could be the last one. Should that happen, we will all be out of work. The king and his family have visited Hohenschwangau seldom as of late, and that is not a good sign!"

Mary desperately tried to hold back her excitement. Helga reached for her hand. "You must stop shaking! Otto's mother will have you thrown off the grounds if she notices that you are still here," Helga whispered in Mary's ear. Her warning did little good.

The carriages finally pulled up. Otto unloaded first. He recently arrived back from the war between Austria and Prussia, in which Bavaria supported the Austrian side. "The hero returns!" Helga uttered to Mary. "I truly do not know who I wanted to win that war, as we seem caught in the middle either way. What will Prussia want from us now?"

"Prussia can wait," Mary replied. She almost lost her footing and resisted the immense temptation to run to Otto as he climbed down from the carriage. "Oh no," Mary whimpered as Otto limped out. "He is using a cane to walk. It is an injury from the war, no doubt."

"Shush Mary. Now is not the time," Helga insisted as she tried to keep Mary's cover.

Otto gave instructions to the servants about what to do with his bags. He then turned and walked past the rest of the crowd. He took the time to smile in both directions, but he saved a special look and grin for Mary.

"There is no doubt the thoughts of you have carried him through many hardships," Helga comforted. A tear of excitement raced down Mary's cheek, which she quickly wiped away. "I would that someday my love would pine for me in such a way," Helga wistfully hoped.

The first carriage rolled away as the next one quickly took its place. The servants stood taller as the door opened, and tension built as the closest servants discovered the identity of the person inside. Out rushed Marie, the mother of King

Ludwig and Prince Otto. Her husband had passed away four years earlier, and she was still sour. She barked orders to the servants, turned, and rushed past the rest and into the castle. "I do not know why we still come here!" she uttered with disdain as she stalked past the line of servants. All who stood there heard her contemptuous words.

The servants dared not to look at her, especially Mary. She kept her head down and hoped to avoid an unpleasant scene. "She did not notice you. You are safe..." Helga assured. After a short pause, she added, "For now."

Lastly, the king's carriage king pulled up. He opened the door on his own and climbed out. He spoke nicely to the servants who carried in his very large number of bags. It took two carriages to manage all of his things. "I have never seen a man so enamored with his appearance. He changes his clothes several times a day, from what I am told," Helga gossiped.

"I suppose what he wears depends on his mood and duties. Is that so strange?" Mary asked as she defended Ludwig.

"No, I guess not," Helga replied. Then she added, "For a woman, it is not strange at all."

"Hush Helga, he is the king!" Mary reminded.

He soon walked past them as all the servants filed in behind him, and they made their way back into the castle to resume their normal duties. Mary hurried to the library. That was the room where she first met Otto years earlier when she tutored him. Her mother used to have the position, but after Mary gained her education, and with her mother's oncoming age, the king allowed Mary to take her place. Mary hurried down the hall to the library, and she fidgeted nervously the entire way. "I have not seen Otto in over two years, with an entire war that has been fought since then. I wonder if he will even feel the same way for me," she quipped.

Just before she reached the library, a hand grabbed her from the side of the hall and pulled her into a small side room study. Otto threw his cane onto the floor and wrapped Mary in his arms, and then he kissed her deeply before she could react.

It seemed to Mary that a lifetime passed in his arms, with so many things said in those silent moments of elation.

"Mary, I have missed you so," Otto confessed as he released the kiss but continued to hold her close. "I thought of you before every battle and prayed I would survive to see you again."

"I worry for you daily and pray for your safety," Mary admitted to him. She then looked at his leg, "You have been injured?"

"My leg is healing nicely. A Prussian soldier stabbed me with his bayonet, but it is almost fully healed. Please, do not worry about me."

"Do not worry? Well, that is impossible," Mary rebutted as she hugged him tightly again. She then let go of him and leaned back, "How much time do we have before you must leave again?"

"A week, maybe a little more, if the army will allow it."

"Only a week?" Mary whimpered.

Otto placed his hands on her neck and raised her eyes. "I can live a lifetime in a week. Concentrate on the time we have, for it will be gone all too soon. Things are happening in the big world, Mary, and we are getting pulled into it."

"What are you talking about?" Mary's concern shifted as the seriousness of his voice stole her attention.

"We lost the war and sided with Austria. Wilhelm will use our allegiance to his enemy against us. He will demand that our loyalty shifts to him, which Ludwig is loath to do. I fear more wars to come. Wilhelm desires to combine all of the Germanic States. His thirst for power knows no bounds."

"Then you will need to leave again soon? To go to another war?" Mary asked as the fear of losing Otto gripped her.

"Not yet, but we will need to stay vigilant. I will go soon to oversee the training of our new troops."

Mary turned away. She walked to a window to look out over one of the gardens below. "Why did you even come back here?" Mary asked. She felt slighted from the short stay.

"If not for me, we would not be here at all. I made Ludwig promise to stop here, if only so that I could see you." Otto turned Mary around. He looked her in the eyes again. "When do you leave to go home?"

"I have several hours of work still," Mary asked. "Will you take me home?"

"I will meet you at the bottom of the hill. Wait for me there." Otto kissed her again. Before he walked back to his room, he picked up his cane. He smiled at Mary, walked back into the hallway, and went to his quarters.

Mary turned and floated to the library to finish her duties for the day. As she entered and walked to her desk, the door shut hard behind her. Mary turned to see Marie, Otto's mother, as she stood there, seething. Her chest rose and fell with each angered breath. "You should not be here! Ludwig promised me that you would be removed!"

"I am sorry, but what did I do to offend you? I shall try to amend it," Mary pleaded as she knelt to the former queen.

"Stand, girl! You have no business here, particularly kneeling to me. Do you honestly believe you have a *right* to be with my son, a Prince of Bavaria?" Her voice was never sharper.

Mary did not know what to say or whether to speak at all.

"Stand!" Marie ordered again. Her voice was quite louder than the first time. "Girl of the field, you will not come back here again. Do you understand?"

"Yes," Mary answered dutifully. Her sorrowful cry touched the cold heart of Marie.

"I understand your attraction to Otto, but you are overreaching. I am doing you a favor. Please, go find a simple man that might provide a more suitable life for your current situation. I have no idea what Otto was thinking by stooping so low."

Tears pooled in Mary's eyes, and no words came to her to use in defense. She could not understand the cruelty of Marie's actions and words.

"You will leave today and never come back again," Marie prompted as she stepped close to Mary.

"Yes," Mary offered. It was as though another person said the answer for her. Marie spun and charged hard for the door. She reached for the handle, but just before she opened it, and without so much as turning back, she added, "You must realize the danger you would be in should you decide to ignore this order. Test me but once, and you will discover the total level of my determination." Marie opened the door and left the room. She briskly covered the length of the hallway before she disappeared around the corner.

Mary waited for her to get out of sight before she dropped to the floor again. She sobbed uncontrollably. Marie blocked her heart's desire from her for reasons Mary did not understand. Her world was in shambles.

Eventually, Mary pulled herself from the floor to finish her day. She stayed clear of everyone in the bustling castle, including Helga. Any interaction would have brought her tears, and she performed every task, even the most mundane, as though she was doing it for the last time. At the end of the day, Mary closed the door to the library and walked down the hall to a side door to the main part of the castle, the same one she used every day.

Helga waited for her there, but Mary sent her on her way home. "I need to be alone. Please go. I will see you tomorrow."

"I will pray for you, be careful on your way home. God bless you," Helga replied before she walked away.

Mary walked out of the gates and looked at the castle one last time. She walked past the guard at the gate and said, "Please tell my uncle that I decided to walk home."

"Ja, Fraulein," the guard answered.

Mary turned and walked down the long windy brick path to the base of the hill, and each step seemed as though it was its own day in her life. She struggled to comprehend how she had arrived at this point and where she had misstepped to cause her current predicament. What should have been a walk of joy upon Otto's arrival became a walk of dread about everything she was losing.

Anxiety gripped her as she rounded the last corner to where Otto said he would be, but he was not there. Mary distraughtly turned and frantically looked for any sign of him. She waited for him for a few excruciating moments before she gave up. "Marie has reached him. He will not come," she muttered to herself. Mary set her chin and turned for the walk home. "It is probably for the best."

Mary heard a horse as it rode up behind her. She turned with an expectant smile as hope rose in her heart. She knew Otto was coming for her and that somehow he would make it all right, but it was only a man who went about his business that met her gaze. She stopped as he rode past her. The man did not even slow down for the pretty girl with a hopeful look. Tears replaced her smile, and a thousand curses toward Marie raced through her mind. She turned and walked again, but this time with a far angrier gait.

Not long after, another horse rode up behind her. Mary refused to fall for that trick of fate again as she marched straight ahead.

"Would the lady want a ride?" the familiar voice reached her ears. Every part of her body was set to deny him, to send him on his way, should he even bother to show up. Should he do anything in any way, she would refute him, as it was much too late. The smallest part of her raging heart that was yet unconquered by her new determination fought valiantly against the rest. It rampaged wildly throughout her body as she forgot her spite and turned to Otto.

He immediately swung down to her. "What is it? What has happened?" Otto asked with great concern. "Why did you not wait as we had discussed?"

She entered his arms, but her thoughts went immediately to Marie. "We must go! We are being watched!"

Otto saw the fear in her eyes. "What has my mother done?" he demanded.

"Please! We need to go!" Mary pleaded. Otto lifted her onto his horse as a cold rain began to fall. Otto climbed behind her and held Mary close as they rode off. The rain fell harder, and it tried to stop them, but the two refused to notice the rain, the land, or the sky as they went. Mary felt safe in Otto's embrace, and he only felt joy in hers.

They rode to the edge of the town as the townspeople ran for cover from the storm. Otto made for a remote building where a local farmer kept hay for his horses. They galloped through the hilly country and rushed to a place of solitude.

Otto slowed the horse as they approached the small shed. He saw no one around as the rain continued its deluge. Otto dismounted and then helped Mary off the horse. Otto led Mary and his steed into the small building. A brick fireplace sat in the corner, and Otto started a small fire to warm them. He then took the saddle off the horse and gave it some hay to eat.

"Otto?" Mary asked. Though she did not know what question to ask, she hoped he had the answer. Otto turned to her and their eyes locked. He walked toward her and took both of her trembling hands. "No one will separate us," he said resolutely. He reached for her neck and pulled her lips toward his. The world stopped. It reluctantly allowed them the time they needed as each of them gave in to their desires and welcomed them to run freely. They held no care for the wants and worries of the outside world.

Mary lay still on the floor and felt only the warmth of Otto's body next to her as she stared into the dwindling light of the fire. Her thoughts then turned back to the big world and the twisted games that continued around them. "What are we going to do? Your mother warned me never to return. I fear for my life should I come back."

"An heir rests on me, for Ludwig will never produce one. Mother is trying to set up a marriage between me and a girl from one of the northern German states, one that will ensure our place in the new German Empire."

"And what do you want?" Mary asked as she turned to look at Otto.

"Only you. If there is to be an heir to the throne of Bavaria, you will be the mother. There will be no other, I promise. I will talk with Ludwig first thing in the morning. He knows my feelings for you, and we will have his blessing. I doubt he has shared that with mother, however. I will talk with her later. Do not come in tomorrow, but please come back the next day, and all will be fine. I promise." Otto kissed Mary again, and she forgot her troubles.

"Though I trust no one more, I cannot see a future where we are together. I am relying on you to make that happen," Mary offered. She laid her head on Otto's chest.

They dressed, and Otto gave Mary a ride to her family home. He let her off a few blocks from her family's meager house. Before Otto left, he bent low and kissed her again. Then he rode off. Mary did as he told her and stayed home the following day. Though she tried to keep busy, her mind bounced back and forth from her dreadful meeting with Marie in the library and then the elation of the moments she spent with Otto. The two ranges of feelings could not have been different, nor more mangled together. She was no different from the rest of the world as she was captured entirely in her own twisted game.

CHAPTER TWENTY-FIVE

THE SECRET MESSAGE

Mary told her parents she was sick. She toiled in her room in complete silence as her hopes and fears battled on their all too familiar ground. As evening approached, she announced herself better and helped with the rest of the chores of the home, as usual.

The next morning Mary's uncle arrived and took her to work. Her nerves ran wild as the horses pulled their carriage up the hill to the front gate. She feared Otto's mother would meet her immediately upon arrival, and in humiliation, send her back home, or worse.

As the carriage grudgingly rolled to a stop, Mary's heart threatened to beat through her chest. Otto stood there and smiled as he waited for her, and her nerves calmed.

"Herr Pankraz, it is good to meet you," Otto welcomed Mary's uncle. He clumsily shook hands with the Prince of Bavaria.

"And a good day to you. God bless you," her uncle replied.

Otto then went to Mary and helped her down from the wagon. Mary's uncle rode away and muttered to himself, "The men at the pub will not believe me when I tell them I shook hands with the prince!"

Otto then led Mary through the gates and into the castle grounds. To Mary's surprise, Ludwig, the King of Bavaria, and Otto's brother, also stood there.

"Mary," he greeted. He took her hand and kissed it. Few were the moments and people who saw Ludwig outside his inner sanctum of the castle, particularly during the light of day. Despite his glamorous dress, everything else about him, particularly his eyes, spoke of a man who despised the early mornings of any day. "I understand you had an unfortunate interaction with our mother a few days ago. For that, I apologize. You are welcome to work here, in the same capacity as you have in the library, for as long as you would like. You have my word as the King of Bavaria. I hope you will stay." Ludwig did not wait for an answer but considered the issue solved. He quickly turned and departed. Ludwig raised his hand to shade his eyes from the rising sun and hurried back to the castle and into his darkened chamber.

Otto led Mary toward the library, and for the first time, he did so with Mary on his arm for all to see. The heads of the staff turned as they walked past. Mary beamed with delight, "I feel like a queen!"

"Someday, you may be one," Otto answered back. He delivered her to the library. "So, there it is. This job is yours for as long as you would like. I expect you will have days off when my mother comes here, which should be quite minimal."

"What happened? Did I create a problem?" Mary asked as she fidgeted again. "We should not have walked as we did, not in front of everyone at the least. They will be talking, and others will find out."

Otto stopped and took her other hand, "Mary, you must stop your worrying. My mother created the problem, and we created an answer by having her leave. She put up her usual fuss, of course, but in the end, she hates it here, and she cannot understand why we like it so much. Both of our likings have mostly to do with the fact that she does not. I, of course, have another reason for wanting to be here more often. As for the others, they can talk as much as they would like, as they matter not."

Otto tried to kiss her, but Mary turned them to head into the library. "We cannot be seen like this too often. You are higher in social stature than I am, and as such, it will create a stir. Please remember that, though my desire to be with you is immense," Mary confessed to Otto, though it pained her to do so.

"I hope there will be a time soon when we can announce our love to everyone. Ludwig is working to keep Bavaria free from King Wilhelm, who is pressuring us to join a new German Empire. We are caught between France, Prussia, and Austria-Hungary, and we seek only to stay independent. That, however, seems less likely every day." Otto then paused, "I should not have told you so much, but there is no one I trust more."

"Then how is this to work? How will we be together?" Mary fretted as they shut the door behind them.

"The sincerity in your eyes touches my soul, Mary, you are such a kind person. We will need to take advantage of our short times together until such a point where we see an opportunity to be together all the time. Our best hope is that Bavaria remains independent and has its own rule. In all other cases, our partner states will arrange marriages to strengthen their positions. But please, Mary, do not worry your heart about that for now. We only have a few more days before I must leave again." Otto kissed her once more, and Mary savored the moments that she knew to be fleeting. He then went on with his day and left Mary behind. She tried to concentrate on her work and tutored the younger children of the castle, but her mind often wandered back to Otto. She prayed for them to be together forever.

Within the week, it came time for Otto to report back for his military duties. The morning of his departure, Mary went into work early and snuck up to Otto's quarters. He was already preparing his things when Mary slipped in the door and closed it quietly behind her.

"Mary, I am so glad you came to see me," Otto said.

"I could not stand to let you go without holding you once more," Mary pouted as she ran into his arms. "I fear I will never see you again!"

"Mary, we will be together again, I promise," Otto swore as he held her tightly. "This mission should not take long. I will be back in no time."

Mary reached up to kiss Otto. She then took a deep look into his eyes, and she studied every line of his face. "You are a good man, Otto, and I love you more than I have ever considered possible. Please, come back to me!"

Otto held her for a while longer. Then a knock at the door interrupted them. Mary stood tall and gathered herself as Otto opened the door. A guard from the castle was there.

"It is time to depart," he uttered. The guard looked toward Mary and saw her strained look. Otto closed the door and went for his bags.

"The staff is talking about us all the time," Mary announced. "Your mother will be furious. We should not have walked together to the library the other day." She frantically tried to think of an excuse as to why she was in his room.

"Nonsense, Mary. I only led you to the library, and there was nothing sinister about it. He is but a guard. Even if he guessed our relationship, who would he tell?" Otto surmised. He set down his bags and gave Mary a last embrace and a kiss before he took his things and marched to his departure.

Mary waited a few painful moments as she looked in the mirror and tidied herself. She then hurried to the library, but she only caught a glimpse of Otto as he boarded the carriage. She watched as it disappeared down the hill. "He's gone," she whispered.

Weeks went by. Mary tried to concentrate on her job from one day to the next, but it was very difficult to do so. One morning, she walked into the castle with Helga, and Mary stumbled to the side of the hallway. "Mary, what is the matter with you?" Helga asked.

"Do not worry. It shall soon pass. Please, get me a drink," Mary replied. "I have had several fainting spells lately. I am not certain just what is wrong with me."

Helga rushed off and then hurried back with a drink of water. "Your color looks better already. You say you have felt like this before?"

"Yes, but just within the last week. It passes quickly, and by late in the day, I feel fine," Mary explained.

"Mary," Helga cautiously began.

"What?" Mary asked.

Helga hesitated again but then asked, "Are you pregnant?"

The words hung in Mary's ears. "No, that cannot be. I am merely ill, nothing more." The thought did not leave her mind, nor did the question of how she could explain it if she was.

After a few weeks, Mary could no longer deny it. "You were right. I am pregnant with Otto's son," Mary admitted to Helga one day while they took a short break.

"I knew you were. This is wonderful," Helga gushed. "Otto will marry you, and no one will be able to stop that."

"Helga!" Mary scolded, "Otto's mother will not allow that to happen. She will kill me if she finds out. No one can know until Otto is back for good. You must promise to keep this a secret."

"I am sorry, Mary, you are right. I will not tell anyone, I promise," Helga agreed. "I am so sorry for you and the predicament you are in. What are you going to do? Soon, everyone will know you are with child."

"It cannot be Otto's. I will make up a man, one from another town. The thought of creating such an elaborate lie, especially to my parents... It wounds me," Mary replied.

"Mary, people will think you a harlot if you do that. Your parents will be shamed," Helga offered.

"Do you have a better idea? I cannot hide it. I have to think of something," Mary cried as she frantically searched for another option.

"You are right again," Helga comforted. "Say that he is a soldier and off to war. At least then you can say you intend to marry when he returns."

"Yes, and then he will be killed before we can marry, and no one will be able to say otherwise. That is the best option," Mary confirmed. "Now, I need to inform Otto that he has a son, but I cannot risk sending him a letter. Anyone might read it."

"Tell King Ludwig. He will be able to get word to Otto," Helga suggested.

Mary pondered the thought. "What will he think of this? He knows of our relationship. Regardless, there is no other way."

✝

"My Lord, may I have a word with you?" Mary asked of the King.

King Ludwig stopped his urgent walk down the hall by his quarters. "I am busy, Mary. Quickly, what is it?"

"It would be best to have this discussion in private," Mary whispered. Ludwig led her into his room. "Please, what is it?" he insisted.

"My King, I am pregnant," Mary uttered.

Ludwig paused. He turned from Mary and walked to the window. He stared out at the world, "It is Otto's, of course." He didn't look back to Mary as he awaited the answer.

"Yes," Mary meekly replied.

"And does Otto know?"

"No, not yet. But I ask for you to relay the message on my behalf. I want him to know that if..." Mary ceased her words as the horrible thought danced across her mind. She then continued, "When he comes home, his baby will be here."

Ludwig turned from the window, "I will send my most trusted messenger only and give him a message to hand off to Otto, even he will not know the contents."

Mary reached into her pocket and pulled out a note. She slowly looked at it before she handed it to Ludwig. "Please, pass this to him."

Ludwig took the note. "It shall be done. I will let you know when the messenger returns." Mary bowed and turned to leave. Ludwig hurried to meet her before she reached the door. He turned her as he whispered, "You carry in you the heir to the throne of Bavaria. God willing, he will someday be the King. As such, you must take the utmost care, Mary. For now, no one can know. You have the responsibility of carrying a future king without any of the safety and precautions that normally would be afforded you. Please, take extreme care."

Mary locked eyes with Ludwig, and she felt the seriousness of his words. Ludwig opened the door and allowed Mary to leave. Ludwig slowly walked back to the window. He opened the letter that Mary wrote for his brother:

My Dearest Otto,

I pray this letter reaches you and that you are alone at its reading. It is with great hope and fear that I tell you I am carrying our baby. I have sought your brother's help to deliver this message to you, and if you are reading it, there is no doubt it is due to him.

Please take the utmost care for your safety at all times until you return, for I have no idea what I would do without you. Our child needs you to return, and the future of our family rests in your determination to come home to us.

Every moment shall pass slowly until your return. Until then, you will be in my every thought and prayer. I need you! Should you be able, please respond to me soon.

With Love,

Mary

"I would that I could confess my love so and have it returned," Ludwig whispered. His breath fogged the window, and then he dipped his head and wiped the fog away. "I shall do all I can to keep this love secret, that it might someday blossom for the betterment of my country and perhaps the entire world." Ludwig folded the letter and went to his desk. He placed the letter in an envelope. He then reached for beeswax, which he dripped onto the flap of the envelope. He pressed his official seal into it and beckoned, "Send a messenger to me at once!"

"He is from a nearby village, and he is away from here serving our country in the war," Mary explained to her parents the next morning. Her father held her mother as the news hit them hard. "I am sorry," Mary added as she took her mother's hand.

Her father spoke first. "When will we meet this young man?" he angrily demanded.

"He will be home soon, and we plan to get married before the child arrives," Mary comforted.

"Our friends at the church will be talking about us, Mary, and it should not be so. You know better than to have done this!" her mother scolded. "This is not how God wants us to have a family. It is not right!"

"I know, mother. As I said, he will be back soon. I promise that you will meet him then!"

✝

Eventually, her parents accepted the situation, as long as they were married when the boy came home. The church families soon noticed Mary's condition, and the rumors flourished about the father's identity. To quell the speculations, Mary went to confession after church. She knelt before the head priest of their church, and Mary told the truth of what had occurred, everything except the father's real identity. In tears, she cried, "Father, the church members are telling rumors about me and hurting my parents. Please, is there anything you can do?"

Father Helmseth consoled her, "Mary, you have confessed your sins to God, and they have been forgiven. I cannot stop the many gossiping men and women of the church, but I may be able to stifle it, at least a little." In the coming weeks, the priest talked directly to several of the more rumor-spreading members, and he told them of Mary's tough situation with the baby's father gone. "I urge you to help stop others from spreading stories about Mary. It is very harmful."

"Father, that is just terrible! I shall certainly tell others to stop if I hear them. It is so sad and unchristian a thing to do," the members said about the rest.

Father also spoke during several homilies of the dangers of gossip and the damage caused by it. "Let us not forget about Jesus's mother and what others must have said about her and Joseph at the time. Damaging, I am sure it was!" Mary was quite pleased that he did not say the Holy Mother's name to avoid the entire congregation staring at her. His intentions were rewarded as the talk of Mary's condition died down, and soon it was not a topic at all.

The parishioners left Mary alone, and her parents helped her through the birth of her baby, a son. She named him Josef, and no other thing in the world brought Mary such delight.

"Mary, what is wrong?" her mother asked when she found Mary alone in her room after work one day. She had been crying.

"He is dead!" Mary wailed. "Josef's father is dead! He died in battle! The names of those lost in the last fight came to the castle today."

Her mother consoled her so, and Mary pretended to cry over a lost love. The thoughts of Otto being gone aided her tears.

"We must go to his family to give our condolences," her mother encouraged.

Mary sat up quickly and wiped off her tears. "No, mother," Mary stammered. "We... we cannot dare to do such a thing. His parents were not even aware of who I was. We cannot show up at his funeral. They will not think well of it. It will do far more harm than good. Please, we just need to leave them alone. I do not want to cause them more harm."

Her mother pulled Mary close, "We shall just pray for him then. I am so sorry, Mary. Your father and I will be here to help you through this."

"Will father understand?" Mary asked. She hated lying to her mother but doubted she could do so at all with her father.

"I will talk with him for you. He will understand."

CHAPTER TWENTY-FIVE

DECISION

Mary sat in the library as she tutored one of the noble's younger children. Her son, now aged 3, sat at another table. Much to her surprise, King Ludwig entered the room. It was something he seldom did. "My Lord," Mary welcomed as everyone stood and bowed.

"Come with me," Ludwig urgently said. He gave no acknowledgment to the others present. They went down the hall to the next room, where Ludwig closed the door behind them.

"How is Josef?" the King asked.

"He is well," Mary answered. "Thank you for asking. Pardon me, King Ludwig, but why have you come for me? You have not asked about Josef before, nor should you have. Is something wrong?"

"The world is moving faster, Mary. !aster than I have ever seen it before. I believe I am wholly inept to do anything about it," Ludwig replied. He stared off into the empty corner of the room. He then focused back on Mary, "We are caught between France and the expanding Prussian state. King Wilhelm pressures us to join him, though I loathe the thought. Bavaria will cease to be important, and it will be swallowed completely in Wilhelm's greed."

"Why are you telling me this? If you are unable to prevent it, what can I do?" Mary meekly asked.

"Otto von Bismarck is coming here, Mary. He is Wilhelm's strong arm. He is coming to investigate our commitment to Prussia and measure our intentions. If I defy him, it will mean war with Prussia. If I join him, we will then be at war with France. In either case, my brother will be put in harm's way." Ludwig trailed off as he looked out the window. "Bismarck cannot learn there is an heir to the throne of Bavaria. It will put you and Josef in danger. Please, you must take him home."

"Of course, I will do so immediately," Mary agreed as she looked at Josef at the table.

"You must not bring him back until I say," Ludwig ordered. "I will let you know when it is safe for him to return. I must go now to make my final preparations." Ludwig left the room and left no opportunity for further argument.

Mary did as she was told. She took Josef back to her home. She returned later that afternoon, and when she arrived, Otto von Bismarck was already there. The tension was thick as she entered the courtyard. The guards of the Prussian state checked everyone who was near the dignitary. Without much delay, the guards allowed Mary to return to her position in the library.

King Ludwig gave Bismarck a customary tour of the castle and ushered him past the library. "What is this?" Bismarck asked as he stopped to look in.

"Our library. The children of the palace receive their education here." Ludwig turned to leave, but Bismarck did not join him. Instead, he approached Mary.

"Fraulein, what do you do here?" he asked with great interest.

"I tutor the children," Mary stuttered nervously.

"And you only do that in the afternoons? I see you have just arrived," he asked with a raised brow of suspicion.

"No, I usually do it all day, Lord. I had to run home for a late meal as my morning was quite busy," Mary replied. She then added, "You are very observant."

"Nothing escapes me. Nothing," Bismarck stated. He then turned and departed. He left the frightful Mary behind.

"I hope you can return when my new castle is complete," Ludwig began as he led Bismarck away.

Time passed achingly slow throughout the rest of the day. Mary saw no more of Bismarck nor Ludwig. When the time came, she descended the stairs and departed the castle. In the courtyard, alone, stood Ludwig. He painfully paced as he awaited his carriage.

Mary would not approach him in public, but much to her surprise, he hailed her to him. "Mary, please ride with me."

"My Lord, are you sure? People will see us," Mary objected.

"We are only going to talk for a short time. You will be getting out soon," Ludwig insisted as he helped Mary into the carriage. Velvet cushions and beautiful curtains for the windows decorated the inside, with fine golden latches for the doors and windows. Mary's heart fluttered with excitement, for though she worked at the castle for several years, she had never ridden in such an ornate carriage.

"This is beautiful," Mary gasped. Ludwig's stifling look captured her attention.

"Mary, the situation is worse than I suspected," Ludwig began.

"What is it?" Mary's fear raged with each passing moment.

"Bismarck insists we join the German Federation. Wilhelm desires to unify all the German states to be the central force in all of Europe. I fear that he will make war on the other states one day, and he will begin with France. I will not be able to hold out much longer. My mother is also pushing me to join them," Ludwig informed.

"You must fight them, Lord. Bavaria deserves to be a free country," Mary argued. She then reconsidered her place as she read the distorted look on King Ludwig's face. "I am sorry, my Lord, it is not my place."

"Nonsense, Mary. I told you for a reason," Ludwig said as he stared out the window. "There is another thing that you should know. Otto will return for a short stay next week."

"That is splendid! I was not aware," Mary smiled. The dour look Ludwig bore stopped her exuberance.

"Bismarck will be here throughout his stay. He seeks to arrange a marriage between Otto and a granddaughter of Wilhelm. It is his way to unify a German pact between Prussia and Bavaria," Ludwig stated.

"No, Otto will never agree to that," an exasperated Mary huffed.

Ludwig leaned close, "You must remain quiet, Mary. Of course, Otto will not agree, but Bismarck is insistent. It will not be safe for you to be here when Otto is, for I fear the danger brought to you should Bismarck discover your relationship. I fear more for the danger brought to Josef should that secret be known. We must handle this carefully."

"I need to go," Mary said as she frantically reached for the door.

Ludwig grabbed her arm and stopped her. "Mary, you must remain calm. I do not tell you these things to scare you, though I know they do. I tell you them so you can protect yourself and Josef. Otto will find time to see you next week, but you must stay home until Otto arranges to see you. Bismarck cannot see Otto and Josef together, ever. If that should happen, the repercussions will be dire. Bismarck is already very suspicious of an heir to the throne that Wilhelm does not dictate."

Mary sat still as her resolve hardened. "If he is suspicious, it is because of things your mother has told him. Please, allow me to leave so that I may look after my son." Mary did not wait for permission. She quickly opened the door and climbed out of the carriage.

Ludwig said nothing. He sat back and allowed Mary to depart.

The thoughts of the interaction ran through Mary's mind on her hurried walk home. She walked ever faster as she urgently rushed to ensure Josef was safe. She dashed through the door of her home and past her mother, who prepared dinner.

"What is wrong?" she asked as Mary pushed by her.

"Where is Josef?" Mary yelled. She did not wait for an answer as she quickly threw open the door to her room. Relief stole Mary as she sat on her bed where Josef lay, fast asleep.

Mary knelt in prayer, "Dear God, please show me a way to save my son. I would give up everything else to keep him safe from the troubles of this world. Lord, show me the way!" She wept out of the fear of losing Josef, and her determination to save him leaped with every passing moment.

The following week passed. Mary avoided both Ludwig and Otto von Bismarck at all costs. The day finally came when Otto arrived. Though it pained her deeply, Mary did as Ludwig requested, and she stayed home. She told her mother she thought Josef was sick and that she would not leave him. As Mary asked, Helga came to see her over the midday break.

"Otto arrived this morning," Helga reported, but Mary cut her off with questions.

"How is he? Has he asked about me? Has he spent time with Bismarck and Ludwig?" Mary queried excitedly, as she was unable to contain her anxious mind.

"I know he was with them late this morning. I was not there when he left, so they may still be meeting. I do not know. He looked fine in mind and spirit, Mary. I am sure he will seek you soon." Helga's words brought Mary comfort.

Mary reached into her pocket. She took a note from it and handed it to Helga. "Please hand this to Otto. I need to see him today if possible."

"Mary, it is too dangerous. I do not want to get caught up in all of this," Helga pleaded.

"Please, Helga, I need to see him. I have no other way to get word to him," Mary begged.

"I shall try, but I can make no promises. I do not even know if I will be near him again," Helga relented. "I must be getting back, for they will be wondering where I am. You worry about Josef, and I will get this note to Otto." Helga left and went back to the castle.

Later that day, Mary readied to go out, and she took Josef with her. She paid for a carriage ride to the building just out of town where she and Otto went on that rainy day, which seemed so long ago. She arrived to see it both empty and dark.

"Fraulein, do you wish me to leave you here?" the carriage driver asked. "I do not believe it is a safe place for you and the child to be."

Mary depended on Helga to give the note to Otto, and she hoped she had. "Yes, thank you." Mary got down as she reached back in for Josef. The carriage departed, and she sat inside the empty and cold building. "Please come for me, Otto," she prayed.

Darkness set in, not only on the day but also Mary's fading hopes that Otto would come. "He may have things to do, or perhaps Helga was not able to deliver the note at all," she said to Josef, who slept quietly in her arms. Mary started to cry as she picked up her bag and prepared to begin the long and lonely walk back.

The clip-clop sound of horse hooves crept to her ears as she left the building. Mary quickly hugged the shadow of the wall to see who was coming. In the darkness, she could not make out who it was, but she knew it was a man who quickly approached on his steed. Mary fought her deep desire to rush to him for fear it was not Otto. Those fears were erased as the horse stopped and the unmistakable voice uttered, "Mary?"

"Otto!" Mary shouted with tears of joy. She rushed to him as he jumped off his horse. The two embraced, and Otto quickly took Josef from Mary. He held his son tight for a moment. He then put an arm back around Mary and led them into the barn. He started a fire, and they huddled together as the light danced across Josef's peaceful face.

"My son," Otto gushed as he saw Josef for the first time. He continually wiped away his own tears of joy.

"He has your eyes," Mary said as she gently squeezed Otto's arm. Otto turned his attention to Mary, and he leaned in and kissed her softly.

"I have missed you so. Ludwig informed me of what has happened. I am sorry for you to have to go through this," Otto said.

Mary read the pain on Otto's face, "What else has occurred? Helga told me you met with your brother and Bismarck this morning."

"Yes. I do not know how long Ludwig will hold out. He is not strong. Eventually, he will cave to their demands."

"And you? Will you give in to their demands?" Mary asked.

Otto lay Josef down and took both of Mary's hands. "I will never go along with their plans, nor will I marry another person to aid them. My heart only beats for you."

"What will we do?" Mary asked, distraught.

"You may need to leave to keep both of you safe."

"To where? Wilhelm will find us wherever we go if he desires to. Where can we go to get away from him?" Mary lamented.

"To the United States," Otto answered.

"When can we leave?" Mary asked. "I have had the same thoughts of us going to Amerika, too, so that we can be..."

Otto stumbled as he interrupted her with his next words. "Not us, Mary. It will only be you and Josef. Wilhelm and Bismarck will stop at nothing to find me if I disappear. I am an heir to the throne should something happen to Ludwig. But if you and Josef go alone, our relationship and the secret of Josef will go with you. Then and only then will you be safe."

Mary whimpered her reply as she leaned hard on Otto, "I cannot stand the thought of going without you."

"It is the only way, Mary. You have to leave here to gain a new start," he argued. "I will follow you later when... If it is safe."

Mary smiled back at Otto, and he wiped her tears away. She could not imagine a time that he could come for her. Otto picked her up and gave her and Joseph a slow ride back into town. He let them off a few houses from her own.

"When will I see you again?" Mary asked as she reached for his hand.

"You cannot come to see me. I must leave in a few days with Bismarck. We are traveling to see Wilhelm in Berlin. Ludwig has asked me to go in his place."

"You have to go with him?" Mary asked distraughtly. "He will try to get you to marry another."

"Trust in me, Mary. My heart only beats for you. I will be back soon, I promise." Otto leaned down and kissed Mary once again as Josef began to cry. "Take care of our son. I will be back soon."

✝

Otto departed with Bismarck just a few days later, and they traveled to Berlin for discussions with Wilhelm. Helga informed Mary to return to work. Her first morning back, she saw Ludwig as he walked the halls.

"It is good to see you back," Ludwig greeted.

"Why did you send Otto away?" Mary demanded in anger. She ignored her manners to the king.

Ludwig grew stiff. "Otto is strong and more than capable of handling Bismarck. They need to know there is strength here, beyond me," he defended.

Mary realized she overstepped, "Of course, Lord. I am only sad he is gone." Mary stifled her true feelings toward what she believed to be a cowardly king.

"We are going to war, Mary. Otto will lead the Bavarian army as we fight alongside Prussia against France. Bismarck promised our sovereignty should we aid them in this fight. After our victory, we will have what we want." Ludwig grinned at his final words. "I have negotiated a victory for Bavaria."

"I fear for this war and that Otto may not survive," Mary confessed. "Good day, my Lord." Out of disdain for Ludwig and his feeble leadership, she did not seek further conversations with the king. She stayed in the library and prayed for Otto's safe return.

Brian Spielbauer

CHAPTER TWENTY-SEVEN

1870

My Dearest Otto,

My heart leaps as the news of each Prussian victory comes back to us, for with each, the hope that we will be a family one day grows. Josef is soon to be four, and he loves to run and play. He also speaks quite well for his age. Ludwig has urged me to provide him a healthy start, and he comes to the library daily with me. He is smart and handsome, just like his father.

I look forward to your return, as you have been gone so long. Please find a way to come back to us soon. Until then, take care to keep yourself in the safest of positions. Your family needs you, and of course, I need you. I hope to hear from you soon.

With Love,

Mary

Mary neatly folded her letter to Otto and placed it in the envelope. "Helga, please find Ludwig and ask him to send this to Otto for me."

"Of course, Mary, I will do so. If the stories of victory are to be believed, the soldiers should return soon," Helga answered. She took the letter and went briskly down the hall. Mary went back into the library and continued to tutor the children.

Before the midday break, Ludwig came to the library. He had not done so in over a year. His appearance brought Mary immediate worry. "God bless you. King Ludwig, is something wrong?" The troubled look on Ludwig's face spoke well before his words came out.

"Otto is injured, Mary. He is returning here to recover. I thought it best for him to do so around you."

"What are his injuries? Was he shot or stabbed?" Mary anxiously asked. Ludwig did not answer right off. Mary pushed him harder, "Please, tell me. Otto is hurt, and my mind is running wild with a thousand thoughts, each one worse than the last!"

"From what I know, he was not wounded. It is a mental illness that seems to be worsening. I will not know for certain until he arrives."

"Has he seen a doctor?" Mary asked. "I have never heard of a soldier sent home for mental illness. Surely there is a wound that must heal."

"Wilhelm had his physician, a Dr. von Gudden, look over Otto. He has been attending to him. I had to be quite forceful for them to allow Otto to come here. Wilhelm insisted his doctor come also." Ludwig wrung his hands as he paced the room. His nervousness was quite evident to Mary.

"There is more? Please, tell me all of it," Mary pressured Ludwig.

"The war is over, Mary. Prussia has the victory," Ludwig offered.

"That is good news, is it not? Then Bavaria will remain independent of Prussia, as Wilhelm promised," Mary stated.

"I fear not. Wilhelm lied to get us to fight with them. He has no intention of allowing Bavaria, or any other German state, to stay sovereign. He is calling for a new German Empire to rule all of central Europe." Ludwig stopped for a moment as he walked toward Mary. "I also fear for the legitimacy of Otto's diagnosis. I pray that when he arrives, we may have our doctor look over my brother. Hopefully, we can find the true reason for his malady."

Mary rushed to Ludwig and wrapped both of her arms around him. It was something she had never done before.

"Mary," he gasped as he awkwardly tried to console her. "You must gain control of yourself."

"Ludwig, please find the strength to defy them and keep Otto safe! I need him alive. He is the father of my son. Only you can help make that so!" she compelled Ludwig. "Stand strong against the German Federation, for Otto's sake; for all of our sakes!" Mary stepped back and looked Ludwig in the eye.

Ludwig turned his head and quipped, "I am the King of Bavaria, but I cannot withstand the challenging stare of a librarian." He slowly dropped his head and turned to leave.

"Please! Help him!" Mary pleaded. Ludwig did not stop as he left the library.

On the day of Otto's arrival, a small crowd gathered to see their war hero return. It was a cold and windy winter day, the few that dared to stand in the cold huddled together. As the carriage pulled up, one of the guards went to open the door. Another person from inside, one Mary had never seen, came out first. He then helped Otto, who slowly stepped down the carriage steps. Otto's legs seemed reluctant to work, and Mary's anxiety over Otto's health soared.

Mary cringed as she saw him step onto the frozen cobblestones. Otto's entire focus seemed directed to the task of walking, and it was as though his legs refused to obey their commands. The crowd, out of duty and respect, gave a modest cheer. It was clear that seeing Otto's humbled state hampered their spirits.

"He was the strong one," more than one onlooker muttered to a friend. "Our hopes for an independent Bavaria dwindle by the day."

Otto stopped. His eyes wandered through the crowd. He looked for someone, and Mary stepped forward just a bit, as she hoped he would see her. She felt his eyes stop on her for a moment, but there was no look of recognition, no thought of love. She mustered all the strength she had to remain in her place and not run to aid him. As quickly as they stopped, the guard urged him forward, and they continued the long grudging walk inside the warmth of the castle and to a room in the rear of the castle made up for Otto.

Mary hurried through the halls, and she was barely able to keep herself together. She went to Otto's room, and she damned the world and secrecy needed. As she turned a corner, she plowed into Ludwig.

"Mary, you cannot be here, not now!" Ludwig chastised. He grabbed her tightly by the arm and took her away, despite her protest.

"I need to see him, please," Mary implored in a calm but firm voice. She gritted her teeth as she tried to pull away from Ludwig, but she could not escape his strong grasp of her arm.

Ludwig pulled her down the hall, and after they turned another corner, he pushed her against the wall. "You will get to see him, but not until later today. Mother is in there now. Your presence will only infuriate her and not help Otto in the least!"

"What is wrong with him? Did he even recognize me?" Mary sobbed.

"I am told he comes and goes. We are hopeful that in time he will return to himself. I know your love will help him come back out to us. Perhaps we can also arrange for Josef to see him? You must remember, though, that my mother knows nothing of Josef. She certainly believes you and Otto have feelings for each other. But should she see Josef, she will make the immediate connection."

Mary calmed down and leaned on Ludwig. "Who is looking him over? Is he a doctor?" At her question, she felt Ludwig stiffen.

"His name is Doctor Bernhard von Gudden. He is the one I spoke about to you. King Wilhelm ordered him to come here with Otto. There are several guards with him also. Doctor von Gudden and many others with him are spies of Wilhelm's."

Ludwig stepped back from Mary, and he looked up and down the quiet halls. He then lifted her chin to gather her focus, "Mary, you must believe me when I say it is not safe for you here, and it is especially not safe for your child."

Mary felt the seriousness in Ludwig's voice. "Why? What do we matter? Josef is but a child." Her body began to shake. Fear for the safety of her child dominated her.

"Mary," Ludwig stated as he grabbed her shoulders. "Your son is the heir to the throne of Bavaria. Otto hoped, as did I, that if we fought with Prussia to win this war, that we would seal our independence. But all we are sealing is our death! Wilhelm is pressuring me to become part of a German Empire led by him. I do not wish to do so, but I cannot hold out much longer. The power he wields grows by the day. Our joining the Empire is inevitable."

Ludwig stopped as he allowed his dark message to sink in with Mary. He then continued, in a far more hushed voice as nurses came and went from the room where Otto lay. "With your son around, the succession of the throne is much different and defined. If there is not a successor, another ruler can be named, should Otto and I fall. Wilhelm will greatly desire that, for he knows full well our opposition to him." His last words settled hard on Mary and took her to the floor. Ludwig immediately reached down and lifted her off the cold stone.

"You must not do this, not now! Not here! Otto needs us to be strong if we are to have any hope of surviving this. Please hold yourself together." The anger in his voice replaced his softer message delivered earlier.

"Yes, for Otto," Mary answered. She wiped her tears away and looked at Ludwig. "I am glad to see you have strength, for earlier I doubted it was there. Please, when can I see Otto?"

"I will come for you this evening. Stay in the library until then. Mother will leave for a while before dinner. That is when I will come for you." Mary nodded and brushed past Ludwig on her way to the library.

It was the longest day of her life as she tutored the young people while she tried to appear busy until Ludwig came for her. Long after the children left and well after she should have gone home, and even after the latest of dinner times, Ludwig finally came to the door. "I am sorry for the delay. I could not get my mother to leave. We can go now."

Mary went to the door and followed Ludwig to Otto's room. Ludwig opened the door, and Mary rushed to Otto's bed. She watched him lay there, motionless. He appeared as if asleep. She asked Ludwig, "Where are his injuries?" She searched for bandages or cuts, but she could see none.

"He does not have any. There is no bullet wound, nor was he stabbed. His injuries are inside and prevent him from partaking in the daily world." Ludwig explained as he used the words told to him by Dr. von Gudden.

Mary placed her hands on Otto's face. Her touch made him stir, and he slowly opened his eyes. Unlike earlier, he recognized Mary immediately.

"Mary, I never thought I would see you again," he gasped with great effort. He slowly reached his shaking hand for hers. Mary leaned down and kissed him. Ludwig also rushed to Otto's side. "How is Josef?" Otto asked as his eyes focused more on Mary.

"He is truly amazing, and he looks more like you every day," Mary gushed. She told Otto everything she could about their son, and Otto basked in every word.

When Mary finished, Otto asked, "May I see him?"

Ludwig answered quickly, "No, Josef cannot come here, not right now at the least. It is not safe." Mary did not like the answer, but she knew Ludwig's concern.

Otto closed his eyes in sadness as tears escaped his closed lids. He gripped Mary's hand. He then looked at her again, "You must go to Amerika. Leave here and never look back." Grief took Otto as he said the words. "My only desire is to be with you, and I will come for you when I can."

"I cannot leave you! I know that if I do, I will never see you again," Mary whispered. She leaned down and kissed him again, "I cannot leave." As she said the words, the door to the room opened. Dr. von Gudden and Marie entered. Marie argued with the doctor over the treatment of her son. Then she saw Mary and stopped cold.

"What is this wretch doing here?" Marie demanded. She stomped hard toward Mary. "I will have you thrown out!"

"Mother," Otto shouted. His voice stopped her violent march. "Do not talk to her so!"

Marie rushed to Otto's side. She stepped between him and Mary. Mary stepped back and tried to stay out of the way. Ludwig motioned for Mary to depart while Marie and Otto argued over her presence. Dr. von Gudden eyed Mary distrustfully as she left. "Who is this girl?" he said aloud for all to hear.

"She is our librarian, and she tutored Otto when he was younger. She knows Otto well and asked to see him," Ludwig answered. His stark look to his mother kept her mouth shut.

"Good evening," Mary bowed as she left the room. She stumbled down the halls and out of the castle, as the information and turn of events that day made her dizzy. Many thoughts clambered through her head as the conversations repeated over again. Slowly, one thought sifted to the top of her jumbled considerations, and it trumped all the others. Ludwig's words 'Josef cannot come here. It is not safe' repeated in her mind. She ran hard and rushed home to her son.

As she worked her way through the people on the way, another memory seeped in, and it was Ludwig's words about spies. Was someone following her even now? If so, was she leading others to the only heir to the Bavarian crown? She slowed her frantic race and looked around her on the busy street as lazy snow fell to the ground. She then stepped quickly into a shop. Once inside, she peered out the window and hoped to see if anyone followed her.

"May I help you?" the man who worked in the shop asked as he broke her trance. Mary snapped from her search.

"No. Thank you." Mary cut out another door, as it was a corner shop, and she went on her way home. She continued to check to see if someone followed her, but she noticed nothing. After she arrived home, Mary was never more excited to see her son, and she refused to set him down the remainder of the evening.

✝

Several minutes after Mary left the shop, a man entered by the same door that she did. He scanned the room as he searched for his target. The business owner came out, "May I help you?"

The man stopped and looked to the owner, "A young woman was just in here. I saw her enter. Where is she?" The business owner slowly answered, "She left a few minutes ago. She went out this door."

The man grimaced as he slapped his gloves against his hands. He then ignored the businessman, who twice again asked if he could help the man. The man stepped out into the busy street and scanned in both directions for the girl he followed. He then uttered, "She is gone."

CHAPTER TWENTY-EIGHT

THE EMPIRE

Mary knew she must leave, and very soon. She prepared to depart for Amerika over the next several days. She told no one of her intentions and only went to work once during that time. Her mission was to see Ludwig and ask for his assistance.

"I am leaving very soon for Amerika. I need your help, Ludwig, as I do not have the currency needed for such a journey," Mary pleaded.

Ludwig answered immediately, "You will want for nothing. Should things change, I will send for you to come back. After all, Josef is the heir." Ludwig brought Mary the coins she needed and told her how to purchase the tickets for her and Josef. He also aided her in other arrangements, for he cared deeply for Mary's safety.

"Where are you going, that I might send for you if needed?" Ludwig asked.

"That is between God and me. I have no intention of returning, nor of seeing Otto again. The safety of my son is above all, even my desires." Mary's heart wrenched at the words, for she only wanted to be with Otto. The world would not allow it. "I will tell no one of my intended destination. I will not even tell my parents that I am leaving. They will be crushed when they find out. Please, help them if you are able."

Ludwig understood. "If I am able, I will. At this moment I wish Otto and I could go with you, though I love my country very much. It will never be the same. I will arrange for an errand wagon to deliver you back to your home today, as it is likely spies are following all of us. You will do well to watch for them."

"I wish none of this had happened, but I doubt I can change any of it now. I would ask one more thing, as I will need a man to help me get to the port of Bremen," Mary asked.

"It will be done. He will meet you out back before you go today," Ludwig replied.

"Thank you for your aid. I will forever be in your debt," Mary replied as she kissed Ludwig on the cheek before she left.

As Ludwig promised, a man took her home that evening, and another met her for the next day. She arranged for the departure time the next day. "You will be gone for several weeks, and secrecy is of most importance. Your reward for it will be high," Mary informed. The man agreed and left to make his arrangements. She then boarded the other wagon and went to her home.

Mary packed only their necessary belongings. She made a nice dinner for her parents to say goodbye, though she never told them of her plans.

"I am taking Josef on a day's trip tomorrow to the lake. We will be back in the late afternoon," she informed her mother. After dinner, Mary cleaned up while her mother took care of Josef. She hugged both of her parents and told them good night, as she knew she would never see them again.

Early the next morning, Mary got Josef ready, and they left well before dawn. The man and his covered wagon sat outside, and he loaded her two bags. One carried their belongings and the other their coins for the trip. Mary fought back tears as they rode away from the only home she had ever known. Josef cuddled next to her in a thick blanket, and he fell fast asleep on her lap. The cover of the wagon did little to keep out the bitter cold.

"Is everything all right, Fraulein? Do we need to go back for something?" the driver asked from in front. Mary heard the compassion in his voice, and she was thankful for his concern.

The cold morning served to numb her senses, and it kept her focus strong. "No, thank you. Please, take me to the palace."

The man replied, "The palace? But that is out of the way?"

"I work there in the library, and I need to get something before we depart. Please, ask me about it no more," Mary sullenly requested.

The man felt the pain in her voice. "What you offered to pay me for this trip was far more than the normal amount. I will bother you no more with unnecessary questions. Only tell me where to go."

They finally reached the castle. Once there, they entered from the back as Mary indicated. Mary took Josef and went inside. She tried to be as quiet as possible in the hopes that no one was awake yet. "I refuse to leave without Otto seeing his son one last time, no matter the risk," she uttered as they walked quickly down the dark and silent halls.

Mary was relieved to discover no one was there and pushed the door open to his room as they entered. The room was empty, except for Otto, who slept in his bed. A small lamp provided dim light. She quietly closed the door to the dark hallway, and Mary walked Josef to his father's side. She lifted the boy and set him next to Otto.

"Who is this?" Josef asked in his small voice. The sound of it stirred Otto, who woke as if from a dream. He then quickly fell into another marvelous dream as his son sat next to him for the first time in over a year. He knew immediately who the boy was.

"This nice man is a friend of mine. His name is Otto." Mary introduced them. Otto reached for Josef's hand, and he was barely able to remain steady. Josef excitedly reached back with no fear of the man who lay close to him.

"Hello, Otto. Are you hurt?" Josef asked. His pure voice washed over Otto.

"No, I am not," Otto answered.

"He is sick, Josef, but he will be better soon. Josef, this man is a brave soldier, and he fights to protect us," Mary explained. Josef's eyes grew wide.

"Did he fight alongside my father?" Josef asked. "Will we come and see him again?"

"Yes, I did. Your father is very brave," Otto responded for her. "And no," his voice cracked, "I doubt we will see each other again."

Mary quivered as she saw the pain in Otto's face.

"Do you carry a gun?" Josef gasped as he leaned close to Otto.

Otto smiled. He pulled himself a little higher in his bed, and he set his little boy on his lap. "This dream has replayed many times in my mind, but now it is happening for the first, and last, time," Otto uttered to Mary. Josef and Otto talked about what Josef was doing, and Mary only interfered to clarify their discussion.

Lights were lit in the hallway. "We must go," Mary interrupted.

Otto reached for Josef as tears filled his eyes. He pulled his son close and held him tight. "Josef, you do everything your mother tells you and grow up to be someone special. Do you hear me?"

"Yes, I will," Josef answered as he hugged the man tight.

"I will be strong soon and get back on my feet," Otto replied. "And who knows, perhaps I will see you again someday?"

"That would be nice," Josef replied. Mary took Josef and set him on the ground. She turned back as Otto tried to stand. "What are you doing?" she asked.

Otto stood tall and answered, "Saying goodbye." Otto whispered the words and pulled Mary close. The two kissed deeply, with Mary draped in Otto's arms. "Please, go," he finally uttered as he broke away from her.

Mary pried herself away as her senses whirled from the many feelings which raced through her body. The desire to save her son again rose to the top and gave her the direction she needed. She took Josef's hand and hurried to the door. As she saw no one in the hall, she rushed down the empty corridor and back toward the door where the wagon waited. She rounded the last corner and rushed into a man, and she almost knocked him to the floor.

"Watch where you are going!" the man scolded in the darkness of the early morning.

After she made sure Josef was fine, Mary stood to see Dr. von Gudden as he stood before her. "Pardon me, we are just leaving," Mary hastily uttered. She then continued their walk with far more casualness than she desired.

"Good day," Dr. von Gudden uttered. He then went on his way, but the look of the two disturbed him, and the picture of Mary and the child did not leave his memory. He continued his walk, but he began to pick up his own pace. He opened Otto's door. Otto sat high in his bed. With the picture of the little boy fresh in his mind and the view of the soldier before him, the doctor shouted, "An heir to the throne of Bavaria is born!"

"Doctor von Gudden!" Otto yelled as the doctor raced down the hall to where he ran into Mary and the boy. He ran faster and yelled, "Wache! Wache!" He tried to alert the guards who should have been at the doors, but they were not yet there. He reached the closest exit of the building and burst through the doors. Though he searched frantically, no one was in sight.

"Wilhelm will want to know! We will need to move fast to catch them!" Dr. von Gudden howled outside the building. "How did I not realize who the woman was? A son is born, an heir to the throne. It cannot be allowed!"

Mary urged the carriage driver forward as they made for the edge of town. She did not allow him to dally and they took only the shortest breaks needed as they raced through the empty countryside. Mary paid him handsomely for the secrecy she needed, and she made him take the least traveled roads as they weaved north and eventually into Prussia.

"I see the urgency in your eyes and know the fear you carry. Please, rest knowing I will tell no one of this trip. You have my word," the driver swore his allegiance to Mary.

"I need you to pretend to be my husband as we go through the towns, should anyone ask. There will be far less to attract attention that way," Mary ordered.

He did as he was asked. When needed, they pretended to be a family. Mary, however, was certain someone followed them. But the farther they went, the less concerned she became. Despite the distance they traveled, Mary would not rest until she reached Amerika. Her son's safety depended on it.

"You will help me find the girl and her son!" Dr. von Gudden ordered Ludwig as they stood in the courtyard of the Castle. The sun had just risen, and the doctor roused the entire castle to find Mary.

"The girl means nothing. I assure you," Ludwig responded.

"But what of her son? A spitting image of his father lying in the bed he is. I have no doubt the identity, and that an heir to the throne of Bavaria is born," Dr. von Gudden exalted, his anger dripping from every word.

"And what if that is so? Where is the harm or concern of yours?" Ludwig dared to challenge.

The words barely left his mouth as the back of von Gudden's hand stung Ludwig's perfect face. The blow knocked him to the ground. The soldiers of Bavaria rushed forward, as did the force which attended to the doctor. Both sides drew their weapons.

"You will not address me so!" von Gudden scorned as he towered over Ludwig. "Tell me where the girl lives!"

"No, I will not!" Ludwig shouted. He rolled to his feet as blood trickled from his mouth.

"What is happening?" Marie responded as she joined the tense scene.

"Your son is being insolent. A son to Otto is born, and I will find him today! Who knows where the girl lives?" von Gudden demanded to the growing crowd. No one stepped forward.

At that moment, Helga entered the packed courtyard. She was completely ignorant as to what had just occurred.

"You! Girl! Come here immediately!" Marie ordered. Helga rushed to them.

"Yes, my Lady," Helga replied with a bow. "How may I help?" Her voice trembled out of fear.

"Tell me now, where does Mary live?" Marie ordered. Helga saw the trepidation in Ludwig's face and the blood on his chin. She also witnessed the intentness of both Marie and the man with her.

"I do not know. I barely know Ma..." Helga began.

A shot cracked in the early morning, and the bullet found its dreadful mark. Helga fell to the ground, dead.

"What have you done?" Ludwig demanded, stunned at what had just played out before him.

Dr. von Gudden lowered his still smoking pistol and holstered it. "Wilhelm will be very disgusted with this. I am taking Otto to Versailles for the coronation of Wilhelm as the Emperor of the German Empire. Will you be attending to answer for yourself?" von Gudden asked.

"I most certainly will not!" Ludwig indignantly replied.

Dr. von Gudden answered. "Very well then, your uncle Luitpold shall attend in your place. At least there are still some men in Bavaria with a spine and loyalty. It is probably best that you stay here in your fairytale castle and dream up your explanation of what happened today," he chastised. "Guards, find the girl Mary. Search all of the roads between here and the borders. Schnell! Schnell!"

The guards with Dr. von Gudden raced out on the main roads to the border and questioned many on the way. They found no one who knew of Mary or her son, and they found no trace of her. They eventually found Mary's parents and brought them to the castle for questioning.

Dr. von Gudden stood over Mary's beaten father, who bled profusely from his mouth. "Where did she go? As you are her father, surely you will know!"

Her father had not the strength to lift his head. Dr. von Gudden grabbed his hair and jerked it up. "Answer me!" he screamed. His eyes bulged and flared in anger.

"I do not know, and neither does my wife," he struggled to answer. He gulped and then slowly continued, "And if I did, I would not tell you, even at the cost of my life..."

Dr. von Gudden pulled his pistol and placed the barrel against the man's head. Mary's father closed his eyes as the doctor notched the gun. Dr. von Gudden quickly lifted the gun and smashed the butt against the man's head, and he fell hard to the ground. "He does not know. Search from here to the borders, and even to the north and on the railways. I doubt she would try to make it through the war front of France. Telegraph the borders and cities in between. We must find the girl!"

Dr. von Gudden went to Ludwig. "We are leaving. Stay here and cower until we return. Otto von Bismarck and Emperor Wilhelm will look forward to Bavaria playing her part as a loyal state of the German Empire. You will lead Bavaria, for now." Dr. von Gudden, Otto, and Luitpold departed. Otto was much more lucid than before he arrived, driven by his interaction with Josef and Mary. Ludwig had agreed that

Bavaria would join them, with assurances from Dr. von Gudden of good care for Otto in exchange.

Brian Spielbauer

CHAPTER TWENTY-NINE

BUENA VISTA

George toiled relentlessly against the grudging land. The fight to clear the trees to make way for the crops he needed never ended. At times, others helped him in his endeavors, but mostly it was only he and his stout team of horses that made it happen. Mathias decided to make his stay in Gutenberg, but George's heart from the start was to live around Buena Vista. He purchased a tract of land in the most southern part of Clayton County, and he was determined to make it work.

The solitude did him well. George did not miss the endless jabbering conversation one would find in a town. He enjoyed hard work, but he equally enjoyed the quiet offered him on his remote farm. He missed Mary terribly, though he knew he would never see her again. From time to time, he traveled into Gutenberg to see his friend Mathias and their new acquaintances, the Tschohls. He also knew the farmers that lived around him and called on them during times of need. His need or theirs mattered little. When need called, it was answered. For the most part, though, George stayed on his small farm and worked hard.

His crops had long been in for the past season. His clearing more timber was for the following year, but it also meant he increased his store of firewood for the winter that was not soon to be over. "You cannot get caught in the middle of winter with no firewood, George! Cut early, and cut often!" Mr. Brimeyer, a neighbor farmer, was fond of saying. George had already witnessed enough winters in Iowa to know the wisdom of that advice, and he took it to heart.

George stood at his only window at the end of an especially warm February day, and he looked at the beautiful sunset. He desired to see each one, for they reminded him of the sunset he saw years ago with Mary at the lake by their hometown. The thoughts of her, and the pain of her rebuke, rushed back to him each lonely night. He desired her companionship. Though Mathias helped him to meet many girls, none of them measured up to his memory of Mary.

George sat down in his chair and started to fall asleep. Exhaustion, as it did every day, took his body. He fidgeted as he dreamt of plowing the spring fields, which he needed to increase in size greatly. The vividness of his dreams masked the sound of the horse-drawn sleigh that pulled up outside. He did not hear the light footsteps as they approached the door, nor did he hear the first series of knocks, which beckoned an answer. A more persistent rattle finally interrupted his dream as he woke suddenly. Out of habit, he first reached for his rifle. Another knock followed, and George slowly walked over to the door. Never before had he received visitors this late?

"Mathias, is that you? Mr. Tschohl?" he asked cautiously.

"It is neither," a soft woman's voice came from the other side. He could not control himself, for there was only one voice in the entire world that could make such a beautiful sound. He quickly set his rifle down and fumbled to open the door.

"Mary?" George cried as he opened the door. They rushed to each other and wrapped themselves in each other's embrace. George closed his eyes and basked in feeling the woman he loved more than any in the world. Surely, she felt the same way to have traveled so far to find him. He whirled her around and around and was unwilling to let her go ever again.

"Mama," a clean voice, one not affected by age or strife, came from outside the open door. George slowly set Mary down, and he looked at her in a new way. He then turned to see the little boy who stood in the doorway.

George looked in astonishment as the driver in the lighted sleigh rode away.

"George," Mary alerted. George turned back to her. His mind spun with the unexpected events. His focus shifted away from the small boy before him and back to the only woman he had ever loved. "This is my son. His name is Josef."

ABOUT THE AUTHOR

Brian Spielbauer grew up on a farm in northeast Iowa. It sat on a hill overlooking Johles Hollow, about two miles north of Osterdock and seven miles west of Guttenberg. He is the sixth of seven children born to Frank and Jackie (Wessels) Spielbauer.

Brian, like all the sons and daughters of Frank and Jackie, played sports growing up. Unlike the rest, he was also in high school plays and was in the band. He also had a vast imagination that allowed him to escape, at times, the bustle of a busy home to withdraw into a different world, one where he took the prominent place in all activities.

He graduated from Guttenberg (now Clayton Ridge) High School in 1991, from William Penn University in 1996, and finally from Bemidji State University in 2002. He taught

Kindergarten through eighth-grade Physical Education and Science, coached high school sports (but mainly basketball), and then he coached and taught at William Penn for ten years.

He married his very supportive and loving wife, Jennifer (Bryant) Spielbauer, in 2001. They live in Fayette, Missouri, with their two wonderful daughters Sydney and Allie.

CPSIA information can be obtained
at www.ICGtesting.com
Printed in the USA
LVHW110929090321
680751LV00004B/8/J